THE
OTHER
JOSEPH

ALSO BY SKIP HORACK

The Eden Hunter
The Southern Cross

THE
OTHER
JOSEPH

SKIP HORACK

ANANSI

This edition published in 2015 by
House of Anansi Press Inc.
110 Spadina Avenue, Suite 801
Toronto, ON, M5V 2K4
Tel. 416-363-4343
Fax 416-363-1017
www.houseofanansi.com

Distributed in Canada by
HarperCollins Canada Ltd.
1995 Markham Road
Scarborough, ON, M1B 5M8
Toll free tel. 1-800-387-0117

House of Anansi Press is committed to protecting our natural environment. As part of our efforts, the interior of this book is printed on paper that contains 100% post-consumer recycled fibres, is acid-free, and is processed chlorine-free.

19 18 17 16 15   1 2 3 4 5

Library and Archives Canada Cataloguing in Publication

Horack, Skip, author
The other Joseph / by Skip Horack.

Issued in print and electronic formats.
ISBN 978-1-77089-425-9 (pbk.).—ISBN 978-1-77089-426-6 (html)

I. Title.

PS3608.O657O84 2015   813'.6   C2014-902784-2
                                             C2014-902785-0

Designed by: Suet Yee Chong

Canada Council   Conseil des Arts   ONTARIO ARTS COUNCIL
for the Arts   du Canada   CONSEIL DES ARTS DE L'ONTARIO
                                          an Ontario government agency
                                          un organisme du gouvernement de l'Ontario

We acknowledge for their financial support of our publishing program the Canada Council for the Arts, the Ontario Arts Council, and the Government of Canada through the Canada Book Fund.

Printed and bound in Canada

MIX
Paper from
responsible sources
FSC
www.fsc.org   FSC® C004071

ANCIENT FOREST ™
FRIENDLY

When we try to pick out anything by itself, we find it hitched to everything else in the universe.

—JOHN MUIR

THE
OTHER
JOSEPH

FOREWORD

On Christmas Day in 2008 two men, one Australian, the other Nigerian, watched a ponytailed American, my little brother Roy, leap from an oil rig into the Gulf of Guinea. Christmas Day— but, to the third- and fourth-century pagan Romans, as our father taught us as boys, Dies Natalis Solis Invicti. The Birthday of the Unconquered Sun.

Nearly three years after Roy made his jump, a woman named Margaret Mokwelu drove from Newark to Walter Reed National Military Medical Center in Bethesda. That was in the second month of my unlocking, back when I—Thomas Joseph, the lost and kidnapped Navy SEAL, free after two decades of imprisonment—was still making headlines. During Roy's own disappearance Margaret had been working in the citizen services office at the U.S. consulate in Lagos. A duffel bag of my brother's effects came into her possession, but attempts to locate any next of kin in the States were unsuccessful. His few things were eventually recycled and released into the world's endless river of need, and even today, somewhere in Nigeria, there is likely an African man wearing his jacket, a child who sleeps in his T-shirt.

But, and bless her for this, there was one item Margaret took an interest in and kept for herself: a three-ring binder containing pages and pages of looping script. Roy's binder sat inside Margaret's desk in Lagos for a year because those reminiscences of his, they touched and haunted her, and she brought it with her when she immigrated to America. Finally Margaret, and that thick gray binder, came to me.

Margaret's former boss in Nigeria is now a D.C. lobbyist, and through his connections she was able to arrange a visit with me at Walter Reed. I had been there a week, awaiting a surgery to remove the inch of knife blade an Arab fisherman had broken off in my hip in January of '91. And although I suspected Margaret might be an intelligence officer, a mind trick designed to ferret out any inconsistencies in my account of the time I'd spent off the grid, after she presented me with Roy's binder my only thoughts were of him. I was twenty and he was twelve when I saw him last. I'm forty-one years old now. If not for Margaret, I might never have met my brother as a man.

I play a part in the story you are about to read, but I already know this won't be the manuscript New York, or anyone, wants from me. You want to read of how I was taken by the sea and coughed up by the sea, sold by fishermen, then Bedouin, before being smuggled out of Saudi Arabia on a night plane and encaged for over twenty years as the private, hidden-away curiosity of a wealthy madman. You want the story of my Arab Spring liberation and of my journey through the desert. I understand. That story will be told one day, but for now, another story. The story of my brother and his search for my daughter. Roy comes first. I owe him that much, as it was on my behalf, or at least in my memory, that he set off on *his* journey. The journey that began with an e-mail from California. The journey that ended with his dive into the Gulf of Guinea.

A confession: I might very well be betraying Roy by letting the world know his secrets, and if that is the case I hope he will forgive me. My only defense is that I believe his trials and tribulations are worth sharing. There is a lot to be learned from the life of Roy Joseph, and this is the best way I can think of to honor him.

So Margaret Mokwelu, thank you. And thank you as well to those who have begun helping me organize and polish Roy's disjointed, untitled "notes" into a book. Also, although a few names must be changed for anonymity, this endeavor never would be possible without the graciousness of the many who have agreed to be identified in these pages. Otherwise, except for my dedication and the occasional epigraph, the words that follow will be his. Speak, Roy.

Thomas M. Joseph
New York City
February 22, 2012

For our family

And they said one to another, Behold, this dreamer cometh.

—GENESIS 37:19

PART I

The Louisiana Notes

*Along with all the other frailties of the average man—
his carelessness, his prankishness, his tobacco habit, his
cola habit, his inclination to rest once in a while and
chat with his neighbor—there must also be expected one
more: his natural human proclivity for sticking his head
in mysterious openings, putting his fingers in front of fan
blades, and pulling wires and pins on strange mechanical objects which he finds.*

—Arthur Larson,
The Law of Workmen's Compensation

M Y NAME IS ROY JOSEPH, AND I HAVE NINE FIN-
gers. Five on my right hand, four on the other.
The pinkie is the one missing. I lost it two sum-
mers ago on a jackup drilling rig that stood in two hundred feet
of green Gulf of Mexico water—about thirty nautical miles south
of Grand Isle, Louisiana, and the Airstream travel trailer I once
called home. I think of melted wax whenever I look at the scar,
or the hard white fat that runs along the side of a raw strip steak.

September 2007. The Loranger Avis. A steel island of heat,
sweat, and noise. Everything is heavy there, and everything can
bite you. The Loranger Avis had been situated where the continental shelf drops off into the Mississippi Canyon. Go a little
farther south and the real deepwater starts—instead of jackups
and fixed platforms, out that way you'll find drill ships and semi-
submersibles, other kinds of floaters.

So there I was on the edge of the North American continent,
twenty-nine years old and working the second morning of a two-
week stint. Three hours into a twelve-hour tower. Just a few days
before, I'd received an e-mail from someone claiming to be my
dead brother's daughter. More about that later, but that's where my
head was. I was layering a fresh spool of quarter-inch wire evenly
across the slow-rolling drum of an electric hoist, and thinking on

that e-mail, when another roughneck—Malcolm, a weight-lifting Cajun—sang out. We were fifty feet above the Gulf, and it was as loud as it always is up top. There was no understanding what Malcolm was saying, but he was pointing behind me. I shut the hoist off and turned around. A long sport fisher was coming up on us, a teal Contender powered by triple 250 Yamahas. Nothing unusual. The legs and substructures of offshore jackups and fixed platforms create sort of a reef beneath the surface, and that shelter brings the forage fish that in turn attract snapper and grouper and sports.

Malcolm came over and we watched the boat drop from its plane, settling into the water as it skidded to a stop. Two-hundred-thousand-dollar setup, and a fucking kid was driving. I figured he was around twenty. His buddy, as well. They were both shirtless, had gelled hair and lifeguard tans. The first-mate pal moved up to the bow holding an aluminum rig hook like a shepherd's staff. He was wearing white shorts and black sunglasses. *Risky Business* Tom Cruise Wayfarers, I think. The driver positioned the Contender on the lee side of the Loranger Avis, and Cruise snagged his hook onto one of the legs of the jackup.

They had a rope tied to the rig hook. The outboards died, and the current pulled the Contender away. Cruise let the rope play out from his hands, and when they were ten yards back he hitched to a front cleat and the rope went tight. Only the bow was facing us, and though I couldn't see an autograph I had a good enough hunch—*Cash Flow, Boy Toy, First Strike*—some bullshit like that. Allowing boats to do this is against policy on most any drilling rig, especially since 9/11, but our toolpusher wasn't up for getting on the loudspeaker and bouncing them yet. We take our shots where we can, and that's a game some pushers enjoy—letting the sports go through the trouble of tying on before hollering at them to break off.

The Gulf was as smooth as a forest lake, and the two rich kids were in the stern being cool together when a sweat-soaked roustabout came sidling up to me and Malcolm. He was new to the oil patch, no older than the boys in the boat. I can't remember his name, and I'm not sure I ever knew it. Worms, we called these greenhorns. They'd shaved most of his hair off the day before; his hard hat was loose and wobbling.

The roustabout pointed at the Contender. "Sweet, huh? That a thirty-six-footer?"

I nodded just to be nice. I was a worm once. All us hands had started out there. "Yeah. That's a thirty-six."

Malcolm was less patient. He was glaring at the kid. "You need something, worm?"

The roustabout took a step back, even blushed a click. "No sir."

Malcolm rolled his cinder-block head around, letting some idea wash over every part of his brain. "Well," he said, "we need something from you. Find Owen and tell him we want the key to the V-door. Don't fuck it up."

The roustabout said, "You bet," and hustled off. It was all grab-ass, snipe-hunt foolishness. Owen would send him to Jimbo, and Jimbo would send him to Mud Duck, and Mud Duck would send him to Darius. Eventually the kid would work his way back to us empty-handed, and if he had any sense at all, realize the V-door of a drilling rig isn't an actual door. No hard feelings. Like I said, we'd all spent time as worms.

I looked down at the Contender. The boys were baiting free lines for amberjack and maybe cobia when the forward cuddy opened and out came two girls. Blondes. I knew then that, policy or no policy, we weren't going to be treated to any runoffs over the loudspeaker from the toolpusher, a man sitting high above us in an air-conditioned office, no doubt studying on those girls same as me. He was hidden behind tinted windows, but I could picture him up there in his clean clothes, binoculars in his hands.

Malcolm was watching the girls too. He'd been clutching the sleeve of my coveralls ever since they appeared. They were wearing purple gym shorts and neon swimsuit tops. One tangerine, the other flamingo. The girls lit cigarettes and popped wine coolers, put their thin arms around each other and began siren-swaying to a song I couldn't hear. The rich boys grinned at them but kept at that tough labor they were doing. They already had two free lines cast, and they were prepping deep-sea rods when the girls grabbed beach towels and danced their way to the bow. *LSU* was written in gold letters on the asses of their shorts, and I imagined scratching out my own message to drop onto them:

> *I used to be a Tiger myself, y'all. Made the Dean's List my first semester and sat in classrooms with princesses like you. So I'm not the born-trash moron you think I am. Hell, a decade ago your kind copied my notes, invited me to parties.*

The girls spread their towels across the flat bow, and I saw one of them had a bottle of suntan lotion tucked in her waistband. That killed me, especially with thirteen days left in my stint. Not lust—just the stinging ache that comes with witnessing the carefree and beautiful and unknowable exist in my same world. But it was also nice, in a way, having them there to help move my thoughts, even if for a moment, away from the out-of-nowhere e-mail that had been tearing at my mind.

So the boys fished, and the girls sunned. And Malcolm and I were looking down on them when the blonder of the blondes smiled up at us. Then she said something to her friend, and they both did a yoga curve, pulled off their shorts. Seeing them in their bikini bottoms was too much for Malcolm. He brought his hard hat against mine and yelled into my ear. "If she winks, she'll screw," he said. "Am I right, Roy?"

If she winks, she'll screw. Rig chatter. That's what we say when we get a seized pipe connection to loosen a bit, means we'll be able to twist it off sooner or later. I shed my work gloves, let my hands breathe. "Yeah," I told him. "They should start climbing to us before long."

Malcolm's face was like a question mark. I can be a soft talker. A mumbler too, at times, but he slapped my chest and wandered off. I stayed put, still looking at the girls. They were propped on their elbows, eyes masked by enormous sunglasses. Enough. I switched the hoist on so it could eat more wire, but then I took another peek at them. The shiny blondes leaned their heads back in sync, showing their throats as they stared at the sun, and I pretended they were watching me like I was watching them. I wondered what they saw. A shaggy-haired, gloves-in-the-mouth gargoyle in steel-toed Red Wings and fire-resistant coveralls, safety glasses and a white hard hat.

Then I did something incredibly stupid. I forgot my surroundings for a second—all it takes—and let my hand rest on the drum of the hoist I was supposed to be watching. I felt nothing really, just a tug and a sudden burn before I jerked away. I looked and saw the thin wire had sheared my little finger off right where it met my hand. My snipped pinkie was lying there on the grate, and even as I was bending to pick it up, I was thinking, No huge deal, the doctors can fix this. I've seen worse out here in the oil patch, much worse.

And I almost had the finger when Malcolm came running. Apparently he'd spotted me there, doubled over and bleeding. He meant well, but that was more bad luck for me. His boots shook the grate, jostling my pinkie, and all I could do was stand there and watch as it slipped through a crack and went plummeting down into the Gulf beneath us, really not so far from where those girls lay sunning.

I sat cross-legged on the grate and let Malcolm hop to. He'd been in the Marine Corps and could play hero when necessary. Someone had tossed him gauze from a first-aid kit, and he held my left arm over my head as he wrapped the hand. The pain had showed up, and the alarm had been sounded. The crew was all gathered around, and a few of them were wearing life jackets because you never know. By then hurt had me blabbering nonsense, and most of the guys were looking away so as not to humiliate me. We weren't allowed to smoke except in the smoking room, but Darius put an unlit cigarette between my lips. I guess he thought that might help me get calm. My right hand had latched onto a pair of scissors that had fallen out of the first-aid kit, and Darius asked if he could take them from me. I nodded, and then I think I was about to really break down when I caught sight of the wide-eyed roustabout. Someone had put one of those little orange safety cones on top of his hard hat without him knowing it. Coned him, as we say on the rigs. Another Loranger Avis game. We'd been doing that to each other all summer. The roustabout was looking at me horrified and wailing, Oh wow, oh wow, oh wow—but I couldn't take a coned worm seriously.

So I started laughing as I went into shock. Laughed even though I hardly ever laugh. Laughed even though I knew I'd gone and fucked myself. It was an hour before the Air Med meat wagon arrived to take me to Lady of the Sea, but the Contender was still attached to us when the helicopter began its slow descent. The girls hurried from the bow as the bird touched down on the heli-deck, the wind from the rotor blades spiraling their yellow hair. I saw the three outboards bubble to life, and Tom Cruise went up front to free the rig hook. Jimbo had given one of the medics my duffel bag, and they were leading me toward the helicopter when the Contender took off west. Finally I glimpsed the name painted across the hull of that big goddamn boat. *The Great Wide Open.* Picture that scrawled in bold, black cursive.

MY BROTHER TOMMY AND I GREW UP ON A FARM in the tiny north Louisiana town of Dry Springs, on eleven acres that bordered a large tract of pine forest belonging to a paper company. Two fenced pastures and a barn, a vegetable garden and a pond and a ranch-style house. My parents were teachers at the high school (Mom, science; Dad, history). Almost-hippie types, at least in a back-to-the-land sort of way, and bookish. Farming was something they enjoyed, and at different times we had cattle and sheep, horses and honeybees. As a boy our dog was a heeler named Blue, and as a teenager, Rocky the Catahoula. There were always chickens and barn cats, and every fall we took three hogs to Mencken's Slaughterhouse.

Both of my parents had been raised in Natchitoches Parish, on opposite sides of the Cane River, the only children of families that had hated each other for generations. Dad was Romeo to Mom's Juliet, and their forbidden teenage romance turned into something even more earnest and determined while they were in college together at Northwestern State. Right before graduation they married at a courthouse, and taking teaching jobs in Dry Springs had been their way of leaving Natchitoches Parish and their snarling kinfolk behind for good. They'd been disowned—orphaned, for all intents and purposes—and Mom was pregnant with Tommy when they moved onto the farm. She gave birth to him at the hospital in Ruston, the closest city to Dry Springs of any real size, and eight years later I came along, their "surprise" baby.

Our farm was flat level except for at the back of one pasture, near the pond, where a tube of ground about six feet high and ten feet wide came snaking out of the pinewoods for thirty yards. For some reason, before I was born even, my father named that mysterious buckle of land after the place he claimed the Civil War had been lost. Cemetery Ridge. Dad used to say that Lee, sickened by the hell at Gettysburg, had leaned way too much on religion, deciding if victory for the South was God's will they'd be able to take that high ground. So a faith experiment, in Dad's opinion. A faith experiment by a man known as much for his self-control as for his piety. A man who had finished West Point without a single demerit. A man not prone to acting rashly. An honorable mistake, but a mistake all the same. "General Lee," Pickett had cried, "I have no division now." Generals gamble, and boys die.

So for years that was my family's joke name for our own minia-ture ridge—all the way up until the winter day in '88 when a briar-scratched graduate student from New Orleans came calling. He went by Ethan, if memory serves, and he was convinced Cemetery Ridge was actually a small section of an ancient Indian mound that lay mostly in those paper company pines. For the past month Ethan had been roaming all through that corporate forest on the sly, surveying and taking soil samples, and now he was hoping we would let him poke around on our land as well.

"Guy's a homo," Tommy whispered to me.

My brother's hair was long and ragged that winter, and when he talked he'd hook a finger through his brown bangs to keep them off his face. That impish grin. High school Tommy always looked like a surfer to me. Some *The Lost Boys,* California kid now stuck in Louisiana.

"A dork," I said, ten years old and wanting to play too.

Tommy snorted, then laughed.

"Frick and Frack," said Dad. "Quiet."

At first I think our father, being a history teacher, was embarrassed he hadn't seen Cemetery Ridge for what it might really have been, but in the end his curiosity won out over his pride, and he threw in with Ethan. Dad and Tommy and I spent the day with him in our pasture, watching the surveying of Cemetery Ridge, and a month later Ethan came to show us an aerial photo that had the contours of the entire spread-eagle hill drawn on it in white grease pencil. We saw the outline of a creature flattened like roadkill in the pinewoods. The hill had four legs and a head, and the tip of a long and curling tail trespassed onto our property. This was maybe a thirty-five-hundred-year-old effigy mound, Ethan told us. A very rare thing. Older than Stonehenge. Older than the Great Pyramid of Giza. In fact, except for a dirt bird over in Poverty Point, he didn't know of another effigy mound in all of Louisiana. I thought I was looking at a weasel, but Ethan was thinking panther. It might even be a prehistoric depiction of the Underwater Panther, he explained—a water monster many Native American tribes were documented to have worshipped.

But after that we never heard from Ethan the grad student again. Maybe he got his Tulane Ph.D. and left for some far-off place. Maybe he stopped believing. At one point Dad was communicating with archeologists from the state, but they were dubious. Though north*east* Louisiana does have a number of Indian mounds, those state archeologists thought our hill in Lincoln Parish sat a shade too far west to be an Indian mound of any sort, much less an effigy mound. Still, they seemed interested enough until the paper company bosses got involved. Political strings were pulled. No one was getting access to their land without a judge's order, and eventually that hill was forgotten by everyone but us Josephs.

And perhaps the hill wasn't some outlier Indian mound but a trick of geography. Maybe a hill was just a hill, I mean. Nevertheless, my father would spend a good portion of the nine years he had left on this earth obsessed. What was once Cemetery Ridge became the tail of the Panther Mound to him, and that same June, the day Tommy departed for basic training—choosing the navy over college and breaking my parents' hearts—Dad gave us each a little steel vial strung on a neck chain. A silver necklace for Mom, dog-tag ball chains for me and him and Tommy. The vials were about an inch and a half long and had been filled with Panther Mound dirt. Tommy is leaving us, said Dad. But this is our home, and this is our family. We'll keep these on us to remember that.

Tommy wept. A thing I'd never seen. Then he hugged our parents good-bye and punched me in the arm. He earned his SEAL Trident at nineteen just like he promised, and less than three years from that arm punch he would deploy during the buildup to Desert Storm. One of those four vials probably tumbles along somewhere in the Persian Gulf now. Another two lie buried in Louisiana. That only leaves mine. And though I'm no warrior, and though I suspect this stolen dirt may be cursed, I'll die too before I let anyone free it from my neck.

A FTER THE 2005 DOUBLE PUNCH OF HURRICANES Katrina and Rita, the good people of Muncie, Indiana, had sent a bookmobile slash computer lab they called a Cybermobile down to Grand Isle for us to use—and in '07 that bus was still parked in the lot of our wrecked library. It had pictures of Garfield the orange cat painted on both sides. He was reading a book while merry mice looked on. When I wasn't offshore that was where I'd go to check my e-mail, but there was seldom any point. I didn't have any family, just a Labrador named Sam, and the few humans I considered friends weren't really big on computers.

But still I would go there, and two days before my accident I'd clicked on the e-mail that would roust me from nearly a decade of hibernation, a summons from the great wide open that, ultimately, would start me on the boomerang journey from Grand Isle to California and back again:

Dear Mr. Joseph,

You don't know me, but I think a navy guy named Thomas Muir Joseph was my birth father. He was born in Ruston, Louisiana, on April 17, 1970, and was living in San Diego in

December 1990. Was that your brother? Please don't be too freaked out. I only want to talk, and I hope you do too. Yes, no, please write me back.

Joni

Holy fuck. It had seemed impossible to believe. The sort of e-mail you might get from some spam-slinging con artist. But this person was definitely describing Tommy—Ruston, the birthday, the hat-tip-to-a-dead-naturalist middle name Mom had chosen for him—and he had indeed been stationed across the bay from San Diego, at Naval Amphibious Base Coronado. I read and reread that e-mail, but before I could decide whether to type a reply to Joni no-last-name at j67789@gmail.com, the librarian told me it was time to lock up the Cybermobile for the day. I spent a mostly sleepless night, then shipped out on a morning crew boat for my hard-luck stint on the Loranger Avis.

BELOW DECK, the crew boat *Deborah Ann* looked like the inside of a passenger jet. Reclining, tray-table-in-front-of-you seats—seven rows of them cut into threes by port and starboard aisles. I was sitting at a port window, surrounded by five of the hands who'd been rotating two weeks on, two weeks off with me the longest. Little Owen and then little Darius to my right. Malcolm, Mud Duck, and Jimbo in the row ahead of us. I avoided people for the most part. These were the only folks I was really at all close to, but they didn't stick around Grand Isle any more than required.

Jimbo and Darius lived in Texas.

Malcolm, Lafayette.

Owen, Kenner.

Mud Duck, Arkansas.

I knew the names of their sons and their daughters, of their girlfriends and their wives and their ex-wives—and though some-times they invited me to leave Grand Isle and visit them in main-land America, I never did. They understood why someone with my past might choose to lie low and live year-round on the island, but what they didn't get was why I took it to such an extreme. Why in general I treated Grand Isle like a penal colony, only ventur-ing across the bridge on rare occasions. It's not that I delight in solitude. I don't, actually. But I'd come to prefer the comfort and security of seclusion over the uncertainty of the unknown, and if the guys called me a hermit for that, so be it.

But then j67789@gmail.com sent me an e-mail and confused things. The *Deborah Ann* was quiet save for some tired, half-hearted conversations—forty or so men trying to sleep or bullshit their way through the two-and-a-half-hour ride to the Loranger Avis—but me, I was slumped against the clammy window and thinking. Bayou Rigaud tracks the north side of Grand Isle, and our hundred-foot slave ship was leaving that channel, coming around the narrow island as we entered Barataria Pass. Strong, deep waters there. Our outlet to the Gulf.

"What's black and blue and hates sex?"

I could hear the grin in Malcolm's voice without needing to see him. These digs were a specialty of his. He knew a book's worth of pedophile jokes, and he'd been rattling them off since before we left the dock. "My God," I said. "Enough already. It's early."

But Malcolm had turned around in his seat to look at me, perching his chin atop the headrest like a sixth-grade bus bully. And though Owen and Darius had their eyes closed, I knew they were listening. Mud Duck and Jimbo too, for that matter.

"The twelve-year-old in Roy's trunk."

The guys all snickered but didn't fall out. They'd heard better from Malcolm, and he slid back down his hole. The Detroit Die-sels had throttled up, and we were full into the pass now, chugging along at fifteen knots, the wake casting out behind us growing to swells of four, five, six feet. To starboard, through the across-the-hull windows: glimpses of the east end of Grand Isle and the coast guard station, the oak and hackberry of the state park. To port, through my own window: the risen sun over Grand Terre Island and the brick, granite, and cemented-shell ruins of Fort Livingston, almost two hundred years old and fading.

Malcolm again. "Say what you want about child molesters, at least Roy drives slowly past schools."

A parting gift, I guess, because he was on his feet, leaving with Mud Duck and Jimbo to go bother the captain in the wheelhouse. I waited until they were in the aisle and gone before bumping at Owen with my elbow, then I reached over to poke Darius on his knee. They really were sleeping this time. Owen wiped at his face. Darius yawned. A small, dark-skinned white man and a small, light-skinned black man. Me, I'm neither big nor small, just five foot ten and wiry. Rig work is a burn-calorie job. I still weighed what I had as a college boy.

"Can I ask something?" I said.

"When you kill him, use a twelve-gauge, brah," said Owen. "A double-barrel so no plastic gets left. Bang, bang. Buckshot, or maybe turkey loads, to his melon."

"Gangster," said Darius. "Cops can't be tracing no shotgun."

I shook my head. "Y'all know I had a brother, right?"

They nodded, and I told them about the e-mail. They both took it all in. Ready for me to let them give counsel, but not interrupting. The Loranger Avis had satellite Internet, plus a couple of computers in the common room for the hands to share, and I was wanting to know if I should send an e-mail of my own when we made the rig. "So?" I said.

"That was yesterday?" Owen asked.

"Yeah."

"Well, well," said Darius.

Their advice was to walk away. "At best you're getting set up for the take," Owen explained. "At worst you're getting a teenager in California."

"You don't want no teenage girl in your life," said Darius. "How'd that work out for you last try, dog?" He laughed and reclined his seat, pulled his Houston Texans hat down like a mask.

I turned back to the window. We were almost out the pass, and some sports in bay boats were clustered near the Grand Terre shoreline, casting sparkle beetles for speckled trout. They quit fishing and motored up as the *Deborah Ann* grew level. Aiming their bows at us, toward that coming wake that might have swamped them or run them aground.

BY THE TIME the *Deborah Ann* reached the Loranger Avis I'd also let Jimbo and Mud Duck and even Malcolm in on my secret, but they were all of the same mind: this was either a scam or a sick prank. Malcolm can be sincere when he's not performing for an audience, and as we watched the others line up to crane-ride the Billy Pugh personnel basket onto the rig he made me promise I'd wait a day or two before rushing to a computer.

And yet on my first night bunking on the Loranger Avis sleep didn't come much better for me than it had in my Airstream on Pearl Lane in Grand Isle. I won't say that Dear Mr. Joseph e-mail was the reason I lost my finger the next day, but in ten years of working the oil patch I'd never once been injured—and only an exhausted man would have been idiotic enough to feed his pinkie to an electric hoist.

I made up my own mind about writing "Joni" while I was at the hospital in Cut Off. Word about maritime injuries and mishaps tends to spread quickly among the people with ties to that dangerous world, but I spent three nights in Lady of the Sea with no visitors other than a Loranger Drilling goblin bent on taking my statement for his incident report. The only person to even call was my neighbor and yellow Lab babysitter Jack Hebert. Jack was retired from flying spotter planes for the pogy fishing fleet, lived with his wife, Ada, and her sister in a Pearl Lane single-wide he'd lifted onto pilings. He collected my mail and, for a hundred dollars a stint, looked after Sam whenever I was away working. Walked him and fed him and such. Jack and I weren't buddy-buddy, but we did have a symbiotic sort of relationship. That is, Jack would do things for me if I threw enough money his way.

So I had nobody, not really—but, I realized, with this Joni here's a slight chance that maybe I do.

The doctors discharged me home, and I hitched a ride south on Highway 1 with a gravel hauler. Thirty-five miles later he dropped me off at the dock so I could retrieve my car—a four-door Chrysler LeBaron I'd had since I was eighteen—then that goofy Cybermobile was the first place I went. Nothing new from j67789@gmail.com. My left hand was a mitten of bandages, but I pecked out a reply with my right: Call me at this number, Joni. I'm skeptical, but I'll talk.

Afterwards I drove to Pearl Lane, and when I pulled in Sam began kangarooing against the front of his kennel, eyes glowing in the headlights. I set him free, gave him some love, scratching at his throat until he was trembling, then I unpacked my duffel bag and shaved, cleaned myself up. I was anxious and restless and thirsty, all on account of that e-mail, and though I felt bad putting Sam back in the kennel so soon after returning to him, at nightfall I went to Carl's Lounge.

ABOUT A WEEK AFTER MY THIRTEENTH BIRTHDAY. January 1991. I'd stayed home from school with a fake cough, and I was taking a break from game shows and my back-of-the-closet *Playboy* when a black car came crunching down the gravel road to our farm. Two men in U.S. Navy dress uniforms climbed out, others watched from the car. I answered the door, understood what it all meant, but they weren't going to tell me anything. The chaplain or maybe both of them were wearing Old Spice, and even now the smell takes me to that day.

My parents were over at the high school still, so the three of us sat outside and waited. We were on the porch swing, and the chaplain put his arm around me when I began to cry. It was cold, but I didn't think to invite them inside and they didn't ask. A snafu on their part, catching me home alone. Then finally my parents came rolling up in the truck. Dad was a gentle man, but he spiderwebbed the windshield with his fist when he saw us. Mom was out the door before the pickup stopped moving. Her legs collapsed under her, and I ran down the steps. I was hugging Mom, and Dad was hugging me. A forlorn tangle of Josephs hearing a voice like God's. Sir, ma'am, there's been a helicopter crash. Your son is missing.

At dark my parents made room for me in their bed and we lay there side by side, out of things to say, holding hands like I was still very young and we were off walking together on some sunny afternoon. I didn't know how bad nightmares could be until that night, and even then I felt as if one Roy Joseph was moving out so another could move in. The child me is someone I can hardly remember.

A YEAR LATER a memorial service was held in the high school gym for my lost-at-sea, body-not-recovered brother. Tommy had been officially declared dead—a non-hostile casualty swallowed up by the Persian Gulf—and after so many unanswered prayers even Mom wanted nothing to do with a church by that point. The same woman who once told me that the more she learned about science, the more she believed in a Creator. And though the navy never gave us any reason to hope, and though by then we'd let go of any delusions Tommy might be found, my parents refused to call that service a funeral, not without any remains to bury. The nearest decent Lincoln Parish cemetery was in Ruston, about eight miles to the west, and we'd gone there the week before so they could choose a site for a memorial stone. They bought a plot in the shade of a grandfather water oak, then put a deposit down on three others adjacent. I probably wasn't supposed to hear that part, but Mom and Dad were living in such a trance in those days sometimes they seemed to forget I was around.

Like I said, a year of desperate, praying-for-a-miracle purgatory followed that visit from the Grim Reaper Corps before my parents gave up on the dream that Tommy, or at least his body, might ever come back to us, and his SEAL team platoon was stateside when we had the memorial service. The full thirteen had flown out to pay their respects, along with some senior officers and enlisted from the higher commands—and all of Dry Springs was in attendance, of course. There was a repast at our farm following the service, and though I should have stayed home with my parents, after the repast I caught a ride to a house across the highway from the Pilgrim's Pride chicken hatchery for another sad party.

The house belonged to an old classmate of Tommy's, and a number of those SEALs had come as well. I got the sense my big brother had been like *their* little brother—he would have easily been five years younger than most of the platoon—and I was sitting on a couch with two of them. One was a tree trunk of a guy from out west, the other had a Hispanic accent. They called him Rico. It seemed a lot of the SEALs went by nicknames, and earlier the big SEAL had told me and my parents that Tommy's had been Orion. He was steadily drinking. I think he might have been the only SEAL who was drinking, in fact. He was the biggest *and* the oldest, about thirty-five. School was his nickname, though once or twice I also heard someone call him Purcell, and after Rico left us for the bathroom he looked over at me. "I have to tell you something," he growled.

"Okay," I said, and he kept staring as I prepared for yet another adult to promise that everything happens for a reason, perhaps share some grief story of his own. Maybe even say that SEAL chant I'd been getting hammered with all day: You've lost a brother, kid, but you've gained a bunch of them too.

But no. "It wasn't just a helo crash," he said. "Well, it was, but it wasn't. Nah, he went out like a hero."

I was shy, but when I saw School was through talking I asked him what he meant. He said he'd spilled too much already, and as hard as it is for me to believe now, I must have screeched then, trying to squeeze more out of him. Tommy's Dry Springs buddies came over, doing their duty, angry that I seemed angry, but the SEALs were kind enough not to laugh at them. These were men, and these were professionals. They didn't make a hobby of fighting, and even School appeared to go from drunk to sober. It was a sight, watching them close ranks and be calm all at the same time. Level voices, thumbs in pockets, ready without looking ready— and that lack of posturing allowed Louisiana tempers to settle.

School and the rest of the SEALs pulled out for their Ruston hotel before I could throw any more questions his way, and I stayed at the house with the Dry Springs folk. Eventually a long-ago girlfriend of Tommy's convinced the others she was all right to drive me home, and in the car I told Camille what the man called School had said to me about Tommy's death. She just pet my brush cut and whispered, Try to put that away, sweetie. That's not gonna make you hurt any less.

Camille was twenty-one to my fourteen, knew more about the ways of the world, so I took those words of caution to heart, at least for a while. Still, I did think to find out School's real name. Camille dropped me off in front of my house at some graveyard-shift-at-the-chicken-hatchery hour, and after Mom finished fussing over me and went back to bed I opened the guestbook from the memorial service, flipping through pages until I hit upon the neat row of thirteen SEALs. Lionel Purcell. I wrote that down on my hand, but there was no need. It would stay burned in my brain from that day forward.

I DIDN'T REALIZE IT WAS LINGERIE NIGHT AT CARL'S Lounge until I walked through the door. To drum up business, on occasion the owner brought in these women to parade around in lingerie and act like they were hawking underwear. I wasn't in the mood for that, but there aren't so many boozing options in Grand Isle. I drank up at the bar for a while, and a skinny girl named Sierra had just come by to wave raffle tickets at me for the third time when someone called my phone. I saw PRIVATE NUMBER and lost my nerve. Yes, I'd written that e-mail, but I also hadn't expected things to happen right away.

"Wanna answer that?" Sierra asked.

I would say Sierra was in her twenties, but not by much. She was from Arabi—St. Bernard Parish—and wearing a red satin thing nearly the same color as her hair. Sometimes drinking can make me almost chummy. I said no, then told her all of it.

"Bad news," she said.

"So what should I do?"

"I'd buy more tickets." She bit down on her lip, twirled a finger in her Kool-Aid hair. She smelled of baby powder. "You sorta look like a guy in that pirate movie."

"Depp? I get that a lot."

"You wish."

"I watch a shit ton of movies. Errol Flynn? I get him too."

"Who? No. Just some dude rocking that same hack-and-whack you got going on. But your pirate isn't ugly. Take a compliment."

She had me marked as a pushover, another horny fool in off-shore Red Wings, but I'd been hoping for a sign and this would have to do. See, I only have a foggy window of boyhood recollections of my brother, and every year I lose more. In maybe my last one I'm twelve years old and we're stuck in a rainstorm together. And in the first, well, there are pirates. The family is in Disney World, and I'm as happy as I've ever been.

"Okay," I said. "Thanks for that." I passed Sierra a twenty, and she smiled. One of her lower canines had been capped in silver, so she was like a pirate herself. She tore four of the raffle tickets from the roll and tucked them into my jeans. I had a pocketful of them now.

"I don't think you need to ever talk to that girl," she said. "I never knew my daddy, and I never wanted to."

But a little later PRIVATE NUMBER called again, and by then I'd pulled myself together. I hurried to the parking lot and picked up. "Hello?" I said.

"Is this Roy Joseph?"

"Joni?"

"This is her mother."

They claim everyone, everywhere, has an accent. That saying a person has no accent is the same as saying a place has no climate. But the precise way that woman spoke did make me think of just such a sterile place. A white room with the thermostat set at seventy-five degrees.

"Are you still there?" she asked.

"Yeah." I walked over to the LeBaron and sat on the trunk.

"My daughter tells me she contacted you. You wrote her this evening?"

"That's right. Is this all some sort of put-on?"

"No, Mr. Joseph. Your brother and I weren't a couple, but yes, we slept together once. He was her father—her biological father."

In Dry Springs Tommy had done his fair share of dating. I'd always assumed he kept at that in the navy, and at thirteen I had been surprised when no Jane Doe surfaced to tell my family she'd lost the love of her life. But this was 2007. "Wait, please, back up," I said. "Just once?"

"We met at a party," she explained. "On the beach. He brought me home and left in the morning. That was all it was supposed to be. I never spoke to him again. But that January I discovered I was pregnant, then I saw on the news about his helicopter. After a lot of thought, I decided to have the baby."

"How old is she?" I'd already done the conception-to-birth math in my head, but I was trying to catch her in a lie.

"She turned sixteen this month."

That hit me like a crane block. September '07, less sixteen birthdays, and around nine months in the womb, would be December 1990. Right when Tommy had deployed. So it was at least possible. "And you're sure she's his?"

"Entirely. There was no one else."

"You're gonna have to prove it."

"Excuse me?"

"Anybody could call and say what you're saying."

"I'm not interested in proving anything to you, Mr. Joseph. And I only called because Joni is insisting." I heard her sigh into the phone. "I didn't mean for that to sound as rude as it did. My point is that we will be leaving you alone now, but please know how sorry we are for the loss of your brother."

"I'm not asking y'all to leave me alone. You really never knew him? Other than that one night?"

"No. No, I didn't. Not my finest hour. I couldn't even remember his last name until I saw his photograph on TV."

"And you're in San Diego?"

"At one time."

"And now?"

"I'd rather not reveal that."

"You won't tell me?"

"No."

I saw a man come stumbling from Carl's with a plastic cup in one hand and a broken cigarette in the other. He had his arms stretched out on either side of him like he was being crucified, and indeed—emaciated, bearded, chestnut hair down to his shoulders—he did resemble Jesus on the cross. Throw me in a Turkish prison, give me a year without scissors, a razor, a square meal, I'd be him.

"How'd you find me?" I asked.

She was quiet for a moment, but then she spoke. "Several months ago we hired someone to help us learn more about your brother, and that led us to you."

"Hired someone?" Jesus had spotted me on the trunk of the LeBaron and was now strutting my way. I tried to wave him off, but he kept coming toward me. He was piss drunk and clucking, making little chicken noises.

"An investigator."

I covered the phone with my bandaged hand and hollered at Jesus. "Come on," I said. "I'm talking here." He stopped about ten steps away and cocked his head, watching, but then I lobbed him one of my Winstons and he went wandering.

"Hello?"

"Hi. Sorry."

She continued. "That was something Joni really wanted. So it was for her—but, to be candid, I had my own concerns."

"Concerns?"

"Medical history. Whether there was anything I should be aware of for her sake, Mr. Joseph. Diseases, for example."

"I'm fine with Roy. Even if you're not gonna tell me *your* name."

"Okay."

"I guess your investigator found out about my parents?"

"He did. How horrible."

"And you learned all this but never called me. Why?"

I was pretty certain why, but she'd put me in one of my martyr moods, and I wanted to make her say sex offender. Or at least I thought I did. She started to speak, but I interrupted her.

"That happened a long time ago," I said. "The girl was in high school, but I was only nineteen myself. That doesn't make it all go away, but you should know how young I was too."

"It isn't necessary for us to discuss that. After you wrote Joni tonight she told me what she had done, and now she understands it was a mistake. I'm very sorry. You must be completely taken aback."

"Hundred percent."

"I'm sure. You have every right to your privacy. We won't be disturbing you again."

"Tommy, my parents, those deaths were all accidents." I didn't really have anything more to add, but I was attempting to keep her from bailing. "Though there is some medical stuff I should mention. Dad's dad passed not long after Tommy went missing, and after that the rest of my grandparents. Heart attacks across the board, I believe. All around age seventy."

"Heart disease, then?"

"I suppose. Mom and Dad didn't get on with their parents. I never even met them."

"I see. Well, that's—" She cleared her throat, and it was as if I could hear her thinking. "Is there anything else that might be important?"

"That was all I had insofar as family. No uncles, no aunts. But y'all already know that, don't you?"

"I should probably tell you good-bye now."

Then I realized something, and suddenly I was angry. "My mom and dad had a right to know they had a granddaughter, lady. That would've meant a lot to them." My voice was rising, but I couldn't stop. If what she was saying was true, for most of the six years my parents had lived after Tommy went, this girl had been out there. "That was a fucked-up thing to keep to yourself. How could you do that?"

The line went dead, and I looked across the parking lot. Jesus was over near Highway 1 watching cars cruise by. And though on some other night I might have gone over and steered him inside before he got clocked, on that night I was feeling selfish and low, and I left him standing there to fend for himself.

I STAYED ON AT CARL'S, drinking and stewing, and later, just as I was about to leave, I won a prize in the lingerie raffle. Sierra brought over a black lace nightie in a cardboard box. She'd changed into jeans and a T-shirt that fit her like a sock. "I made it so you'd win," she said. "Yep, yep. So you gotta tell me what happened to your hand."

She had asked me this already, but I'd told her I didn't want to talk about it. "Broken finger," I said now.

"Aw, poor baby." She looked around like she was making sure no one was eavesdropping on us. "You got a place? A real place? Not some fish camp in the marsh?"

"Real enough."

"ATM by the jukebox. Gimme ten more Jacksons, I'll make breakfast for you."

"I'm speaking to a cook?"

"Quit messing."

Every now and then, like maybe six times in the past decade— during the rowdiness of the annual Tarpon Rodeo, usually—I would find myself binging beside a flirtatious out-of-towner and we'd wind up in a bed together. But this business with Sierra, I had never really done anything like that before. I was her sucker, the chump she'd chosen to bleed dry, and cards were coming at me fast. Between the beers and the painkillers my thinking was off. *Here* was someone who didn't seem repulsed or frightened by me, so I summoned some cash and walked with her to the LeBaron.

PEARL LANE. SIERRA sat in one of my lawn chairs while I saw to Sam in his kennel, making sure he was set with food and water since he wouldn't be sleeping in the Airstream. He was four years old, around my age in dog years but a puppy in these moments still, realizing I had come home, and his whinings went from excited to wounded, shaming his jailer as I walked away.

When I got back Sierra started saying something about me taking a shower, but I wasn't too high on letting her out of my sight. Apparently she could see that. "I'm not planning to rob you," she said, standing. "Where am I gonna run?"

"It's not that."

"Then shower up. I'm not asking. I'm telling."

"I already had one today. I even shaved."

"So? Shower again. It's a new day today, anyways. Past midnight, Cinderella."

I pulled the door open, and she followed me inside. After I switched on the lights she shimmied onto the counter beside the sink, keeping herself hunched so her skull wouldn't rub against the ceiling.

"This ain't so awful," she said.

"Thanks." It was hot in the Airstream. I went by her and put the AC on at full blast.

"You got any music?"

I didn't have a CD collection or a stereo or such. They had

music stations with my satellite-television package, and that was enough. Classic country and classic rock. I usually went for one or the other, depending upon my mood. I handed Sierra the remote control. "Check out the up channels," I told her.

I made to kiss her then, but she turned her head. "Shower time," she said. "You gotta, baby." She slid off the counter and grabbed at my cheek. "Scrape those teeth too. But there's not gonna be any kissing."

"Really?"

"Really. That goes for any part of me, not just my mouth."

I still didn't love the idea of leaving her alone with my things, but I knotted plastic grocery bags over my bandaged hand and ducked into the bathroom, chomping on a toothbrush as I waited for the water to run warm. Soon my tile of a mirror began to fog, but I knew what I looked like. There are two basic cuts of roughneck—the neat-as-a-cat, military-esque type and the more unkempt, Roy Joseph sort—but, regardless, all of us who've been stinting long enough have the same weathered, high-mileage face. The same permanent squint.

I showered as quickly as I could while Sierra flipped around on the TV for a song she approved of. When I came out, rainy-haired and towel-wrapped, some boy-band tune was on and she was wearing the nightie I'd won. She had her own hair up in one fist like a bright red squid and was spinning in a slow circle. I threw the plastic bags in the trash, and she tossed me a condom from a pink backpack she'd brought along with her from Carl's.

"That's better," she said. "See?"

"I guess so."

She plucked at the steel vial of Panther Mound dirt hanging from the chain around my damp neck. "What you got in there? Bumps?"

"Dirt. Dirt from where I grew up." The vial had been threaded

to seize closed forever. I couldn't have unscrewed it even if I'd
wanted to.

"Dirt?"

"It's like a memento."

She frowned. She wasn't interested in that. "You swear to God?"

"That it's not coke? Yes. I swear to God."

"Too bad. Coke would get you kissed." She tugged at the towel
hitched to my waist, and I tried to stop her but she got it off.
"What's wrong? Stiffen up, limpy."

"Give me a second."

"Tick tock. There's no waking me once I fall asleep."

She let my towel drag behind her as she made for the bedroom
in the back. I followed, then sat on the bed when she began dancing again.

"You think you could just lie next to me?" I asked.

"That's how it works."

I gave the condom back to her. "And sleep, I mean. Just sleep.
Maybe let me hold you."

That stopped her. First she looked puzzled, but then she looked
pissed. Seeing that transformation play out was like watching a
snake coil up. "Listen here," she said. "I don't give no refunds."

"I'm not angling for one."

"You a fag or something?"

"No."

The nightie was too big for her, and one of the straps was
hanging off her shoulder. She relaxed, then shrugged. "When I
started doing this on the side everyone said that—that there'd be
dates who'd only wanna talk—but I ain't never seen it till now.
Congrats." She brushed at the other strap with her hand, and the
nightie dropped around her ankles. She was all bones and hard
edges. The AC had cooled the Airstream way down, and her
skin was splotchy and covered with goose pimples.

"I could maybe try," I said.

"Up to you. I'm happy not to get dripped on."

"But you'll stay?"

She collapsed behind me onto the bed, and I turned to look at her. She spoke into the space above her like some dying girl. "Fine. Hug on me, weirdo."

"I've just got a lot on my mind."

"That niecey, you mean. Did she call again?"

"Kind of. Earlier, back at the bar."

"Told you not to talk to her, dummy."

I lay down alongside Sierra, breathing her in, and after a few minutes of that I had a change of heart. I began to pull at myself with my good hand. My eyes were closed, but I could feel her watching. I heard a noise like cellophane crinkling, realized she was tearing at the condom wrapper. I opened my eyes.

"Oh well," she said. "You're looking ready now. Lucky, lucky me. You got lube here? I lost mine."

I shook my head.

"KY? Astroglide?"

"No."

"Great." She slipped the condom over me and fell back. The hair between her legs had been waxed away. "Let's go, but take it easy."

I crawled on top of her, and she grunted. "Sorry," I said. I got all the way inside, and her hip bones stabbed at me as we locked together. My bandage swiped across the headboard, and a shock of pain went racing up my arm. I flinched but kept on. "Is this okay?"

"Don't quiz me. Fuck me."

I don't know if it was from the drinking or the Vicodin or what, but I didn't feel anything at all. I pushed against her and pushed against her for song after song, and though I thought talking would maybe help me get finished, every time I'd speak

Sierra would order me to shut up. Finally she told me we had to quit.

"You pumped your money's worth," she said. "We're done."

THE NEXT MORNING Sierra left the Airstream wearing my raffle prize under an old long-sleeved work shirt I'd given her as well. The day was already on broil. Jack Hebert opened the door of his stilt-mounted trailer-in-the-sky and hollered down attaboy as Sierra and I walked to the LeBaron, his live-in sister-in-law, Tricia, smirking beside him. Tricia was a hairdresser in a past life. I'd pay her to trim my mop, shave my neck. Jack once told me they sometimes fooled around while Ada was off getting dialysis. Perfect neighbors for a guy like me.

I drove Sierra to the motel on Highway 1 where she said her crew of lingerie gypsies was staying. They toured around the parishes like that, hopping from dump to dump. I tried to talk to her, but she just stared out the window. She had scuffed heels on, and the rest of her clothes were in that pink backpack. She got out the LeBaron without saying good-bye, but I stayed parked there in the open. Like I wanted the whole island to know what I'd been at.

My mouth tasted like ashes, and I had a sour, empty stomach. It felt as if something was chewing on my brain. Dad had been a Catholic, but in name only. And though Mom raised her sons to be Methodists like her, after Tommy was taken from us our church-going came to an end. Still, I've always believed that somewhere Tommy is watching. My parents, too. I do a lot of shit I'd rather not have any of them see, but to believe otherwise would make my life unbearable. I'm lonely enough as it is. I used to feel certain a day had never passed without me missing Mom, Dad, Tommy, but eventually I saw enough sunsets to realize that couldn't be true. If heaven exists I'm sure the cloud-sitters smile at being remembered, but the truth is I forget the three of them plenty. There's a betrayal in that, of course. Maybe Joni's mother didn't want me in their lives, but this extended beyond the living. Tommy was dead at twenty, yet in my head he will forever be older and wiser and braver than me, his odd little brother. Parked outside that motel, I asked the question I'd avoided asking ever since I'd read Joni's e-mail—Tommy, what do you want me to do?

So I drove from Sierra to the Cybermobile and typed another e-mail to Joni:

> I spoke to your mother, and I'm glad y'all found me. I'm willing to trust you, and I thank you for reaching out. If you ever want to write me or call me, you do that. We don't have to kill this unless that's what YOU choose.

A T THE TIME OF MY ACCIDENT ON THE LORANGER
Avis, I was at least secure in the knowledge that
I would be a rich man fairly soon. I'm not talk-
ing about the injury. Since, for a roughneck, no disability could
be attributed to the loss of a pinkie, I suspected I'd only bank ten
to fifteen grand once I got around to filing my comp claim. No,
my forthcoming fortune would be the result of people dying too
young. I'd be a tragedy tycoon.

My parents had hired a personal financial specialist after
Tommy's death was finally made official, a backslapping guy
from over in Ruston. Donny Lee Scott, CPA/PFS. Sort of an
accountant/adviser, Mr. Donny Lee helped them pool my brother's savings with the quarter million or so they received in death
benefit and life insurance payouts, said he'd handle everything
until they were ready to retire from teaching at the high school.
Five years went by, then in '97 they died. I was a spring-semester
freshman at LSU when a grief counselor knocked on the door
of my dorm room. The guy told of a slick bridge and a flipped
car and a deep creek, and then he tried to hug me. How do you
describe how it feels to have everyone taken from you? To have
no family left? To have no one to share the pain with except a
fucking grief counselor? I won't even try.

I was devastated, wet-faced and sucking for air, yet there was also a flicker of something else beneath that crushing pain. Something I'm ashamed to admit, but here it is: at nineteen years old I also felt a stunned sense of relief. My parents were the kindest of people. I'd seen them destroyed by losing Tommy, and I didn't realize until right then in that cube of a dorm room that, ever since, I'd been living with only one real goal—just don't let yourself die before they do, Roy. They've had enough hurt.

AS FOR MY OWN HURT, responsibilities called. There was nothing for me to do but stand up and stagger forward, so I dropped out of LSU and moved home to Dry Springs. Everything my parents left behind went to me, and I finished out that spring on the farm, sleeping and drinking and crying, boxing up things little by little, selling equipment and livestock and whatnot as I prepared to put the place on the market at some point. Our Catahoula, Rocky, soon vanished into the coyote pinewoods, wandered off as if searching for Mom and Dad, and after buyers came to trailer away our four Beefmaster steers, then a trio of Duroc hogs, all I had to keep me company was a pride of half-feral, unnamed barn cats and a coop full of chickens.

But then, as summer came on during that bad year, a sturdy brunette girl in a softball jersey rode up to the house on a quarter horse. Eliza Sprague. She was balancing a pan of lasagna on her wide thigh.

"No one ever sees you," she said. "They're worried all you're eating is eggs."

"Who's worried?"

"Everyone."

"So they sent you?"

"I sent me." Eliza's round face was pancaked with makeup, and she was staring at the beer in my hand. "Think I could have one?" she asked. And instead of just taking the lasagna from her I invited her inside.

I didn't know Eliza well. For most of my life she'd been the pigtailed kid on the school bus who lived one dirt road over from mine off the highway. She was in high school now, but though I wish I could claim she was sixteen going on thirty or some such, that's not really true. She was sixteen and looked it, and nineteen is nineteen. I get that, and it seemed that way even when, eyes glistening, she dared me to kiss her a couple of beers later. That was before I let my hair become ratty, before I started hiding my own face behind patchy stubble for days at a time. Despite the depressed darkness of that summer I was still trying to look like Navy Tommy back then. Clean-cut, a bit of a pretty boy, to be honest. But due mostly to my shyness I'd also not yet managed to shuck my virginity.

All I can really say is I wanted her. That the hot months in Dry Springs could kill you with boredom. That I was out of my mind. Tommy made SEAL and died serving his country by twenty. Went out like a hero, according to Lionel Purcell. Me, at nineteen I had quick and clumsy sex with a minor.

From then on Eliza would often ride by after her parents left for work. We only let it happen all the way between us a few more times, and on each occasion I swore that would be the end of that. But maybe I also thought the universe owed me something in return for all my hardships. That's a dangerous line of thinking, and one August morning Eliza was standing in my kitchen, sobbing and telling me she was pregnant. She asked me to pray with her, but the dominoes fell swiftly. There was an ugly scene with her parents, then an abortion in Shreveport I didn't learn about until after the fact.

It was all supposed to have been kept a secret, but Dry Springs never did too well with those. Still, my brother had made the town proud by dying, and Mom and Dad had put in a lot of years at the high school. For those reasons the Lincoln Parish D.A. had been willing to look the other way, but Eliza's parents were out for my head once everyone knew their business. The D.A. dragged his feet until December, but when the Spragues refused to forgive me, neither could the state.

Door number one: Cop to a single felony count of carnal knowledge of a juvenile in exchange for probation and, for the ensuing ten years, registration as a sex offender with local authorities, but no prison spell.

Door number two: Stand trial and risk being hauled to some gladiator camp.

My public defender struck the plea deal. I pulled six years of probation (two supervised, four unsupervised) and was marked down as a felon and a sex offender—and with that finalized I figured I should hurry up and split Dry Springs. That same week I rented a storage unit in Ruston and emptied out the rest of the house, and when I turned twenty that January I had the farm sold. I signed half the proceeds check and all my inheritance, as well as both payouts from my parents' life insurance policies, over to Mr. Donny Lee to transform into an "investment portfolio." I wanted nothing to do with that blood money yet, and since thirty seemed like a nice, round, far-off age to a twenty-year-old, and the first new millennium birthday I'd be celebrating free and clear of Louisiana's sex offender laws and conditions, I asked if he could grow it for me until then. Mr. Donny Lee assured me he could indeed, said if I'd really let him tie that money up he'd make me a millionaire.

Don't rush the monkey and you'll get a better show, sonny. Just mind where you stick your pecker for a decade, and let's see what that century brings.

Then, because I knew it was what my parents would have wanted, I phoned LSU about starting up again in Baton Rouge following the winter break—but the university wouldn't let a threat like me re-enroll. I was to be suspended pending the outcome of a student conduct hearing, and that first spit in the face, that first taste and dawning of how the world was going to treat a registered sex offender, left me terrified. Baton Rouge was the only place other than Lincoln Parish I'd ever lived. I wanted to run, yet I had nowhere to go except a Ruston hotel.

But one night, eating dinner alone at a Burger King, dreaming up escape fantasy after escape fantasy, I saw an ad in the *Daily Leader*. OFFSHORE VACANCIES: TERRIFIC PAY! NO EXPERIENCE NECESSARY! The ad was by a drilling company down in Terrebonne Parish, and I had a what-the-hell moment. Anything different seemed good at that juncture, and demand must have been high because they called me in. I was given a physical and had my back x-rayed, pissed in a cup and got hired on as a roustabout. Next, I found a landlord in the bad end of Houma greedy enough to rent to my type, and three weeks later I boarded the crew boat in Grand Isle that would take me to my inaugural rig.

Grand Isle is the sole inhabited barrier island in the state, a seven-mile cigarette of terra firma connected to the mainland by the Highway 1 bridge over Caminada Pass. To a pinewoods, north Louisiana native Grand Isle felt like a lost colony, a hidden secret I'd heard about but never seen. And at the end of that maiden stint, on the hour-plus drive back to the month-to-month apartment in Houma, exhausted and aching but feeling like a man, I found myself missing the island. The sunrises and sunsets that scorched the horizon, the varnished sleekness of the dolphins feeding just beyond the surf, even the baby cries of gulls harassing shrimp boats. Apparently I was a water person without ever having known it, and after a few more stints I decided to simplify things. Not quite everything had been passed along to Mr. Donny Lee, and I used some of what farm-sale money I'd pocketed to lease the lot on Pearl Lane—then to purchase, from a dentist in Thibodaux, a twenty-five-foot 1988 Airstream Excella. This had been his tailgating trailer for LSU games, but he told me he was looking to upgrade to an RV for football Saturdays. The LeBaron was useless for towing, and though the dentist wanted ninety-five hundred for the Airstream, wouldn't come off that price any, he was willing to haul it down to Grand Isle for me.

So the boy whose father once gave him a metal vial came to live in a metal vial. When I moved to Grand Isle—and before that, to Houma—the superintendent of the parish school district, as well as every residence and business within about a quarter mile of my new address, received a postcard from the state of Louisiana introducing me to my neighbors. Community notification. A thing like that will quiet any wanderlust in a man, and Grand Isle appeared to be as good a spot as any to pretend, at least for the ten years ticking away on my pariah clock, that no other worlds existed.

Such is the allure of living on islands, I suppose. Eventually I was bumped up from roustabout to roughneck, but on account of my record I was doubtful I'd ever rise any higher. Two weeks of breaking my back on a rig for about 3K a stint, to start; two weeks of no-paycheck rest and recovery in Grand Isle. The pretty boy evolving now, his features becoming drawn and wolfish and worn. He is never not red-eyed and tired, this sunned and sinewy man.

THE YEARS WENT BY, then in the fall of 2003 I saw a puppy frolicking on the side of Highway 1. A duck dog—a purebred, and neutered, yellow Lab from the looks of him. He was four months old or so, and since he was the kind of dog assholes might steal, I figured I'd better grab him out of the puddle he was splashing around in. He wasn't wearing a collar, and they didn't have a pound on the island, but I stopped by the police station to tell the chief I had someone's pet. I was the only registered and reporting sex offender among the fifteen hundred residents of Grand Isle, so the chief knew me well, made a point of staring me down every time we crossed paths. I always hated talking to the man, usually tried my best to avoid him, but the last thing I needed was to get pinched for a puppy theft.

Still, a week passed without anybody ringing to claim Sam—I'd already started calling him that—then the day came for me to go back offshore. Jack Hebert said (for a neighborly fee, of course) he'd watch him for me, and while I was on stint I began to hope that bungling Lab pup would be waiting when I got back. And he was. But that wasn't fair to Sam really, being stuck with me. He was never meant to chase tennis balls on Pearl Lane. He was born to spend cold and rainy mornings in a marsh blind, retrieving shotgunned teal and wigeon, gadwall and pintail. I was a hunter once, growing up that was maybe my favorite thing to do, but it wouldn't be until 2013 before the law might allow felon me to own a gun again, and whenever I threw a ball for Sam I was reminded of that. Made me feel like I had been neutered myself, not being able to take my hunting dog hunting, but at least I could give him somewhere to stay. Pearl Lane. The Airstream.

I'd torn out the stained carpets and put in hardwood floors that matched the Airstream's oak cabinets and paneling, then replaced the twin mattresses in the bedroom with a pillow-top full. Over time I bought new curtains and cushions, a better AC and a microwave and a TV, a DVD player and satellite television and a couch. I kept things more than tidy—constantly vacuuming and sweeping and mopping, polishing and dusting—and I would give the aluminum hull a monthly bath to prevent it from corroding. I had received permission to pour a concrete foundation out back for a shed that housed a washer/dryer and a hot-water heater, my tools and ice chests and so on. And later, after Sam joined me, I set up the chain-link kennel and a doghouse on a side slab. My sewage, gas, and electric were tied in with the town systems, but I could be ready to roll in a snap. Ahead of

Katrina and then Rita, as well as a number of hurricanes and storms before those bitch sisters, Malcolm drove down in his pickup and bailed me out, towing the Airstream to his deer lease near St. Francisville while I followed after him in the LeBaron. Otherwise, to ensure the moving parts stayed in working order, each spring I'd grease the wheel bearings and negotiate with Jack Hebert for the use of his F-250, then make a trip to Lake Claiborne in north Louisiana, one of the few places other than Grand Isle where I could feel anything like peace. I would spend an April week there before turning back, and on my last whip-poorwill night at the lake I'd always empty a can of RC into its dark waters to mark Tommy's birthday.

The secret to living well in a trailer is in not letting posses-sions pile up on you. I bought my groceries one bag at a time at the Sureway, and each Christmas any pair of shoes or piece of clothing I hadn't worn in a year got boxed and left on the door-step of this church or that church, me playing Santa whether the congregation wanted castoffs from Roy Joseph or not. Two plates, two forks, two glasses, etc. That's the discipline it takes, and for a long while that suited me. Life stayed simple, and as I waited for my thirtieth birthday—January 4, 2008, my windfall—I just ac-cepted that, until then, I could do a whole lot worse than simple. After my six years of probation wrapped I could have left Loui-siana, tried to find a more lenient, forgiving state, or even some foreign country, where I could avoid having to continue pervert-reporting annually with the police. And I'm not sure why I never did exactly that. Maybe because I was settled in Grand Isle and working. Maybe because Louisiana was the devil I knew.

So I was biding my time, but I still had that storage unit. Though I stayed clear of Dry Springs, every April, on my way to Lake Claiborne, I'd pass through Ruston and go by Peach City Self Storage to check on my survivor spoils. I assumed one day I'd want at least some of what I was holding on to. The family photos and a lot of the furniture, sure—but also Mom's homemade quilts and framed Audubon prints, Dad's coffee tins full of musket balls and Caddo arrowheads, Tommy's yard-sale pedestal globe and the flag America traded us for him.

I'll always remember what I was thinking on that helicopter ride to Lady of the Sea. Hang in there, I was telling myself. You're not quite thirty yet, but in three months your scarlet letter can be burned, and in four months, yes, happy birthday, you'll be an honest-to-God millionaire. You can start a new life in some new place.

And though I hadn't decided where that new place would be, there was one thing I did know for certain about my future. That I was finally through with the oil patch. I was done. Retired. They took my finger, but they wouldn't take me.

CONVALESCENCE. HEALING, ONE-HANDED DAYS spent hoping Joni would resurface. Almost every night, the same nightmare. I'm bleeding on the Loranger Avis, but this time no one can help me. I am pale and then dizzy and then dead. A doctor had warned me anxiety and even flashbacks wouldn't be uncommon after such an injury, but I'd made it to twenty-nine without going down the therapy-and-Prozac rabbit hole, and I was afraid to start now.

Then, October. I was asleep in the Airstream and never heard my phone ring, but in the morning I saw a missed, 2 A.M. call from an area code I didn't recognize. Nearly two weeks had elapsed since I wrote that e-mail to Joni behind her mother's back, the short note urging her to get in touch with me if she wanted. To the Cybermobile. I reverse-searched the number on a white pages site and found out it belonged to a San Francisco cell phone, then $4.95 on my credit card bought me a person. Nancy Hammons. But "Joni" might have been an alias, I realized. Then again, Nancy Hammons might be the mother. Maybe she hadn't said all she wanted to say to me. Or maybe it *was* Joni who called, but her phone was in Mother Nancy's name. Or maybe it was only a misdial.

I hardly knew more than a fence post about social networks,

but there were MySpace and Facebook accounts for a lives-in-San-Francisco Joni Hammons. The profile pictures were just of a sunset, or a sunrise, and security locks excluded outsiders and the uninvited. But I was like Sam on a scent trail by that point, and though I didn't find anything else encouraging for *"Joni Hammons" San Francisco* online, *"Nancy Hammons" San Francisco* brought better luck, some credible hits. I learned there was a Nancy Hammons who taught poetry at San Francisco State and had published a few books of poems. That a Nancy Hammons ran lots of Bay Area 5Ks. That, as a concerned parent (a concerned "single" parent, in fact), a Nancy Hammons had once written a letter to the *San Francisco Chronicle* complaining about budget cuts affecting George Washington High School. Then, eureka. She mentioned her daughter Joni in that letter—horrifying the teenager, I'm sure, but abetting me. An English department faculty page and a literary journal's website both led me to the same photo. This Nancy Hammons seemed to be in her later thirties, just as Tommy would have been, and had boy-short hair dyed to an extreme blond. Attractive, but in a leave-me-the-fuck-alone way. I typed *Nancy Hammons* and *San Francisco* into the white pages site, and that gave me a phone number and address for a house on a street named Marvel Court.

After that phone call—maybe from Nancy Hammons, maybe from Joni Hammons—I waited for someone to write or call me again. Joni was pretty much all I could think about, but I didn't know what else to do. I could have tried that cell phone or Marvel Court number and pled my case to mother and/or daughter, but what if they told me to leave them be? What move would I have left then? But I wasn't beaten yet. I had her last name, and I had her address. And thanks to my lost finger I had the free time. If Joni wouldn't come to me—if she was through with e-mailing and calling, that is—maybe I could come to her.

First, however, I had to find out a few things about California law. As best I could deduce, as a nonresident, visiting registered sex offender, RSO Roy Joseph would be required to register locally, or at a minimum report to a police station to be "assessed and cleared" should I remain in any California city or county for more than five "working" days. So I could have one week in San Francisco without being notched and branded. Five working days, plus a Saturday and a Sunday, to locate Joni and meet her. And though by the middle of December I wouldn't have to worry about such legal bullshit in Louisiana or anywhere else, December was too far away to wait on. That missed phone call had revved an engine that must have been idling quietly inside me, and I didn't want second thoughts and excuses to shut me down. As soon as my hand was healed, my post-op appointments through, I had to solve the mystery of this supposed niece of mine—even if that meant sidestepping Nancy Hammons.

Go, Tommy whispered in that smooth voice of his. Go.

YEARS BACK, once I'd gained an appreciation of the Internet and its capabilities, every so often I would try looking for Navy SEAL Lionel "your brother went out like a hero" Purcell on the computers in Grand Isle's pre-Cybermobile library. And in 2003 I was directed to a crude, slapdash website. Apparently someone by that same name ran a guide service out of Battle Mountain, Nevada. I scrolled through photographs of hunters with bloody-mouthed antelope and mule deer, and then I saw him. Older and heavier than the SEAL I'd met when I was fourteen, but even behind the gunslinger mustache I could tell it was him. He was sitting astride a collapsed buck and frowning at the camera. There was an e-mail address, but I could never get past the idea that writing Lionel Purcell might result in him doing some *where has life taken that guy?* sleuthing of his own. Orion's little brother, the sex offender. Not too long after I first came across the website it disappeared, and I took that as a warning I should remember what Tommy's old sweetheart Camille had told me way back when about how some things are best left alone.

But then Joni happened. That e-mail of hers couldn't have been easy to send, and I felt ashamed for having put Lionel Purcell on the shelf. He knew things, and if a teenager could be brave enough to hunt for news of Tommy, I could do the same. I imagined Joni would be asking a lot of questions if and when I found her, and I wanted to be able to give her more than my foggy boyhood memories of my brother. The Battle Born Outfitters website was still missing, but I pulled a map up and finished hatching my plan—on the drive to California I'd stray north, then take I-80 west to Battle Mountain. I would stop there and see what came of it. Nothing perhaps, but at least I could tell Joni I'd tried turning that rock over. Eventually I would need to find a place to stay in San Francisco, yet that could wait. I just wanted to be on the highways that would begin taking me to Nevada and Lionel Purcell, California and Joni Hammons. And with all that decided, those bleeding-out-on-the-Loranger-Avis nightmares came to an end.

THE LEBARON WAS A MAROON '94 model with over two hundred thousand miles on the odometer, but she'd also been a gift from my parents and that had made her hard to part with. The frame was well rusted due to the salt of Grand Isle, and there was a gray patch on the center of the hood where the paint had burned away from the primer. Counting on the LeBaron to get me all the way to Nevada, much less California, was a gamble, but I reckoned if I was meant to ever reach either place I'd make it okay.

Though, before that, north Louisiana. In Ruston:

A raid on Peach City Self Storage to grab a photo album I wanted to bring to San Francisco with me.

A dutiful-son appearance at the Joseph plots in Oak Crest Cemetery.

A face-to-face, state-of-my-finances meeting with accountant/adviser Mr. Donny Lee. Assuming Mr. Donny Lee had no surprises for me, in January I'd be thirty years old and rich and no longer an RSO. After San Francisco I intended to take the quickest and easiest route back to Grand Isle, then spend the next two months preparing for the beyond-Louisiana place where I could begin my third act.

And the drive to Ruston would take me past the exit for Dry Springs. I'd avoided Dry Springs altogether since my exile, but now I would make my return. Already I was recalling things I hadn't mulled over in years. What it had been like to help my parents take apart Tommy's bedroom. What it had been like for me to take apart theirs. The guilt I'd felt when I sold. Those first lines from my mother's journal, the two sentences I couldn't read past—words buried somewhere in my storage unit. *To be a parent is to always wonder whether the world sees your children the way you see them. My son is gone.*

The farm was the only real home Tommy or I had ever known. And though in some ways the thought of visiting Dry Springs had me feeling more uneasy than pondering Battle Mountain or even San Francisco did, it was an embarrassment that I hadn't been there in ten years. My brother was whispering to me again. Go, Roy. See, feel, learn. Before the month was out the stump on my left hand was fully healed, covered by an itchy patch of marbled skin, and I crossed over Caminada Pass at dawn on an October Thursday, Sam lying beside me on the LeBaron's bench seat like a roll of yellow rug, some clothes and a sleeping bag stuffed into my offshore duffel bag.

Sam slept and I drove, following the Highway 1 two-lane through the low, chartreuse and khaki sponge-lands of flat marsh and open water between Grand Isle and Leeville. On shell and asphalt shoulders, families fishing blue crab and redfish, five-gallon buckets and tailgates and folding chairs, thawed chicken necks and soggy shrimp, popping corks and cast nets, jean shorts and rubber boots, white people and black people and more, the last names often the same or similar save for the Vietnamese over three decades here now, refugees like me, all of them close enough to blow a wake of hot wind over as I rocketed past in the LeBaron, the phone and the radio and the thoughts of my maybe niece and of Tommy and of a SEAL called School all distractions threatening to make me slip from the road and become a sideswiping killer of fishermen. And when others speak of Louisiana as backwater or third-world they usually mean places like these, places that are falling, sinking, eroding into the suck of slinking salt waters, and nowhere as badly or as quickly as the fading fifteen crow-fly miles between my island and the harder ground that finally appeared after the Bayou Lafourche lift bridge. All that was behind me would one day be gone. The marsh, the highway, Grand Isle. But I was safe now. Acadiana. Some trees. Oaks, even. Commerce and industry and telephone-pole signs. INJURED OFFSHORE? . . . I BUY GARFISH . . . PROP REPAIR. Homes and businesses and solid ground, yes, but now that dark bayou to follow as well. Diesel rainbows, eddies of foamed trash. Ahead: Golden Meadow, Galliano, Cut Off, Larose, then another big bridge. The crossing of the Intracoastal. Agriculture, sugarcane. The backwater becoming a banana republic here. Some of the farmers burning their fields preharvest. The land all around me on fire and smoking.

PART II

The Road Notes

*Stand by your brother, for he who is brotherless is like
the fighter who goes to battle without arms.*

—ARAB PROVERB

WEST OF NEW ORLEANS SAM AND I QUIT THE highways for the interstates. I-55 took us up to Hammond, and we left crawfish and boudin and the Catholic majority behind. In Louisiana you drive north to get South, trading Cajun Country for Dixie somewhere just below here—in Ponchatoula, maybe Manchac—and we were in the hardpan pinewoods now, sweet tea and barbeque country, Bible Belt towns that looked and felt like the Dry Springs I remembered.

In Tangipahoa Parish, three enormous white crosses in a dairy pasture, and billboard after billboard. AIDS: JUDGMENT DAY HAS COME . . . ORIENTAL SPA AND MASSAGE: TRUCKERS ENCOURAGED! Then, gas in Kentwood, where a sign welcomed me to THE HOME OF BRITNEY SPEARS. For over a year Malcolm had us believing her mom gave him a Jesus-camp hand job once, back when Britney was still a Mouseketeer. A lie, but a good lie. The interstate again. Into Mississippi. We passed a caravan of dove hunters on their way to rain lead onto sunny fields of sorghum and millet. Two retrievers were slithering in the bed of a Ford, jockeying for the best wind, while a third sat stone still and watched me and Sam go by. A black Lab staring at us like a dog of war.

IT WAS A BIT PAST NOON when I hit Jackson and hooked onto I-20, and forty miles later I arrived in Vicksburg, on the east bank of the Mississippi River. Vicksburg is across the bridge from the upper part of Louisiana, lies along the usual route I'd take each April to call on Lake Claiborne with the Airstream. Tomorrow I'd be in Dry Springs and then Ruston, and though I'd never spent the night in Vicksburg before, this was a good place to break for the day. I hadn't made it very far, but the most necessary step, actually leaving, had been accomplished.

I checked into a hotel near the interstate. I had an ice chest filled with dry dog food in the trunk, as well as another containing tennis balls and towels and pet shampoo, bowls and a few jugs of water, and once Sam was situated I sat down on the bed in our room. But I wasn't tired yet. I wanted out. I needed to come up with something to help eat away the hours, and in Vicksburg that meant either the casino boats or the military park—site of the forty-seven-day siege of that fortress city on the Mississippi. Pemberton had ridden beyond the works to meet with Grant under an oak soon to be butchered by souvenir-seeking soldiers, then surrendered on the Fourth of July, one day after Lee retreated from Gettysburg. "The Father of Waters again goes unvexed to the sea," said Lincoln. I get no thrill from stabbing at a draw-to-deal button on a video poker machine, so I had a hamburger and a beer in the hotel restaurant before driving off for Civil War parkland.

If it was my mother who taught me the most about science and nature, it was my father who taught me about history. When Tommy was a boy Dad used to take him to Vicksburg, and after Tommy got too teenage cool for those trips it was my turn. My father loved exploring that park, at least until the sad times came, and there was one spot in particular he always brought me—a big grassy hill on Confederate Avenue. All through the park the states that had troops at Vicksburg erected separate monuments in memory of their fallen soldiers, and atop that hill I could see Louisiana's memorial to its cannon fodder. An eighty-foot column of granite crowned with a carved-stone flame.

I left the LeBaron and hiked to the top of the hill. It was well into October, but still fairly hot outside. I was breathing heavy from the climb, wearing jeans and my Red Wings because I almost always wear jeans and my Red Wings, and a T-shirt was pasted flat to my back. I looked around and saw black vultures or maybe turkey buzzards circling off to the west. This seemed to be the highest point in the entire brother-against-brother park. Good ground, those dead generals might have called the hill, same as Cemetery Ridge. You'd think there would be a constant breeze in such a high place, but there wasn't, not on that day.

A slice of shade had sundialed out from the monument, and I stood within that long shadow and lit a cigarette. My head started to spin, but I kept smoking. Another drag and I gagged. I dropped the Winston and pressed my hand against the monument to steady myself. The granite was warm, and my eyes focused on where stone met grass. Much of that cut rock lay underground, hidden like the substructure of an oil rig beneath the surface of the Gulf.

I stayed that way, nauseous and propped up by a memorial stone, until I heard someone yell. I turned to look. A platoon of after-school Boy Scouts was charging the hill. I wiped the spit from my lips and watched them come. A dozen or more boys with bright, beautiful, wiseass faces like Tommy's. All of them running, all of them attacking.

AFTER THE MILITARY PARK I walked Sam back and forth on the hotel's parched kidney of lawn. I was obsessing over what my north Louisiana tomorrow might bring, and I took a nap that brought the first dream, good *or* bad, I'd had in weeks. Instead of the Loranger

Avis, instead of a nightmare, I'm on the farm in Dry Springs. Four riders on four horses are moving across our land, waving as they come, and though I am apart from them and watching I think they are us, the Josephs, my family. That there are two versions of me. One who carries on, and this one who waits.

So, not a nightmare—more like something inside me was in fact trying to fix itself while I'd been sleeping. Or maybe I just woke before things could get ugly. It was nine o'clock when I opened my eyes, and I swapped my T-shirt for an oxford, then went by the front desk to ask where I might still be able to find a decent dinner. A girl with a canary-yellow handkerchief tied around her neck was working the counter, and she was somehow both freckled and tan. Besides the casino boats, all she had to recommend was a place downtown that had charbroiled steaks. She scratched out directions. "But you should hurry, sir," she said. "Have a blessed evening."

Downtown was quiet and had the stepping-back-in-time, movie-set look of many a downtown in my reconstructed South. A look that suggested it had once been prosperous and flourishing, but long ago withered. Still, Vicksburg's seemed to be doing better than most, and that was probably due to the money and the people those casinos brought in. A portion of downtown had been cleaned up, restored, and along the brick-paved and lamppost-lit main drag there were closed-for-the-night antique shops and art galleries, that sort of thing. Riverboat gambling, the answer to all our problems.

The steak restaurant I was searching for sat on the river side of the street, and I was able to park at the curb. The hostess did her best to smile when I came in, but I could tell her heart wasn't in it. That her thoughts were on the punch clock already. Her name tag said Mindy, and she could have been the cousin of the girl at the front desk of my hotel. I envisioned their common ancestor, an Irish cotton buyer.

"One?" she asked.

"Yeah. Sorry. I know I'm pushing it." There was a bar in the back, and a black man with wild white hair was washing glasses at the sink. I pointed at him. "Can I just eat up there?"

Mindy dealt me a menu from the stack on her podium. She seemed relieved. "Absolutely," she said, before sliding around me to flip the sign on the door. "Mr. Charlie will take good care of you."

I made my way to the bar and settled onto a stool. The bartender Mr. Charlie dried his hands slowly with a towel, but he didn't acknowledge me. He was staring off into space while I read through the menu. "All right, then," I said. "Hi."

Mr. Charlie was wearing a black bow tie and vest, a white shirt, and had a flat boxer's nose. He looked exhausted. He was too old to be up that late, much less tending a bar. "You ready?" he asked.

On the Gulf rigs Tuesdays and Saturdays are steak night. Friday, seafood. But I was a free man now, could eat steak whenever I wished. "So I guess I'll have that T-bone," I said. "Medium rare, please. And I can pass on the salad."

"It's free."

"I don't want to keep you any longer than I have to."

"Naw. What dressing you like? Italian?"

"Sure. I appreciate it."

Mr. Charlie took the menu and went into the kitchen. When he came back he put the salad in front of me. I thanked him again and asked for a double bourbon and an ice water.

He started to grab a whiskey glass but then stopped himself. "ID?" he said.

Jack Hebert's sister-in-law/concubine Tricia hadn't put blades to me since before the Loranger Avis—my hair was to my eyebrows, halfway past my ears and lapping at my collar—so I lifted my bangs off my forehead so Mr. Charlie could truly see me. My squinting roughneck face. "Come on, sir," I said. "I'm just about thirty."

He shrugged. "That's a kid to this gramps. I don't take chances no more."

I almost told him to forget the bourbon, but finally I pulled out my wallet. I handed him my driver's license, and his eyes jumped when he saw the SEX OFFENDER printed in orange letters under my photo. A recent development. Nearly every year the Louisiana legislature came up with some new degradation, and as of 2006 I had a pervert driver's license to go along with the sex offender identification card I was required to always have on my person. They love me at the DMV.

I got my well bourbon and my ice water, but Mr. Charlie fixed them in silence. I asked him to just go ahead and box up the T-bone when it was ready, and he disappeared into the kitchen. There was a TV behind the bar. I watched an NFL week-in-review while I picked at my salad, all my appetite gone. The Saints had beaten the Falcons in the Dome on Sunday, but that only put them at two and four for the season. The Saints. It was heartbreak every year with them.

After a while Mr. Charlie brought the T-bone, then he took my money and returned to the kitchen, still playing the mime. Mindy was gone as well, and I stepped out onto the sidewalk with my steak, looked left and right down the street. The LeBaron was the only car around, but I thought I heard music. I glanced up. There were speakers fastened atop the cast-iron lampposts that lined both sides of the road, and I walked into the middle of the street and listened. It was calliope music. The paddleboat and circus kind. Those lamppost speakers seemed like something the government would install in anticipation of a disaster, a way to help calm the masses and keep them from rioting. In a deserted downtown that campy music was eerie as hell, made me think the world had ended while I'd been inside. That the four riders from my dream had actually been the horsemen of the apocalypse. I drove to the hotel, and that was the night I first called Viktor Fedorov.

VIKTOR FEDOROV was an international marriage broker. He also owned a car service. Years back, long before Joni's e-mail, I'd learned of him from the captain of one of the crew boats that sometimes motored me to and from certain rigs. Captain Terry had a Russian wife who was a celebrity among us hands. Larissa was her name. She would always see Terry off from the dock—often making her the last flesh-and-blood female we'd lay eyes on for two weeks—and I'm sure I wasn't the only one who kept a mental picture of her filed away for the shower. I'm not saying Larissa was a goddess (fried blond hair, old-world teeth), but she was definitely out of Terry's league. Some of the guys had taken to calling her the Coke Bottle on account of her figure, and what always ate at me most was when, returning to Grand Isle at the end of a stint, I'd spot her waiting along Bayou Rigaud for Terry. There I'd be with nothing to look forward to but Sam and my empty Airstream, now stuck having to think on rat-faced Terry getting to go home with a woman. Another reminder that a matrimony of any sort might be forever out of the question for me.

But, to his credit, Terry wasn't shy about the truth behind that marriage of his. There's this Viktor out in San Francisco, he told me on the crew boat one day. Viktor runs a first-class operation. None of that mail-order-bride bullshit. No flying all the way to an ass-fuck corner of Russia to meet a roomful of white-slave farm girls. Viktor matches his clients up with gals already here on work visas. Intelligent, pretty gals like Larissa. Women who know the language. Women who will ink a prenup and are less likely to get homesick. Sure, she's in it for the permanent visa, but everybody wants something out of a marriage.

Terry was aware of my past, of course. He knew the reason I lived half of each month offshore, the other half holed up on Pearl Lane. The reason I had few friends and kept so much to myself. The reason why on occasion I'd receive anonymous letters warning me to leave Grand Isle. But Viktor will work with you, Terry assured. Just be up front, because the feds will be checking on that if y'all make it to the marriage-visa stage. Full disclosure for foreign brides. That's the law these days, Roy.

Indeed, Terry knew so much about the law it made me wonder about *his* past. At the time I'd told him I wasn't interested—but now I was bound for San Francisco, and I was feeding most of a twenty-five-dollar steak to Sam inside that Vicksburg hotel room, lonely and depressed, when one Terry story rose up in bits from the dark depths of my memory. Something about a homeless guy who challenged him to a footrace through Golden Gate Park. Town's like a cereal bowl, Terry had said to me. Fruits and nuts and flakes.

Except for the Russian who'd introduced him to Larissa, that is. Terry could have been president of his fan club. And though in Grand Isle we made our share of cracks about Terry and the Coke Bottle, I'd seen something once that came bubbling to the surface next. They were parked in Terry's truck at the Sureway. I couldn't hear what they were saying, but Larissa was laughing, flashing the new braces on her tangled teeth, and there was nothing fake about it. They were happy. And alone in my hotel room, I wanted that too. Suddenly the coincidence of Terry's marriage broker and Joni both being in San Francisco felt almost like a sign.

So I called Terry and woke him, asking for his man's number, and that same night, before I could change my mind, I introduced myself to Viktor Fedorov. He was an Ivan, all right. Spoke with the same gruff accent and short, to-the-point sentences as a helicopter pilot Russian I knew from the oil patch. I told Viktor I was coming out to San Francisco for a week of vacation and would like to have a sit-down, and things took on their own momentum after that. I e-mailed him a webcam photo from a computer in the hotel lobby—one of a roughneck sitting at a computer in a hotel lobby—then wrote a humiliating little essay explaining both my circumstances and my plans for the future. Viktor said to check back in a couple of days, before I even reached the city, and he would rustle up a few women who were willing to consider me. I'd pay him $250 for each one I met. An actual marriage would cost five grand.

ON FRIDAY MORNING I HOPPED THE MISSISSIPPI River into Louisiana, then pulled into the welcome center to slap myself in the face. Well rested and lucid, I could see the foolishness of the night before. Had I really thought I'd meet some Russian woman and, in a week, fall in love? Marry her? Have her shipped to Grand Isle? Move her into the Airstream? Look, wife. Right across the highway is the beach. You can sunbathe on our dirty sand. You can sit yourself down among the debris that has drifted ashore from the Gulf. You can even fish and crab, if you want. Did you ever notice I only have nine fingers? I'm not rich yet, but I will be come January. You'll just have to trust me on that.

So from the welcome center I sent Viktor a text asking him to call off his search, and since this blunder seemed easy enough to put the brakes on compared to some of my former sins of impulse, I was able to shake my head and advance. I got back on I-20, and as north Louisiana miles rushed by I was almost feeling eager. A stubborn and excited curiosity to see the old home and let the hurt come.

DRY SPRINGS. POPULATION 582. A hundred miles west of Mississippi, a hundred miles east of Texas. Sam was standing on the bench seat. Usually he was happy to just stretch out and relax, but now he was showing great interest. Ronnie's Quickstop had evolved into a Chevron that also housed a Subway, but otherwise Dry Springs seemed much as I'd left it. The town hall, the post office, the volunteer fire department. A service station and a Dollar General. Carrington's Seed, Feed, & Hardware. The Bank of Dry Springs. Doolittle's Diner. All clustered around the sleepy four-way intersection where Elmer Street crosses the Dixie Overland Highway. I turned right, and soon we passed the high school where my parents had taught. Pinewoods, fields, and pastureland now. Farms and nurseries, the chicken hatchery and some timber operations.

My family's old farm was just outside Dry Springs proper, at the end of a mile of gravel that, the year after Tommy died—and on the same day as his memorial service at the high school—went from a no-name stop on Rural Route 4 to being christened Thomas Joseph Road. That hadn't been our idea, but we couldn't refuse. Fifty balloons sailed into an oystery Louisiana sky that afternoon as we were all leaving the gym. One for each state, I guess. Before night fell I'm sure most of them were lost to pines and power lines, but I imagined a sort of resurrection. Something better than a sainthood sign on a dead-end road. A single balloon catching an air current and traveling farther than anyone might believe. To a place well beyond where America ends and the seas begin. Finally the limp, latex corpse of *that* balloon settles atop blue waters, a mock jellyfish to be eaten by an ancient loggerhead—yet somehow it brings the turtle no harm, and together they swim on.

I turned off the highway and drove my brother's gravel road. Our barn was standing, but the house was gone. A blacktop driveway began at an electronic gate and passed straight through the grassed-over foundation where our house once stood, then continued on to the far end of the property. There was a new house back there. A bantam mansion, really. It had high, white columns, wide porches across the first and second floors. Iron letters on the gate read RES IPSA PLANTATION.

I'd sold the farm to a young lawyer couple from Ruston with a toddler son. I was ripe to be picked, a freshly minted felon, yet they paid about what I was asking, didn't try to take advantage of a bottomed-out kid. It was hard to accept that now, a decade later, the farm was as much their home as it had ever been mine. Other families had lived here before the Josephs came, and before all of us, Caddo, maybe mound builders. I'd been nothing but a minute to these eleven acres. At best this land had merely tolerated me.

I got out of the LeBaron, then climbed onto the blotched hood. The lawyers had also taken down a fence and sacrificed a pasture in order to accomplish their *Gone with the Wind* fantasy, and what at one time had been a ryegrass field seeded here and there with turnip was now as smooth and clipped as the fairway of a private golf course. I stared out over the sole remaining pasture like a meerkat, half expecting to see cotton and slaves, but no, about two hundred yards off was a herd of brown-and-white somethings huddled by the bank of the pond. Not far from the rise in the land where my father collected the dirt still trapped in my vial. I stood there until I realized what I was seeing. Jesus Christ. Llamas.

BACK AT THE FOUR-WAY I turned south onto Elmer Street, then just before the train tracks I made one left, then another. Eliza Sprague's house would be to my right on the odd-numbered side of Ballpark Drive, and I let off the gas and began reading mailboxes, pushing Sam flat on the bench seat so he wouldn't block my view.

My high school was so small we didn't even field a football

team, and though I had a handful of friends growing up, I'd done nothing to keep in touch with them. In fact, the only person from Dry Springs I'd had any contact with since running away was Eliza, of all people. I'm not sure how she found me, but not long after my move to Grand Isle she sent a letter to Pearl Lane. She told me she wanted to say she was sorry. That what had come down on me was her parents' doing. That she wished we could go back to how it was before anybody knew about us but us. That part of her loved me and probably always would.

I held on to that letter, but I didn't write Eliza. My probation officer had made it clear I'd better stay away from her—insofar as the law was concerned, Eliza's feelings about what had happened wouldn't alter my situation. But her words did bring me some comfort. I didn't love her, and I doubted she actually loved *me,* but maybe that could have come in time. Maybe all we had needed was to be allowed to figure things out for ourselves. In a parallel life Eliza and I are married and living in Dry Springs. We had that kid and are beating the odds.

It was over seven years before I heard from Eliza again. I'd evacuated from Grand Isle for Katrina, come back to a war zone, then repeated the whole damn drill a few weeks later for Rita. After I returned for good a letter from Eliza *Hayes* appeared in my bent-crooked-by-tidal-surge mailbox. Apparently Eliza had found the Lord, and she claimed writing me had been her preacher's idea. A tollbooth on her road to salvation, was the way he'd put it to her:

> I looked online and saw you were still living down south. I was praying so hard for you during those storms, Roy. I really hope you made it through them okay.

She also wanted to tell me that I should forget her and forgive myself for what I'd done, turn to the Bible if I hadn't already because we are all sinners. I'm married, she added. My husband

Carver is a wonderful man, and we have two precious boys—three-year-old twins. Smile upon the Lord, Roy, and He will surely smile upon you as well.

So the strangest Dear John letter the world has ever seen: a homework assignment for an evangelical. I'd known a Carver Hayes in high school. He was a year or two older than me, and not the sort to venture far from Lincoln Parish. And despite having promised myself I wouldn't be making *this* detour, after my visit to the farm I had pulled onto the highway and called information for an address. The puppet of some sick god, on a homework assignment of my own.

The house was a one-story red-brick with three tall pines in the front yard. And behind those longleafs, a very pregnant woman in gingham, bandanna in her dark hair. She was on her knees, pruning an azalea bush, two young boys sitting in the grass with her. Eliza, but an adult Eliza. She was sideways to me, the long dress a puddle around her. A shepherdess with lambs, and soon another would come. And I wondered what the outcast creeping his shitty car down Ballpark Drive might have lost by not ignoring his probation officer. If I could have been Carver. A home-owning, churchgoing man. The father of twins, plus one, with a *She's the real boss of this family* wife. Hearing a car approach, Eliza sat back on her heels and raised a casual hand. A hello or a good-bye, she really wasn't paying me any mind. To her I was just a passerby. To her I could have been anyone. A final, parting fuck you from Dry Springs.

And later, on my way to Ruston and Peach City Self Storage, a text from Viktor Fedorov: No? I have women wanting to meet you. You are sure?

I SEARCHED THROUGH my storage unit while Sam patrolled a climate-controlled labyrinth of humming, fluorescent-lit hallways.

Seeing all that furniture, all those boxes, always makes me feel like a pharaoh reviewing a ten-by-twenty burial chamber. Like I should curl up with Sam and my possessions and wait for the afterlife. Being reminded I still have so many *things* to be responsible for pricks at me. I hope I will have use for them someday, but then why do I daydream about a fire at Peach City Self Storage? A raging blaze that will take that weight off my shoulders? I love the sound the rolling door makes when it rumbles down, the snap of the padlock.

Finally I found the photo album I was hunting. It was about an inch thick and bound in oxblood leather, FOR OUR TOMMY pyrographed into the calfskin by my father. The album went into my duffel bag unopened. I would show Joni her father, but I wouldn't be looking at those photos before I absolutely had to.

OAK CREST CEMETERY had once been a hardwood forest, and though the land lacked any sort of crest, enough of the trees had been spared for the name to make *some* sense. At a flower shop in town I'd bought three bundles of carnations, and the petals were already starting to wilt at the edges. There was always a lengthy gap between these visits—and here I was, thinking it might be years and years before I returned—but I could never bring myself to buy plastic-and-silk roses and calla lilies. Even dying flowers aren't as gloomy as those fake ones.

I'm sure Dry Springs had been expecting a big double funeral, but I buried Mom and Dad without any kind of ceremony. Though that probably came across as cold, they'd both drawn up wills and that was what they had requested. They didn't explain, but I understood. Tommy didn't get a proper funeral, so they didn't want one themselves. My parents now lie on either side of Tommy's vacant grave, and to the left of Mom is the spot reserved for me.

The closest thing *I* had to a will was a business card from Mr. Donny Lee I kept in my wallet, and on the back of the card I'd written:

> *If I'm dead please call this man.*
> *Bury me at Oak Crest Cemetery in Ruston.*
> *I have a plot there.*

I did that years ago, after Malcolm got a FUCK YOU, TOE-TAGGER! tattoo on the bottom of his foot. It was dumb, a joke of my own really—but that note was also perhaps the only way anyone would know what to do with me.

The Joseph plots were near the front, by the sprawling water oak. I left Sam in the LeBaron so he wouldn't piss on any headstones, but I didn't last much longer at Oak Crest than the ten minutes or so it took for me to smoke a cigarette. I rarely did. Some people find solace in cemeteries, some people don't. And the thought of spending forever planted in the same quiet place made me glad, if my brother had to die, he at least escaped that infinite finale. Even if that means the grave between Mom and Dad is a sham. That we never got to press our hands atop a coffin and know he was home. That even now I'll sometimes see his young face in crowds.

I left Oak Crest weeping in the LeBaron, hoping all three of them understood why this had to be farewell for a while, maybe a long while. Sam had his head on my thigh, and I put my knuckles to his wet nose. *None* of them are here, buddy. I need to keep telling myself that. I can be anywhere and think of Tommy's arm around my neck. Mom's warm smile. Dad's ever curious eyes.

A feeling, then—not freedom, exactly. More like a sorrowful slackening. And as I was driving away I reflected on the note in my wallet and wondered, not for the first time, if it would be too huge of a betrayal if I just asked to be burned and scattered.

MY LAST STOP in Ruston. It had been a couple of years since I'd met with Mr. Donny Lee in person, but he was locking the door to his office downtown as I pulled up. We did most of our business on the phone or through the mail—me giving him permission to do this or that with my money; the signing of tax returns, disclosure forms, and the like—and when I called to him from the LeBaron it was clear he didn't recognize me any more than Eliza had. He looked like a very different man himself. A dove-gray Stetson and lizard boots, a bolo tie with a silver clasp. Mr. Donny Lee was dressed as an oilman.

I stepped out, one hand on Sam's collar. "Roy Joseph," I said.

He grinned at me from the sidewalk, his confusion gone. "Don't I know! Roy Boy and Lil' Yella Sambo! Gaw, sonny, get a haircut. You're a Huckleberry Finn."

"Sorry for not calling ahead. You off somewhere?"

"Not at all. Lunch with a seventy-year-old woman." He checked his watch, removed his Stetson. *His* hair seemed shoe-polished, jet-black now instead of possum hoary. "Let Miss Linda wait. I can always spare clock for an old friend like you."

His office was sandwiched between a defunct clothing store and a place that bought gold. There was no receptionist or waiting area, just a carpeted and wood-paneled room. A veneer desk occupied the end of the office like a glued-maple altar, separating a pair of fabric armchairs from a burgundy wingback, and I took a seat as he powered up his computer. Standing there, behind that massive desk, he could have been a captain at the controls of a ship.

"Okay," he said, finding whatever he was looking for. "You want the State of the Union or something more specific?"

There were a row of filing cabinets and a gurgling water cooler against the far wall. And above them: a framed Louisiana Tech diploma and various certificates; a greenhead in flight but cupped to land, duck call hanging by a lanyard from its yellow bill. Entering, Sam had barked at the full-strut wild turkey in the corner. So now he was on his belly under the street-front plate glass, chin on paws and eyeing that longbeard, daring the puffed tom to move or even cluck.

"State of the Union," I said. "You remember how I—"

"What happened to your goddamn finger? That new?"

I told him the story, then explained I was through with working. That as soon as I turned thirty I'd be ready for him to start freeing up some of my money. "I think I'll need, I don't know, forty or fifty grand a year to live on," I said. "And a bunch more than that early on to buy a house with. Wheels too, probably. Basically, I need it to be where I can settle down somewhere and retire."

"Retire! Been working since I was eleven."

"Yes sir. But all the same."

He nodded and began tapping at the keyboard, pausing sporadically to punch numbers into a desk calculator. I held my breath and waited, nervous as hell that at any moment he would look at me and apologize, tell me my January dream was a delusion. That my Airstream, Pearl Lane, Grand Isle days wouldn't be coming to an end.

But instead he whistled.

"Something wrong?" I asked. "About two million, right?"

"Afraid not." On a stand next to his desk was a football he'd once showed me that had been autographed by a college Terry Bradshaw. He picked the ball up, smiled, then pump-faked. Spry for his age, my accountant/adviser. "Try two and a quarter," he said.

"What?" I was smiling now too. "Really?"

"You watch TV? Dow's been breaking records lately. Even my grandkids know that. But thank Gil Bean, not me. Busy as a dog with fleas, Bean. He's aggressive, but he's safe. Bean wears suspenders *and* a belt."

"Who's Gil Bean?"

"Come now." He shook his head. "That Dallas guy I told you about in the spring? Got most of my fat cats with Bean. He's done well by us. Very well. You want me taking your money out his hands? Beanie doesn't play with less than two million."

"Well, do thank him for me." I shrugged. "But, you know, I have all these plans."

"With respect, that's small thinking."

"Yes sir. Again, nothing needs to change till January. But beyond that, I'll be needing income. I can't live on a number."

Mr. Donny Lee came around from his desk. He smelled like saddle leather. "And the tax men shall rejoice. They've been awaiting." He laughed, said he would leave trying to sway me for another day. "Call me after your thirtieth, and we'll sort this all out. I'll quit making you richer if that's what you really want." Then he slapped me on the back. He was done with me, and now I was done with Ruston.

I WOULD SPEND the rest of the afternoon hiking green pinewoods with Sam. My good memories of Lake Claiborne State Park—a smiling me walking barefoot along a concrete bulkhead, tagging behind Tommy and wishing I was him; jars full of fireflies; hot dogs dangling from coat hangers; my family happy and together and sucking at honeysuckle—had kept me coming up there for Tommy's birthday every April, so after Ruston I bought groceries and drove the twenty-five miles northwest.

With summer over I had the park pretty much to myself, and I dropped a hundred bucks for a cabin on the lake. The water was shining in the sun, and I imagined Tommy swimming around and around forever, a frogman crossing salt waters to ascend Louisiana rivers. The Atchafalaya and then the Red, the Black, and the Ouachita. Bayou D'Arbonne, finally. Bass, bluegill, catfish, sacalait. My brother slipped through a dam conduit to bring himself to Lake Claiborne, close to his home and with me, and he was staged in those six thousand man-made acres of blocked-up bayou, waiting for my next move, safe even among occasional gators, the Underwater Panther always somewhere, but not here, at least not now.

Sam and I saw wood ducks and deer, a coral snake and a road-runner, and though I usually try to keep an even keel, tending to view too much happiness and hopefulness as dangerous, as a setup for a fall, that last evening in Louisiana—grilling corn and onions and country ribs on the back porch with Sam, listening to the trillings of toads and the chirpings of crickets, the booming *Who cooks for you? Who cooks for you all?* of a hoot owl as I planned to sleep, not in a travel trailer or on a rig or in a hotel, but in something like a house—I stared up at the star-splashed sky and was certain I was getting my first taste of how life would one day be for Roy Joseph, millionaire.

I RODE THROUGH TEXAS AND OKLAHOMA WITH THE radio off, and though I spent plenty of time pondering Lionel Purcell—and of course, Joni Hammons— Viktor Fedorov had come to dominate my thoughts. Which is to say I passed most of the drive thinking about women. Russian women. Marriage. A wife. Viktor had rung me twice already that day. He was harder to blow off than I'd thought. No messages, but those calls could only mean he was hoping I would reconsider.

For so long the main focus of my life had been to keep to a routine and avoid the unexpected by clinging to my island and my oil rigs. Yes, maybe it was foolish to have ever dialed Viktor's number, but when I reached Kansas I was actually starting to see the wisdom of giving myself a non-Joni motive to explain my presence in San Francisco. I wasn't violating any laws just by looking for her, but it couldn't hurt to have a verifiable, cover-my-ass story as to what I was doing in that city. I came to find a wife, officers. Nothing more, nothing less. Five working days, says the law. Five working days.

From a Holiday Inn in Wichita, I called Viktor and flip-flopped. Again. He had three candidates for me to meet. "It might be very difficult to pick," he kept telling me. "I have done a good job for you." I told him I'd make California on Thursday, and then I took care of the rest. Step One: A computer in the Holiday Inn's business center. Step Two: Select a dog-friendly San Francisco studio apartment on Craigslist to sublet. Step Three: Swap some e-mails with the current tenant, Karen Yang, negotiating seven nights of Thursday-to-Thursday rent (six hundred dollars, plus a three-hundred-dollar damage deposit—good Lord). Step Four: Overnight Karen a two-hundred-dollar check so she'd hold the place for me.

TWO DAYS LATER, somewhere in Wyoming, I swung into an I-80 rest stop to let Sam run around. Morning still, a dandelion sun. It was only me and a couple of truckers who were napping in their rigs. A dry, chill wind was lashing the parking lot, but the barren and brown land stretching all around us was as level as the Gulf before a storm.

The rest stop itself was brick restrooms and some picnic tables, and I couldn't shake the feeling that horrible crimes had happened there. That after miles of lonesome but beautiful scenery I'd arrived upon a murder stadium, a rape arena. It was as if, with no obvious place to visit evil on each other, man had to go blueprint one. I walked to the edge of the parking lot and watched Sam snake through the sagebrush and clump grass. To my right a slanted signboard sat bolted to a rusting pedestal, and sealed beneath dusty Plexiglas was a photo of an antelope and a drawing of a gaunt man dragging a two-wheeled handcart. Science for my mother, history for my father. Positioned between antelope and man: a paragraph informing me I was standing in the largest unfenced area in the Lower 48. The Red Desert. Millions of acres of high-altitude desert that separated the southern Rockies from the central Rockies, home to over fifty thousand pronghorn antelope, as well as a rare desert elk herd. Shoshone and Ute had roamed here, and later, passing through like me, mountain men and pioneers, Pony Express riders and Mormons.

On the drive I had often fixed on some solitary house I could see from the interstate. A clapboard two-story walled in by Great Plains cornfields. An assembly-line modular anchored in the shadow of a western butte. A nation of immigrants, sure, but the exploring days of most Americans are well behind them, if they ever even explored at all. Perhaps some eccentric forefather had been a nomad, but now there his children remained. The shy kittens of a legendary alley cat. The Roy Josephs to that brave man's Tommy, wasting away in their own versions of my Airstream. Pioneers. It's easy to forget that even in the old times such venturesome spirits had been the exceptions. The vast majority kept on with their lives in well-settled lands—scratch-farming, drafting contracts, making hats—but you don't hear much about the shopkeepers and whatnot who never left home. Those trailblazers we celebrate, the ones chasing after someplace better, were outcasts, outliers, and outlaws.

Then came the Google car. I watched a white Chevy Cobalt veer onto the exit for the rest stop, eventually pulling into a spot a few spaces over from the LeBaron. The car had a contraption periscoping from its roof like the mast of a sailboat, and a logo on the door read GOOGLE in a rainbow of letters. A chinless, balding man wearing khakis and a lime-green polo stepped out. I was at the edge of the lot still, waiting for Sam. The man nodded at me and I nodded back, then he started walking toward the restrooms. I heard the Cobalt give a quick yelp as the doors locked.

I called Sam in, and once the man was gone we went over to his car to see what was what. The roof contraption was a kind of steel boom, and atop it were cameras aimed in all different directions. A bright glare was coming off the passenger-side window, and I touched my forehead to the glass so I could peer inside. A laptop computer was attached to the console, and the backseat was buried under crumpled fast-food bags and popped cans of Red

Bull. The laptop was open, but I couldn't read the screen. There was a metallic tick issuing from under the trunk—the exhaust system, cooling.

When I turned around I saw the Google man approaching. I put my hands up to let him see I meant no harm. He smiled. He was older, and a tube of fat ran above the waistband of his khakis. Something about him made me think family man, nice guy.

"My bad," I said.

"Part of the job," said the man. "Folks are always curious."

"So this is how it's done?"

He chuckled, but then the phone on his belt holster chimed. "Just a sec," he told me.

Sam had wandered. He was back in the desert, investigating, making discoveries, and I jogged over to get him while the man dealt with his phone call. That didn't take me long, but maybe some all-seeing, Silicon Valley royal was tracking his knight's progress and telling him to quit fucking around. Get on with it, make new friends on your own time. Whatever the reason, the man was in a hurry now. I watched from the desert as the Google car went gliding to the interstate, those cameras ready to tame everything. To continue shrinking the world even as I was trying to explore it.

B ATTLE MOUNTAIN SAT ON A HIGH-DESERT HIGHWAY that ran along I-80 in northern Nevada. There wasn't much there, and what *was* left looked to be fighting for its life. A railroad cut through town before continuing on west with the interstate, and the businesses I saw were mostly what I'd expected. Gas stations and trucker motels and baby casinos, some sad bars and a few dingy restaurants. No shortage of trailers in Battle Mountain, and on the slope of a faraway hill some irony-deficient crew of civic-proud dolts had spelled BM in enormous block letters fashioned from whitewashed rock. The work that must have gone into that. These are my people, I was thinking. I didn't know what battle was ever fought atop that brown hill, but if this town held the victors I never wanted to see the place the defeated were sent to live.

I spent my first BM evening in a motel-casino-restaurant-bar in the center of town. It was Monday, so I had two full days to devote to Lionel Purcell before I was due in San Francisco. In the nightstand I'd found a tattered Lander County phone book lying between the Bible and the Book of Mormon, but no Purcells were listed. In the morning, after some breakfast in the restaurant, I went and saw the leathery woman at the front desk to see if she could help.

"What you wanting with Lionel?" she asked.

"It's a private matter. So you know him?"

She sniffed and gave me an I-can-be-that-way-too look. "Sorry, mister," she said. "*That's* a private matter." Her nose was shriveled like a dried fig, as if God had cursed her for sticking it in everyone's business.

To hell with her. There were over three thousand other people living in Battle Mountain, no need to keep matching wits with this sphinx. I went back to my room to take a shower, and I'd just toweled off and dressed when there was a knock at the door.

Lionel Purcell. He was as big as I remembered him. Tall—every bit of six four—and built like a steer-dogger. And indeed, he was outfitted for a rodeo. Black Justin Roper boots and a straw cowboy hat. Dark blue Wranglers and a starched turquoise shirt.

"You're Lionel," I said, dumbstruck.

The man looked past me, searching the room with flat gray eyes. He had the same mustache I recalled from the photo I'd seen online four years ago—a thick yellow horseshoe like the one Hulk Hogan sports—but there was some silver in it now, and he was in the neighborhood of fifty. Those eyes settled back on me. "I am, I am," he said, his voice deep and gravelly. "And I'm betting you're Ahab's kid brother."

I'd thought Tommy's nickname was Orion—that was what Lionel himself had told me and my parents—but when he was alive my brother never said anything to us about a nickname, Orion or Ahab or otherwise. "You mean Tommy?" I asked.

"Right. Ahab. So are you or aren't you?"

I nodded.

"You echo him, dude. An older, civilian model. Great to see you again." He held out his hand, palm up, and I shook it. Sam had been asleep on the bathroom linoleum, but now he came out to see who was at the door. Lionel dropped to a knee and pulled him close, started jingling the tags on his collar. "Heya, prowler. I like a Lab. What's *his* handle?"

"Sam . . . how'd you know I was here?"

"Bev called about twenty minutes ago, said a Roy Pickett Joseph with Louisiana plates was asking after me. Curious as a bag of cats, tough as a pine knot, Bev. I reckoned you might be some kin of Ahab's. He was the only Joseph I ever knew."

Small towns are all the same, in certain respects. I told him I was passing through Battle Mountain on my way to visit San Francisco. That I'd seen his website years back and was hoping to talk to him.

Lionel grinned. "Doing the Kerouac thing?"

"I guess."

"I've tried that. You leaving today?"

"Hope not."

"So don't." He slapped at Sam's ribs and stood. "You two come with me. No sense in staying at this shithole."

Then Lionel was gone before I could even thank him. I moved my bags and the dog bowls to my trunk, and he sat in his diesel dually pickup while I went to see Bev. She lit a long cigarette when I came through the door, looked put out that Lionel hadn't murdered me. I laid my key on the counter, and she pointed her cigarette at me like a wand. I waited for her to speak, but she never did. The glowing tip of her menthol was tracing tiny circles in the air between us.

"All right," I told her. "This has been fun."

The weather outside was nice. Cold but not too cold. I started the LeBaron and followed Lionel onto the highway, then we cut left and crossed over the railroad tracks. He was driving a red Dodge. A sunbaked sticker on the bumper read KEEP NEVADA WILD!, and the double tires on the rear axle gave the dually a tarantula quality. It was a giant red spider, skittering.

Sam had his head hanging out the window, taking it all in with me. The day before, the salt flats of Utah had rattled him. As we crossed that white wasteland from time to time he would peek at me with a look like, Hey, um, are you seeing all this?

And that was the same look he gave me when we reached Lionel's trailer. It sat on a dust lot next door to a small vinyl-sided building doing business as Rhonda's Ranch. A ramshackle scrap-wood deck wrapped around the trailer, as if the single-wide had come crashing down atop a kid's clubhouse. Upright sheets of corrugated tin fenced the length of one property line—a wind-break, I figured—but Lionel's border with Rhonda's Ranch was free and clear.

Lionel parked his truck by some cinder-block steps that led up to the deck, and I stopped in the road. He slid from the cab onto the hardpan, then kicked a ball of chicken wire that went bounc-ing across the lot like a silver tumbleweed. A pair of soil-filled washtubs were sprouting high thistle, and he signaled for me to squeeze the LeBaron in between them, pumping both arms, a mar-shaler directing a plane into a hangar.

A cockroach came struggling out of a dashboard vent, one of those thumb-sized, hairy-legged tree roaches. A stowaway that had probably been living within the guts of the LeBaron since before I left Grand Isle. I looked over at Sam, expecting him to pounce, but he was still watching me. "We're doing this," I said. And Sam kept on staring, listening but not understanding, as I lifted my foot off the brake and we made our way forward.

TWO COUCHES TOOK UP most of the space in the living room of the trailer, but there were also books and bookshelves every-where. There was no TV, just a radio in one corner playing outlaw country, a computer looping through a psychedelic screen saver in the other. Both couches were covered in a brown, leatherette material that was ripped in places and showing synthetic clouds of white batting. Thin gold curtains masked the windows, tinting the sunlight amber, and stationed between the couches was a long, low coffee table made entirely of welded iron.

Lionel pointed at the table. "Watch out for that," he said. "It's a shin buster, savvy?"

We each sat down on a couch, and Sam laid himself on the caramel carpet, his back pushed against the door. Lionel took off his cowboy hat and placed it among the paperbacks spread across the iron coffee table. Thrillers and mysteries mainly, plus some field guides for animals and plants. His blond hair was longer than I'd realized—longer than mine, even—but he had it tied up in a messy screw of a topknot. A ceiling fan above us was rotating slowly, and all those books gave the trailer the musty smell of a library, a Cybermobile. Sam had shut his eyes, and I asked if it was all right for him to be in there with us.

"Leave him be," said Lionel. "He's fine."

"You really don't care?"

"I really don't."

"It'll be two nights at most. If that's okay, I mean."

He nodded and removed a can of Copenhagen from the front pocket of his shirt. "You thirsty? Water? Pop? Milk?" He tapped the side of the can against his belt buckle, then whipped his hand, thumping his index finger on the lid to pack the tobacco tight. He waved the can at me, but I passed.

"Maybe some water," I said.

"Sure thing."

He twisted the metal lid off the can, then maneuvered a wedge of Copenhagen behind his bottom lip. Once he had his dip situated he replaced the lid and snapped his fingers to clean them. Specks of fine cut careened off the coffee table like fleas at war. He'd already grabbed himself a Dixie cup to spit in, lining the inside with a paper towel to keep it from spilling or splashing, and now he went into the kitchen and filled a plastic bowl with water. He placed the bowl on the carpet beside Sam, doubled back to the sink and topped off a glass jar for me.

"Thanks," I said, taking the water from him.

"Yup." Lionel returned to the couch opposite mine. He'd untied his hair, and it was hanging in his face now. He flicked his head back, then spit into his cup. "Ouch. How'd you lose that?" He was looking at my left hand.

"Working. Out on a rig in the Gulf."

"I imagine that'd do it." He rolled the spit cup against his cheek and frowned. "So you've come to talk to me about your brother."

"Yeah. And again, I'm sorry for dropping in on you like this. Just seemed easier than calling or writing or whatever."

"Driving to Nevada is easier?"

"No. But I don't have to be in San Francisco till Thursday, and I thought you might still be living here. It wasn't that far out my way to swing by."

"Not truly *on* your way though neither. Not from Louisiana. And how come now? All these years later?"

I took a sip of water. "Because Tommy has maybe got a kid in San Francisco, and I wanted—"

"A kid? What?"

"The mother tracked me down six weeks ago."

He rocked back on the couch, laughing. "You're lying! That smooth-dog!"

I shook my head. "She says Tommy went home with her from some beach party in San Diego one night, and y'all shipped out not long after that."

"And you've been talking to them?"

There was no soft way to explain all my amateur detective work, so I kept things vague. "Not that much with the daughter. But yeah, the mother and I have been."

"They're needing money, that or one of your kidneys. You're caught in some psyops."

"It was all my idea, going out there."

"It's still fucking weird." He ran his hand across his mustache. "What all you know about the mother?"

"She's a poet. Teaches at San Francisco State."

"Oh boy. She married?"

"Doesn't look like it."

"What's her name? I was king of the beach party." He picked up one of the books on the coffee table. *The Shape of the Journey*, it was called. "And I read some poetry now and again too."

"Nancy Hammons."

"Never heard of her. Christ. San Francisco, poet. Gonna be a wild ride."

"You've been there?"

"I've been everywhere, man." He tossed *The Shape of the Journey* back on the table. "Suppose it's true what's she's claiming—want some advice?"

"Yeah. I know. Run the other way."

"Then I won't say no more." He scratched at the side of his neck. "You seem like a frayed rope. How old are you?"

"Thirty in January."

He smiled. "That mama chose a bad time to fling this at you. Thirty packs a sting. Shit, I was a Mormon before I turned thirty. A good one, in fact. I'd door-to-doored for the LDS in God-awful, fecking Belfast for two years."

"I'm working through it."

"It's the day-to-day living that wears you out. Any idiot can face a crisis."

I nodded. "True enough."

"Chekhov. Read them Russkies, Roy. Dostoyevsky, Tolstoy. They teach us how to suffer like men. Copy?"

"Copy," I said, thinking of *my* Russian. Viktor.

Lionel whacked at the coffee table with the toe of his boot. "I don't have any pictures of him or the guys or nothing. I was never keen on all that."

"That's okay," I said. Hell, I couldn't even look at that FOR OUR TOMMY album yet. "I just thought we could talk some."

"I'm in." He put on his hat. "But let's go out back."

I followed him outside and saw five long dog kennels lined up across the rear of his property, right where the dust of his lot ended and flat scrubland began. As Sam presented behind us there came the howl of multiple hounds, heads bent back as they moaned, but Lionel whistled and they quit. He sank into a rusty folding chair, and I did the same. We were sitting side by side now. Rhonda's Ranch was off to the left, close enough to hit with a rock.

Sam lay down on the deck between us, contemplating the hounds, caged brothers and sisters who seemed to want him for their prison gang. "My mountain lion dogs," said Lionel. He skipped his thumb along Sam's spine. "Treeing Walkers."

"You're still a hunting guide?"

"Only sometimes. Trying to get back into it, by and by. I let life get away from me for a while there, spent some lost years in the bottle." He wiggled his spit cup. "Things I could keep a grip on in the navy eventually got too slippery."

I was fishing for something to say but coming up empty.

"Are *you* a drinker?" he asked.

"Not to where I can't not."

"Good man."

Morning had faded and the day was warming, the sky a few shades lighter than Lionel's turquoise shirt. Not far from the kennels stood a large work shed constructed from the same corrugated tin as the windbreak running to our right. The shed's wide doors were chained and padlocked. I looked over at Lionel. "Why did you call him Ahab earlier?"

"Ahab was what he went by."

"But what about Orion?"

"The constellation?"

"No. As his nickname."

He shook his head. "No way anybody would ever get called that. We weren't X-Men."

"You told us it was Orion. I'm not wrong."

"Who's *us*?"

"Me and my parents."

"Nice folks, your parents. They know you're here?"

I told him about Mom and Dad, and he winced.

"Fuck, man. Orion? Don't recall ever saying that. Sorry. Sixteen years is a long time."

I was getting frustrated. "Tell me about *Ahab*, then. Why that?"

A Peterbilt had rolled into the gravel lot behind Rhonda's Ranch. I watched the rig's rawboned driver walk around to the front door of the windowless building and go inside. A long while passed before Lionel spoke. Long enough to make me wonder if he was about to lie to me.

"Okay," he said. "You need to understand, those names some of us got pinned with, they didn't mean jack, not really. School, they called me. As in Old School, because I was older. Before that it was Cowboy." He plucked his finger against the brim of his hat. "So I want you to know it's not rocket surgery."

Just then, beneath a WIFI AVAILABLE HERE sign, a side door to Rhonda's Ranch opened and a grown woman in pigtails waved at us. She was wearing a short plaid skirt and white knee socks.

"Trick or treat," said Lionel.

"That's tomorrow."

"Every day be Halloween over there. They got costume after costume."

The trucker came out with the woman, and they walked to his rig, climbed up into the cab. The door slammed shut, and Lionel spit. "If the gal's willing, some dudes prefer that," he explained. "Don't like making it on a whorehouse mattress."

I didn't say anything. I was thinking about that lingerie girl Sierra. What a world. A place where money can buy you pretty much whatever. A bride, even.

The Walker hounds were at it again, but this time Lionel didn't hush them. "I'd been nine years on the West Coast when your brother was awarded his Trident and assigned to my platoon in Team FIVE," he said. "Then the kid was on operator fast track once Saddam invaded Kuwait. Most of the already-deployed SEALs were stuck in the Philippines or floating on amphibs with Marines, and none of them were gonna be sprung for the desert. So uncommitted, on-deck stateside platoons were the first ones to go, by and large, and we got sped through the final phases of our pre-deployment workup so we could head over." Lionel turned his chair to face mine. "He was my baby boy. I was the one who dubbed him Ahab."

"Ahab like in *Moby Dick*?"

"Nah. Ahab like in 'Ahab the A-rab' by Ray Stevens."

"The country singer who had all the joke songs?"

"They weren't all joke songs. The man recorded 'Sunday Mornin' Comin' Down' before either Kristofferson *or* Cash." Lionel made double fists and started punching them together. "So there was a one-star carrier group commander up at North Island, old Vietnam jet-jock type, uglier than a hat full of assholes, but he had this daughter. Misty. Crazy gal, but a fine thing. She came home from college for the summer and was living with Daddy in Coronado. Ahab wouldn't ever talk about it, but rumor was MPs caught him and Misty somewhere they had no business being, doing the deed. They decided to spare him from having his balls cut off—but then one of them told me, and from then on, I'd see your brother, especially around any officers, I'd sing a Ray Stevens song. Not 'Misty,' that would've been too obvious, but the rest of them. 'The Streak,' 'Harry the Hairy Ape,' that one about the squirrel getting loose in the church."

"And 'Ahab the A-rab.'"

"Bingo. Before long we all just settled on that. He pulled chicks, Ahab. He could get laid in the middle of Temple Square."

I waited for Lionel to keep going, but he was through. It was only the hounds now. They worked themselves into one last frenzy, then shut down as well.

"Yup," said Lionel. "It's a nothing story. I probably thought Orion would seem bigger."

I nodded, but in truth I did like hearing about Tommy sneaking around with a girl. The chapter of his life that came after Dry Springs but before he was summoned to war. There were two Tommys. The rural, bangs-in-the-face rebel I am so afraid of forgetting, and the on-top-of-the-world, cut-from-iron SEAL I barely even knew.

"Okay, but that wasn't all you said to me. You remember?"

He shrugged. "I did a lot of drinking that trip. I remember *that*."

"You said he went out like a hero. Those were your exact words, more or less."

"Really?"

"If there's stuff you're not supposed to tell, I understand—but I swear it would stay with me."

Lionel crossed his arms and leaned forward. "There's nothing to tell. It was after dark, and we were on a mission rehearsal when a chip light came on in our helo. Mayday, autorotation. But the pilots still had some control over her, so the crew chief ordered us out with him before they'd have to ditch and do their egress. Ahab must've hit the water too hard and blacked, got swept off by the current. I don't know."

"That's the same as what the navy told us."

"Well, that was what happened. I'm sorry, man. You were just a kid. It's like me saying his name was Orion, I'd wager. My drunk ass thinking something bigger might be better for you."

I made a quick, laughing sound. "For half my life I've been carrying around what you told me that night."

"Fuck." Lionel stomped his boot on the plywood of the deck. "Still, that don't mean he wasn't a hero—having it go like it did."

He seemed upset, and I doubted he was acting. Not now, at least. His eyes were on the deck, and he looked as if he was waiting to be sentenced. This wasn't what I had wanted. I had no intention of crossing the country just to spread poison. Lionel had been Tommy's friend. For all I knew he had told me what I'd needed to hear back then.

"It's all right," I said. "You didn't do anything wrong."

I PASSED MOST OF THE DAY in the shed with Lionel, helping him install KC lights across the hardtop of a jeep he kept parked in there. A two-seater military Willys from the forties, about as simple to monkey with as a lawn mower.

It was nice to take it easy and work at a problem I knew could be solved. Earlier Lionel had pointed to a far range of high mountains and told me they were the Rubies. Apparently he spent a lot of time with his Willys in those mountains, and I'd been lucky to catch him in town. He said he paid a kid down the road to collect his mail and tend to the hounds whenever he was away—his own little Jack Hebert—and besides monthly bills to send out and retirement checks to deposit, that was about it for Lionel's obligations and responsibilities.

I've heard some say that there are water people and mountain people, and though a man might certainly enjoy both, his soul is forever aligned with one or the other. If that is true, then with me it's water. I appreciate the beauty of mountains, but after a while among them I'm sure I would ache from an awareness of being landlocked, hemmed in. Even on an oil rig, with all of us living on top of one another, no real privacy to be found, I could look at Gulf waters and feel a loosening.

Lionel, on the other hand, clung to mountains. He'd let on that he was almost two years sober thanks to AA, and that once he got sick and tired of always being sick and tired, nature— more specifically, the Ruby Mountains—had been his choice for a higher power. Something greater than himself. He told me he found solitude without loneliness in the mountains, and I re- member the way he squinted at those distant Rubies while we talked. Like he couldn't wait for our conversation to end so he could bolt up there before winter snows came. I sensed he had gotten more than his fill of water during his career in the navy, and I'll admit that what freedom I see in sparkling depths is mostly an illusion. That water traps me more than it liberates me. That gazing from some island or some rig, I'm not any more free than a man staring out the window of a jail cell. But you are what you are.

IT WAS MAYBE five o'clock when we finished installing and wiring the KC lights. The temperature was dropping, and I went with Sam to let him run the scrubland. When we returned I saw Lionel standing at his property line. He was talking to one of the women from Rhonda's Ranch. Despite the cold she was dressed as a pink genie, had on a bubble-gum-colored veil and so forth. Platform heels. Lionel waved when he saw me, then said something to the genie. She rubbed her naked arms and hugged him before wob- bling back inside.

I waited on the deck of the trailer as Lionel came striding over. "You hungry?" he asked.

"Starved." Except for a few strips of venison jerky he'd given me in the shed earlier, I hadn't eaten since breakfast. "Can I buy you dinner somewhere?"

"We just got invited to supper at Rhonda's."

"Was that Rhonda?"

"There's not a Rhonda. Not no more."

"They serve food there?"

"Microwave pizzas and shit. Jell-O. Whipped cream."

"I'm not looking for anything but dinner."

He laughed and climbed the steps to join me. "You think I am? I get to see all the mouth breathers coming in and out of there." He went to the edge of the deck. The sun was setting, and he went quiet to watch. For a moment the world was red. "San Francisco. You're sure you wanna go?"

"Yeah. Thursday. That girl, you know? I feel like I've got to."

Lionel nodded, then vaulted off the deck, spreading his long arms like he was a batman. His boots landed hard in the dirt, and he stumbled. I could tell he'd hurt himself. It was a dumb thing to do; he wasn't a young guy. He turned and started limping sideways toward the shed. "Then forget Rhonda's," he said. "Let me show you my mountains."

L IONEL HAD PAINTED THE WILLYS DULL BROWN AND mounted electric winches to the front and rear bumpers. The tires were wide rock-crawlers, and there was a spare and a fuel canister anchored to the swinging tailgate. The Rubies lay to the east of Battle Mountain, back the way I'd already come, and when we were through eating at an interstate McDonald's Lionel drove seventy I-80 miles to the city of Elko. The hardtop was fairly light-gauge steel, and though the Willys could only do about sixty, tops, between the wind and the whine of those off-road tires it was too noisy for much talking. Instead I just sipped my hot coffee as every car passed us.

In Elko we left I-80 and went south for a long stretch. It was a black night, and once the lights of the city were behind us the sky became pinholed with stars. The highway, then a road, then another road, one that kinked and twisted as it rose into the Rubies. It was very cold out now, at least for my Louisiana blood, and the Willys didn't have a heater. Before we left I'd put on a flannel shirt, tugged a pair of sweatpants over my jeans, and Lionel had given me a knit hat and a heavy Carhartt coat to wear as well. I thought about Sam, locked in a kennel beside one of those rangy lion dogs. Stay warm too, buddy. Try to eat your food, and I'll be back tomorrow. This is just something I think I need to be doing.

We made sharp turn after sharp turn, then the headlights of the Willys played across the smooth white trunks of aspens. Lionel slowed down, and we left the blacktop for a narrow dirt road that led into the aspen grove. We were surrounded by Forest Service land, but Lionel told me this road, and the mountaintop acreage it would take us to, had belonged to the Purcell family for generations. He was like me. A rich poor man or a poor rich man, depending on how you wanted to look at it.

"My sod," he said. "My birthright." He flipped his new KC lights on, and more of the aspens were revealed. "And away we go. Hold on, little brother."

We started off all right, but as the grade steepened the dirt road gave way to rocks, the Willys bucking and bouncing as we crept over them. I could see then why Lionel had said we shouldn't bring Sam. He'd have hated the hell out of this.

After a breakneck fifteen minutes the aspens thinned and pines appeared. My ears popped, and Lionel told me we were pretty high now, around eight thousand feet. "Not much farther," he said.

There was a final series of hairpin switchbacks, followed by a straight climb that pinned my head against the seat. I couldn't see past the hood of the Willys, and lying back like that—feeling the weight of my own body as we pushed directly up the slope, watching stars slide across the windshield—I felt like an astronaut. The Willys churned along, and on either side of us the ground fell away into blackness. On neighboring mountains a few campfires were burning.

"Deer hunters," said Lionel, and when at last we leveled he looked at me and smiled. "We're here. Come sunup you'll shit seeing what we just did."

We drove on through pines and came to a small meadow.

It was close to ten o'clock, and I was sapped. Lionel killed the engine but left the KC lights on. I helped him make camp. He unfolded two plastic ground cloths from the back of the Willys, then we set up a pair of one-man tents that were like neon cocoons. He punted my sleeping bag to me.

"There you go," he said. "I'm gonna build a fire."

I freed the sleeping bag from a stuff sack and squared it out inside my tent—but now, with my bed all situated and waiting, for some reason I wasn't as tired as before. Lionel was hunched down next to a ring of stones, organizing logs atop kindling within, and I went over to him. He handed me a long black flashlight and pointed off into the darkness. "Follow that trail till you reach the first pine tree," he said. "I've got a cache of wood under some Visqueen. Grab us another armload?"

By the time I returned a fire was crackling, softening the cold, and Lionel had shut all the lights on the Willys. I dumped my wood beside the fire and sat on the ground. "So," I said.

"Yup," he said. "So." He had his boots off. The grass around the fire ring had been beaten down, and he lay back, tilting his cowboy hat until the brim covered his eyes. "I fall asleep you let me be. I'll make it to my tent."

I nodded and lit a cigarette from the punk end of a kindling twig. Peaceful, calm. I watched the fire for a while, the sparks chasing sparks as Lionel began to snore, and pretended Tommy was asleep in some third tent and would see me in the morning.

He took me camping once. We were in Arkansas, near a place Hernando de Soto was said to have sojourned the summer before his men sank his corpse into the Mississippi River. I was no more than nine, Tommy's hair was still long, and a girl in my class had died that same week. Meningitis. She was a friend, but either I didn't want to go to the funeral with my parents, or Mom and Dad thought I was too young to be there. So instead I went with my brother to Arkansas, and that night, by a fire that looked a lot like this fire, Tommy taught me how to whistle. Teasing me until I had it down. And though we talked about everything but death, I knew he was watching me. That the whole reason we'd come was so he could make sure I was okay.

THE NEXT DAY I woke confused. I'd shed my Red Wings and sweat-pants, Lionel's canvas Carhartt, but I was still in my jeans and flannel shirt. I felt greasy and feverish. My head was killing me due to the altitude, and even my hair reeked of stale wood-smoke. Then there was a sound like quiet thunder. It was only when I heard a second far-off and echoing boom that I realized someone was firing a high-powered rifle. Somewhere a mule deer was prob-ably dead or dying.

I crawled out of the tent and pulled on my boots. The morn-ing was gorgeous and crisp, but the thin, dry air was tough for me to breathe. Birds were calling, the sky as blue as I'd ever seen it anywhere. Our campsite was on the flat of a sort of plateau, and the snowcapped peaks of taller mountains crowded against us. We were in the last of the alpine tree line; our meadow was encircled by tart-smelling pines. Just six days ago I'd set off from the marsh-lands of Louisiana, and tomorrow I'd begin searching for Joni in San Francisco. America. Amazing.

Lionel didn't look to be stirring, so I walked to the Willys. Time to explore some. I followed our tire tracks into the pines for about a hundred yards, then stopped where the land dropped off but the jeep trail kept on, running down the slender backbone of a steep ridge. Deep gullies flanked the ridge, and the sheer slopes were scaled with loose plates of shale. A few feet to the left or right of those twin ruts and the Willys would have rolled, no problem. Rolled, then plummeted. Far below that Nevada ridge I thought I could see an asphalt ribbon of road, but from where I was standing it seemed no wider than the veins in my wrist.

Place me at the top of a ladder, or even the railing of an oil rig, my legs almost always get weak. It's like I don't trust myself not to lurch forward or fall. It's like that is completely out of my control. My stomach did a dizzy jump, and I turned away before my knees buckled. We would have to leave the way we came, but there was no point in fretting over that yet.

Lionel's tent was still zipped when I got back to camp, and I opened the lid of the steel box that took up the rear of the Willys. I'd brought a few things along with me, and Lionel had all sorts of supplies stored in there as well. I sat on the bumper, brushed my teeth and washed my face with water from a gallon jug—then stripped off my clothes and slapped on some deodorant, changed socks and jockeys before putting the same jeans and flannel shirt back on again. With nothing else to do I went over to the fire ring. Several orange coals were half buried in ashes, and I pushed them together with a machete Lionel had left stabbed into the dirt. Next, I cut slivers from a dry log, adding the shavings and blowing softly until I'd coaxed a flame. Once I had that good and going I fed twigs and then sticks and then logs.

For a thousand years or more, long before this meadow had come to be Lionel's, men had maybe lazed hereabouts doing what I was doing then. And I was musing on that when I saw Lionel emerge from the pines. He was walking toward me, and strapped to his back was a coffin-shaped camouflage bag that looked big enough to hold golf clubs. I guess he'd brought that bag with us in the Willys, but I hadn't seen it before now.

"Happy Halloween," he said.

I rose and swatted the ash and dust from my jeans. "I thought you were still asleep."

"Been up since dawn." He shrugged the bag off, then hung it from the nub of a broken pine limb. "Pretty here, right?"

I nodded. It was.

He came and stood by the fire. "I'll brew us some coffee. And there's eggs and bacon in one of them Igloos."

"What's that?" I asked, pointing over at the bag.

"You call that a drag bag. But inside, hooyah, an SR-25. My precious. Semiautomatic, .308 sniper rifle. Almost eight grand she cost, pimped and scoped."

I watched him to see if he was kidding, but he didn't appear to be. "That was you shooting earlier?"

"Just keeping sharp, sending a few downrange. Target practice."

"Two shots were all I heard."

He laughed. "Don't need much practice. Not at a buck a blast." He went to the Willys and began digging around in the back. "Let's eat. I'll give you a demo later."

AFTER BREAKFAST we hiked about a half mile from camp. Lionel still seemed to be limping slightly from his batman deck-leap at the trailer, and though, as a felon, playing gun bearer made me nervous, I'd volunteered to lug his sniper rifle. With gun, gear, and ammo, the drag bag weighed at least thirty pounds, but the shoulder straps and waist belt allowed for easy enough carrying.

A little after nine o'clock we came to a shelf of granite that looked down onto a deep valley separating us from the next mountain over. We were even with the spot on that other mountain where its own trees petered out, surrendering to a steep, rocky summit dotted with patches of green grass and dirty snow. Lionel took the drag bag from me. Stacked boughs of recently snapped pine had been arranged along the rim of the rock shelf, and I realized this was a blind of sorts he must have built that morning. He opened the drag bag. The SR-25 was about four feet long, and except for the rifle scope, the matte-black .308 resembled a machine gun.

Lionel danced his fingers across a length of steel tubing that had been fixed to the muzzle. "A suppressor," he said. "Helps knock down the recoil, but also hides the muzzle flash and cuts back on my dust signature, that and toys with the sound of the report quite a bit." He gave me a look like a patient teacher. "So then no one knows where you're shooting from."

"I take it you wouldn't want them to?"

"I surely wouldn't."

"That's legal? A suppressor?"

"Is in the Silver State."

He pushed a box magazine into the bottom of the rifle, then slammed one of his dollar rounds into the chamber. Unzipped, the drag bag had butterflied into two padded shooting mats, and he positioned the .308 between them, propping it up on the legs of a folding bipod.

"Ever hear of a snow cock?" he asked.

I stood watching as he removed a large pair of binoculars and a handheld spotting scope from a day pack he'd brought along. "Snow cock?"

"A Himalayan snow cock. It's a bird. About the size of a chicken." He told me to lie down, and we both wriggled onto a shooting mat. Him to the left of the rifle, me to the right. "They're from Asia," he said. "When I was a kid the state got some from Pakistan and started releasing them all through the Rubies. They reckon we have upwards of a thousand now. Our own resident population here in Nevada."

"And you like to shoot them? Is that what we're doing?" Snipe hunt, I was thinking—but I'd let him clown me.

"At them. I miss way more than I hit, if we're being honest. A chicken at six, seven hundred yards? Wind blowing? Good luck." He took out his can of Copenhagen. "Beats paper targets, though. Look around you, dude. Sweet as anything still left in this country."

"No doubt."

"Then tell me, tell me what breed of man sees these mountains and says to himself, Shucks, we don't have any Pakistani birds—who thinks that way?" He worked a pinch of tobacco into his mouth, then returned the can to his shirt pocket. "People need to learn how to leave things alone. And if they can't do that they should be putting wolves back in the Rubies. Even the elk and bear are all gone. Grizzlies and blacks, both." He spit into the pine boughs bunched around us. "But wolves and bears would be too fucking real. It's all got to do with creating the illusion of wilderness now."

"You ever been married, Lionel? Have children?"

"Nope. You?"

"No."

"Why you asking?"

"Just wondering." I pointed across the valley. "That your land too?"

"You know it's not."

"But what about the law? I know *this* can't be legal."

He glanced over at me. "You on the lam or something? And what kind of law you mean anyway?"

"The kind with the badges and the guns."

"Meh. On the one side there's the government and its piles and piles of laws, but on the other side you have what some call Natural Law." He formed his hands into a V. "When they diverge I go with the Greeks. End of story."

I nodded like I knew what he was talking about.

"Get comfortable." He patted my shooting mat. "It's the right thing, trust me. This is a noble endeavor. Civil disobedience, Thoreau, et cetera, et cetera." He sighed. "They'll find a way to steal it from me one day, Roy."

Again I nodded, only this time I understood exactly what he was saying. That in the end they will take whatever they want.

FOR THE BETTER PART of an hour we lay in the sniper's nest, glassing above the tree line on the opposite mountainside with the binoculars and the spotting scope. Lionel swore that while I'd slept that morning he had seen a half-dozen snow cocks on the mountain we were watching, claimed he'd let loose at two of them before the flock scattered. He thought they should be in the area still, that the birds might return to resume feeding as the day wore on.

So we waited. Lionel had the spotting scope, and I concentrated the heavy binoculars on a grassy fissure that ran in a jagged zigzag up to the summit.

"You haven't made them sheep yet?" he asked.

"What sheep?"

He directed me to three bighorn sheep bedded among the rocks, and finally I was able to pinpoint them with the binoculars. They were like rocks themselves. I set down the binoculars, and Lionel looked up from the spotting scope. "How far off you think they are?"

"You plan to shoot one?"

"I'm not some everyday fucking poacher. How far?"

Without the binoculars I couldn't see those brown sheep at all, but I had their approximate location high on the mountain marked in my head. I drew a mental line across the valley from me to them, then started laying football fields out from end to end through the sky that separated us.

"Beats me," I said. "Five hundred yards?"

"Five even?"

"Sure." I wasn't doing much more than guessing.

"I'll say six-forty. Let's see." He reached into his day pack and pulled out what looked like a small video camera. "Laser range finder," he explained. "Cheating." He lifted the range finder to his eye, and a few seconds passed as he searched around for the bighorns. "You were too low. Want a mulligan?"

"Six-forty."

He dropped the range finder next to the rifle. "Six hundred eleven."

"Isn't there anything more you can tell me about Tommy?"

"Like war stories? That what you're after?" He put a hand up in helpless defeat. "We trained together for almost a year, then our platoon spent about a month deployed before he died. I'm sorry, but again, there's really nothing else to tell. Truly."

I didn't want to believe him, didn't want to accept I was going to leave this mountain no more enlightened than when I'd come. "But was he happy?" I asked.

"Happy? How would I know? I thought a lot of him, though. Ahab was a good kid."

"Did he seem to like his life? That's all I mean."

"What a question." He bobbed his head as if thinking hard about it. "Well, I'm pretty sure he liked wearing the Trident."

"Yeah?"

"It's tough to say. He was a free spirit, at least for an operator. Was why I enjoyed him. Close with his cards, but in a trickster way. Not so serious like you. We'd badger him with those Ray Stevens songs, but he gave as good as he got."

"I'm not all that serious."

"Fine. You're a comedian." Lionel handed me the binoculars and grinned. "Now let's get back to me and a Joseph boy, fighting the enemy."

IT WAS ALMOST NOON when Lionel announced that several snow cocks had appeared. I wasn't able to find them with the binoculars, but he passed me the spotting scope so I could get a better look. An I'll-be-damned moment. This wasn't a snipe hunt after all. There were six of them, each a mix of gray and black and brown with some white along the throat and head, and they were indeed the size of chickens. Lionel thought this was most likely the flock he'd busted that morning, and I watched one of them through the spotting scope while he consulted the range finder. It stood motionless on the slope as the others fed nearby.

"Which you on?" Lionel asked.

"The highest."

He peered back into the range finder. "Got it."

"How far? Six hundred?"

"Seven hundred three." There were foam earplugs lying next to the rifle, and we both slipped a pair in. "We're talking a Hail Mary shot here, but you good?"

I nodded. His voice was muffled now, but I could still hear him okay. He pushed his cowboy hat back. Grabbed ahold of the .308's pistol grip with his trigger hand. Flipped the lens caps on the rifle scope. His cheek was settled against the stock, and he began to sight on the snow cock. "Doping the scope," he said, as he clicked at two dials to match the yardage from the range finder and, I assumed, account for the slight breeze blowing across the valley. He finished with his adjustments but kept talking. "I'm locked at a hundred, so at this distance my bullet drops about thirteen feet. The skinny air here will flatten that arc out some, but not lots." He switched the safety off with his thumb. "And uphill, no less. You watching?"

I put the spotting scope back on the snow cock. It was staring straight up at the blue sky, looking out for danger. Hawks, eagles. "Yeah," I said.

"Don't blink."

His breathing became steady and even, and just when I thought he might not shoot there was a pneumatic yawp from the rifle like a nail gun punching on top of the roaring whip crack of the bullet breaking the sound barrier as it made the lobbing trip, then a quick puff of rock dust and maybe feathers. Something—a spent cartridge, I realized—had bounced off the side of the spotting scope. I began to search for snow cocks and saw only a lone bird moving up the summit, confused and desperate, scrambling for the safety of the reverse slope.

"Son of a bitch," I whispered. "Did you actually hit it?"

Lionel dropped the magazine from the rifle. He was on his knees, and he took the spotting scope from me, storing it in the day pack along with the binoculars and the range finder. "We probably shouldn't dawdle," he said.

I started to stand, but then he stayed where he was. "Everything okay?" I asked.

"I'm an asshole."

"What?"

He ejected the round still chambered in the rifle, began to spin the cartridge in his hand. We were both on our knees now, and from across the valley, in the scope of some other hunter, it would have looked as if we were praying.

"There *was* a crash," said Lionel.

"I believe you. I never meant—"

"Stop. Let me talk. January '91, well over a month before the ground campaign. Iraqi troops were occupying an offshore oil field east of Kuwait, and on the eighteenth the navy would be going in to clear them. That was the Battle of Ad-Dawrah. You familiar?"

"No."

"Doesn't matter. But that was what we were practicing for. SEALs might be needed for fast-rope inserts onto some of those oil rigs, so they had eight of us flying from a destroyer to an abandoned Aramco platform. Dress rehearsal for the op."

"Where?"

"In the Persian Gulf, off the Saudi coast. You got the truth from the navy, just not the goatfuck particulars." He shook his head. "Like how there should have been another helo with us, but the ship's CO needed the other SH-60 for mine watch. So it was decided we would Charlie Mike and run the rehearsal with the single helo, and yup, corners were cut. Still—friendly waters, nothing too complicated. We'd done the same run twice already, but of course something went wonky with the 60's hydraulics on this one. We were flying doors open, seats out, and wearing flight suits and helmets, light tactical setup, MP5s and pistols, our climbing harnesses clipped to floor fittings. The pilots were getting us lower, coming down in a swoop, and me and Ahab were to be the first pair off. Nighttime, easy seas, but not much moon. Couldn't see dick, couldn't hardly hear the crew chief's commands, so I told Ahab, Unclip your carabiner. When we feel the spray hit our face, we jump."

Lionel ran his tongue across his front teeth, and then the cartridge he'd been holding went sailing into the valley unfired. He was speaking like a hypnotized man, channeling another Lionel Purcell. A version he didn't know anymore. A minute could have passed, and in that quiet minute he was hands on his thighs and chest to the world—a knelt samurai preparing to die with honor. I knew I shouldn't ask him to go on. I shouldn't, but I did.

"So what happened?"

He closed his eyes, then opened them, returning to the here and now. "Don't really know. Chaos and Murphy happened. Everybody was busy, so nobody quite saw, but I guess Ahab either got bucked or jumped too early, too high. I glanced over to check on him, but he was already out. I jumped, the rest jumped, and we collected up. We each had our own flotation, but he never showed. He wasn't anywhere."

I felt like I'd been smashed against that mountain, crushed by that sky. "The navy looked for him, though, right?" I asked. "Later?"

"They looked, but we'd gone into the water ten klicks seaward and a windstorm blew in that lasted almost two days." Lionel's shoulders slumped, as if sharing that memory had only made it heavier somehow. "That was that."

After all those years, I had a story. The same story, but with details. A story I'd have to tell Joni—how there was a good possibility her boy SEAL father had made a mistake. Or maybe Joni would get old pictures from a photo album and the simpler story. The fleeting story Lionel had told me in the very beginning. He was aiming his finger at me now, and I wondered if he was reading my mind.

"Who cares how it played?" he asked. "Just know this—you die in the line, you're a hero. That's who your brother is to me, Roy. And I'm sorry, but I won't ever talk about that night again."

I T WAS NEARLY DUSK BY THE TIME WE HAD THE WILLYS
parked back inside Lionel's shed. The Walker hounds
were at full volume, and when I let Sam out of his
kennel he touched noses through the chain-link with one of the
hounds, then hopped around like he hadn't seen me in a year. I
rubbed at his ears to calm him, and he followed me to the shed.

Lionel handed me a Coke from an ice chest and cracked one
for himself. "You still leaving tomorrow?" he asked.

"Yeah. But I appreciate you taking me in, telling me what
you did."

We settled into lawn chairs, and he drained his Coke in two
slams. "I'm glad you came looking."

"Me too," I said. And in spite of everything, I meant it.

"Don't let it be another sixteen years."

"I won't."

"Sure you won't." He stood. "I need to snag something. Sit tight."

He jogged off to the trailer in his limping canter, and I started
picking kennel hay from Sam's blond coat. When Lionel rejoined
us he had a pistol in his hand. A small black automatic. I had a
panicked thought that for some Natural Law reason he was about
to shoot me, but instead he spit the magazine and racked the slide
to show me the pistol was unloaded.

"Here," he said, popping the empty mag back in place. "That's for you, little brother."

My eyes stayed on the gun.

"Chop chop. Free gat. Thank you for your service."

"But why?"

"Just take it already."

Finally I reached out and accepted the pistol. I'd been forced to sell off all Joseph guns prior to striking my plea deal with the D.A., and it felt awkward in my hand. Lionel returned to his lawn chair, and I sat down across from him, examining the pistol in the light. I didn't recognize the make or the model or even the caliber, but according to the markings on the barrel this was a Walther PPK in 7.65 mil.

"Same as James Bond used," said Lionel. "And same as what Hitler put to his head." He removed his hat, and his hair fell loose as he hooked the crown over his knee. Between that hair and his horseshoe mustache he looked sullen. A half-yeti already missing his mountains. "Ahab gave that to me."

"Come on."

"It's a fact." He pulled a rubber band off his wrist and tied his hair up. "We'd always spring some gag or another on newbies. The guys told him he had to buy the oldest man a present out of respect, something expensive. Said that was a Team FIVE tradition."

"And Tommy bought you this?" My brother the worm.

Lionel nodded. "I told him they'd been jerking his chain, but I think he knew that. He wouldn't take it back, so now I'm giving it to you." He pointed at the ceiling of the shed. "Hooyah. I win, Ahab."

"I can't take it either."

"Nope. You can and you will. That's a direct order."

"I'm a felon."

He floated one of his eyebrows. "No lie?"

"I got into some trouble when I was young."

He waved me quiet. "Not any of my concern. You've seen I kick the chalk off the sidelines myself."

"I had sex with a minor. She was sixteen. I was nineteen."

He waved his hand again. "I absolve you. It's not how you start, it's how you finish. Fake it till you make it."

AA platitudes, I supposed. I looked down at the Walther. It was against the law for me to be holding a gun, but this was something different. Tommy had held that pistol, and I could sense him now, in the shed with us. This was like a holy relic. Those tangible reminders that dead saints once walked the earth as people. Twenty-year-old boys don't leave much behind when they die. Here was an artifact to be cared for and venerated. A splinter from the True Cross, the finger of Doubting Thomas.

"Screw 'em, Roy. Don't beat yourself up over the past. There's no bottom to that."

"Okay," I said.

"Take it one day at a time. The only easy day was yesterday."

"You're fucking with me."

He laughed. "Who says I'm talking to you? I might still have a box of ammo for her. I could look."

"That's all right."

"Now you listen. I wrestled over whether to give that to you because I can tell you're a bit unglued. I don't want you getting itchy, hurting yourself."

"You don't need to worry about that."

"Well, I do. Don't make a jackass of me."

He stood, and I realized he was asking me to shake on it. To promise I wouldn't go out like Hitler, a coward in his bunker. I stood up myself, and he grabbed my hand as if I was falling and he was there catching me, steadying me. After that we talked some more, but not about anything important, not about anything I can remember now. Words I forgot almost as I was saying them.

He'd given me all he could, and we each drank another Coke, then called it a night. I thanked Lionel again for everything, and he told me to keep careful, that a strange and crowded city like San Francisco was no place to be. The last thing he said to me was maybe *you* are Orion. Happy hunting.

On Thursday I would ride out of Battle Mountain with the rising sun, and though I think Lionel probably heard me and Sam bumping around, he didn't emerge from his bedroom to see us off. I left the Walther lying among the books on the iron coffee table. For now that relic would remain with him for safekeeping. Though I didn't question that Tommy would have wanted me to have that gun, if I got caught with it I could be looking at prison. And despite my occasional displays of bullshit swagger and disregard, and the hero I'd apparently had for a brother, the reality is that life had made me a good slave. That in any real moment of truth, I was never not afraid.

PART III

The San Francisco Notes

So this is the battlefield?

—Red Dawn (1984)

BEYOND THE SOFT, BUTTERY SUNLIGHT OF POSTCARD San Francisco is a low-slung and oftentimes foggy neighborhood locals refer to as the Outer Richmond. My sublet was on Forty-Sixth Avenue, in the bottom floor of a guacamole-green building between Fulton and Cabrillo Streets. About a quarter mile from the ice-cold Pacific, and a half block north of Golden Gate Park. Many of my neighbors were Chinese or Russian, and our stretch of Forty-Sixth Avenue was nothing but salt-mellowed two- and three-stories crammed together like the worn toy cubes of a child. I'd hate to see what a fire might do there. A thrifty lady buys a used toaster, then everyone dies.

Viktor Fedorov's house was just eight blocks away from my tiny apartment, and during our Kansas phone call we had arranged to meet in the park the morning after I got into town. "I will see you at nine thirty," he'd said on the phone. "By the windmill at the end of JFK Drive."

And though Joni wasn't for Viktor to know about, the apartment was also a mile and a half from Marvel Court. Thursday, my date of arrival, wouldn't count toward my five working days of amnesty, but starting tomorrow I'd be on the clock. I only had a week to both find Joni and charm her, so after my check-for-key exchange with the serene, apple-cheeked Karen Yang, I left Sam in the apartment and trudged up Cabrillo, then Thirty-Second Avenue, alone.

The Hammons house was a yellow, entrance-beside-garage stucco, flat across the front save for ten feet of balcony built into the second floor. It sat wedged between a pair of similar two-story stuccos on Marvel Court, not far from where that short, dead-end lane hit up against a steep and bushy hillside belonging to a park called Lincoln Park. A trail through the trees and scrub along the eastern portion of Lincoln Park brought me to the hill above Marvel Court. I could see the house from there, and I reckoned if I returned tomorrow and waited long enough I'd spot Joni coming home from school. That tomorrow I would know what she looked like.

FRIDAY MORNING, and an overcast sky. Golden Gate Park. A thousand-acre rectangle of land running from the middle of the city to the ocean. Way west by the quiet Outer Richmond the park felt unfinished. Wild, almost. There were sad cases who dwelled within its thickets: addicts in blanket tents, loner combat vets, small homeless confederations. So, condoms and needles, trash and misery, but also things I never expected to find in a big American city. Peace and beauty. Raccoon, possum, and skunk tracks. Various songbirds, raptors, and waterfowl. Ravens and crows. There was a restaurant that looked over the Great Highway and the Pacific, two dormant windmills and an archery range, some soccer fields, and even a nine-hole golf course—but pretty much everything else was forest.

The windmill on JFK Drive was only a ten-minute walk from the apartment, and I found it without any trouble. A Brothers Grimm windmill, about seven stories high with brown shingles and four still sails. We were early, so I figured I had let Sam nose the green hedges of the tulip garden there. And I had just taken him off leash when I saw a silver-haired man coming up the sidewalk with a dog of his own. A Saluki—like a greyhound, but with a feathered and fawn-colored coat. The man saw Sam roaming loose and stopped. His Saluki was leashed, so I was the one in the wrong, no argument there. I hollered for Sam, but it was too late. He'd seen the sight hound and was bounding over to say hello. I kept yelling, but Sam wasn't listening.

A dog will sometimes become nervous if it's on a leash and gets approached by a rowdy Fido that isn't, and once the man saw Sam wasn't going to peel off he dropped his Saluki's lead so she wouldn't fluster. At first the two dogs were only sniffing each other, and I'd almost reached them when the Saluki bit Sam on the ear. Sam made a sound like tires squealing. Now *he* was pissed. The Saluki hauled ass, and Sam tore after her—but she was the fastest dog ever. The man was shouting in Russian and I was shouting in English, until finally we got our dogs in check.

Sam was pawing at his ear and whimpering. I knelt beside him, then looked to the Russian. He was pushing sixty, moonfaced and bull-necked, about my height but way broader and with short, Caesar-cut hair, a downturned mouth, and half-lidded eyes. He was wearing a black leather jacket and black pants, and had the Saluki sitting between his splayed feet.

"Are you Viktor?" I asked.

"Yes," he said. "You are Roy? Is she all right?" A statement of concern, but in the same bored monotone I'd heard on the phone. Like he was flipping each word over for a tedious inspection. "I am very sorry. I have never seen Dina bite."

"It's not your fault." And it wasn't, of course. Still, it made me sick to see Sam hurting. I examined a small cut on the inside of his left ear. "It's *he*," I said. "Sam."

Viktor nodded. "I believe your Sam will be fine."

In my sweatshirt I found a wad of napkins I'd pocketed at some point, and I was wiping the blood from Sam's ear when he slipped away, tail wagging, and went back over to the Saluki. Soon they were rolling around together near the tulip garden, all forgiven. Viktor laughed, and I stood.

"Dina and Sam," he said. "You see? They are falling in love now." He took my wrist in his hand, avoiding the blood-smeared napkins. "How was your trip?"

"It went okay. No problems till yesterday."

"Something is a problem?"

Last night I had planned to go searching for a diner, but the LeBaron wouldn't crank. "My car," I said. "I need to replace the battery, I think."

"I just saw a Louisiana car. The red BMW on Cabrillo?"

"The Chrysler on Fulton."

"A 300?"

"An old LeBaron."

He frowned. "You are missing a finger."

"I am." My left hand was in the pouch of my sweatshirt, but he must have noticed the clipped knuckle while I was seeing to Sam's ear.

"This happened on an oil rig?"

"Yep."

"You did not tell me this."

"Does it matter?"

"Probably no."

"But possibly yes?"

He stuck his own meaty thumb in my face like a hitchhiker, an artist measuring proportion. "I had an uncle in Leningrad who lost his thumb. Do you forget sometimes it is gone?"

"What?"

"My uncle, his missing thumb, it would tingle."

"Oh. No. Not really."

"Maybe it is not gone long enough?"

"Could be."

His arm fell. "How is our friend Terry? He is still with Larissa?" But without waiting for my answer he glanced at his watch. It was as shiny as a gold disco ball. "Let us walk," he said.

There were only a few roads on this end of Golden Gate Park. Paved, gray arteries and veins in a choke of green. We leashed the dogs and headed in the direction I'd come from the apartment. Past the archery range, on Forty-Seventh Avenue, was an exit from the park onto Fulton. On the corner to our right was a grass acre field. Viktor brought me halfway across it and stopped.

"Yesterday they found a body here," he said. "But today you cannot even tell this."

"I'm sorry?"

"Right here. In the early, early morning after Halloween. A homeless woman. She had overdosed herself."

I'd been asleep in a Battle Mountain trailer, but as Viktor moved on I was picturing a scabby, rotten-toothed woman collapsing in the wet grass of that little field. She's vomiting. She's seizing. There is the faint roar of the nearby ocean, a cold night breeze. She lies dead for hours before anyone even knows.

From the killing acre we took a dirt trail that led through a forest. Eucalyptus trees with leaves like narrow lance tips, the bark shedding from their creamy trunks in long, spiraling strips. Cypress. Pine. An understory of rhododendron and azalea and ivy, dark topsoil and thicket. From somewhere in the brush a radio was playing.

Viktor was doing all the talking, rambling on about a guy he'd seen in that same forest over the weekend. A falconer hunting squirrels. The morning was misty and chilled, but he seemed to be warming to me, his monotone lifting on occasion as he spun his tale, and I followed along, half listening, smelling the dank of the moist woods and the salt of the Pacific, sporadic whiffs of urine and shit. I was wondering what I'd gotten myself into. *Probably no*, he'd said regarding my finger being a deal breaker.

Kiss my ass. No doubt I could come up with a less depraved and creepy cover story to explain my presence in San Francisco than bride shopping.

"What a thing," said Viktor. "To see a *sokolnik* and his bird in this park."

"Terry said you have a car service? Limos?" I've learned asking questions helps keep the focus off me.

Viktor nodded. "I have four limousines and a Mercedes."

"How long have you been in America?"

"I got out in 1973 with nothing but my wife. I was just twenty-four. But a smart man can make his living here, raise a family."

"So y'all have kids, then?"

"We have a daughter in St. Louis and a son in Seattle."

That seemed crazy to me—the Americans created by this Russian. A family transforming and morphing into something completely different than it had once been. The new family becomes the real family; the old family becomes trivia. If Nancy Hammons was to be believed, Tommy had spent one night with her in San Diego, and now the only other descendant of the Dry Springs Josephs left in the world was here in California. We walked on in silence.

Eventually the forest opened, and we came to a long, tapering pond hemmed by willows, water grasses, blackberry bushes. Along a blacktop path was a bench hidden within all that jungle between us and the pond, and we stopped there to sit. Sam sprawled out at my feet. Dina came over and lay by Viktor. There were mallards and wigeon and pouldeau in the pond. Red-winged blackbirds were bouncing on willow limbs.

I lit a Winston; Viktor was working on a cigar. "We watch now," he said. "The Russian nannies. They come here and they gossip."

"Nannies?"

After a few minutes they began to file in—five youngish women pushing baby strollers the size of shopping carts. The nannies collected on a small gravel-and-sand beach on the other side of the pond, their strollers parked like circled wagons as they smoked cigarettes and talked.

"There she is," said Viktor.

"Who?"

"In the white sweater. The blue jeans. Do you see her?"

She was far away, but I did. Her chin-length hair was a coppery color, and she was apart from the group, scraping sand off her black boots with a long stick. Once she finished she went to join the others. Her body was full, compact but curved, and the way her chest pushed against the front of her wool sweater made me think of those Fox News anchors the guys on the rigs liked to leer at. Free porn, we'd call Fox News.

"Yeah," I said. "I see her."

"Marina Katanova." Viktor tapped the ashes from his cigar. "From Moscow. One of the three women I have spoken to for you. The best one, probably. And they are like wives and mothers already, these nannies."

I felt something inside me shifting. This was the difference between hearing Lionel Purcell speak of unlikely creatures and seeing them appear on a mountainside myself. The difference between having an address and seeing a house. My father happened to be born just across the Cane River from the girl he was meant to be with, and if that isn't fate I don't know what is. But, hell, perhaps this was fate too. That the search for a lost niece in San Francisco and the long-ago blatherings of a crew boat captain would bring Viktor, then this woman, into my life.

"You will be meeting her tonight," said Viktor. "That is the soonest she can get away from her work."

"Does she live there too? At the place she works?"

"Exactly."

"That's near here?"

"No. But she comes on the bus with the baby. She is lonesome."

"And she knows about me?"

"She does—though we should go before she sees us."

"About that stuff I wrote to you in my e-mail, I mean."

"Ah. Yes. Some of it. The good things, those I told her."

"But not everything."

He shook his head. "Let her learn for herself that you are nice, that you have means. If there is a later, then yes, we will tell her everything. But for now that can wait, okay?"

I was still watching Marina Katanova as he stood. I would have traded another finger for binoculars right then.

Viktor looked down at me. "You are not happy? We could begin with one of the other two. Do you want that instead?"

Marina was no less Russian than the rest of those across-the-pond nannies, far as I knew, but even at that range, and even though she was among baby strollers, a single dopey thought would not leave my brain. Maybe she's like a Cane River girl for *me,* I was thinking.

"No," I said. "I'd rather get to know that one first. Marina."

WITH THE LEBARON'S battery dead I was left riding the bus to travel any fair distance, lurching from stop to stop on those rattle-trap barges. Marco Polo in jeans and a gray sweatshirt, adrift in the washed-out and faded pastels of a new world. And after my walk with Viktor I set out for the bayfront shipyards. I'd seen them from the bridge as I had crossed into the city, and though I'm not sure why, I thought going there today might somehow inspire me, help me lay out my plans.

So I was eastbound on a bus called the 5 Fulton. At five-thirty I would be meeting Marina Katanova, and before that, when school let out, I'd try to steal my first glimpse of Joni. With that accomplished I was confident the rest of my plan would form in my mind. Somehow I'd have to introduce myself to Joni, but that clearly couldn't happen at Marvel Court, the home turf of Nancy Hammons. I had to find a way that wouldn't spook her. A way that wouldn't end with me being driven to a police station. The best way for Joni, but also the best way for me.

In a half hour I was downtown, and I quit that bus to wait for another. Glass and concrete. Tall buildings and bike messengers. A different terrarium here than the Outer Richmond. Warmer. The sky not overcast but cornflower and streaked with the cotton contrails of planes. Classy, on-the-go women and men with all ten of their fingers marched by. In their smooth dresses and suits they were like some different species.

When I reached the shipyards I saw longshoremen and dockworkers gathered by the bay. They were throwing crusts to seagulls as they finished their lunches. I went into a corner store and bought a Mountain Dew, some Funyuns, and a ham sandwich secured inside a triangle of plastic, then found a bench and ate. To my left the I-80 bridge looked like a spiderweb dropping into the water, and I could see across the bay to Oakland and Alameda. Tommy had cooled his heels for a few weeks at an Alameda naval base after completing boot camp in Illinois. His only stop before, on his road to becoming a SEAL, he went to Coronado for BUD/S training. A tanker was heading north, a container ship was coming south, and I imagined my brother tracking them from his side of the bay. Maybe it wasn't such a bad way to go, drowning. Maybe Tommy held his breath until a peaceful euphoria slid over him and he couldn't resist that last, fatal swallow. Then, no more struggling, no more suffering, no more fear. Just blackness without pain except, at the very end, when there was a starburst of light and his thoughts went to us, his family.

Or, better still, maybe he never even woke up from his fall.

BY THREE O'CLOCK I'd walked from a bus stop to Lincoln Park, and I found a spot on the bushy hill above Marvel Court where I could sit. After an hour a green Subaru Forester pulled into the garage, and then a woman came jogging out to grab the newspaper from the driveway before retreating into the house. And though she was too quick for me to make out much of her face, she had the same close-cropped platinum hair as in the photo of Nancy Hammons I'd brought up in the Cybermobile. But she also appeared to be older. Tommy would have been thirty-seven. This woman looked at least forty-five.

There was a rainbow sticker on the bumper of the Subaru, but on Thursday I'd managed to locate a collection of Nancy's poetry in the "local authors" section of a bookstore, and several of the poems in *Salted Waters* had more or less outed her already. I'll admit to feeling a twinge of disappointment Nancy wasn't closer to my age and straight. Ever since I'd learned of Joni I think part of me had been hoping all she was missing in her life was a father, and that the woman who'd given birth to my brother's daughter was thirty-six or thirty-seven and as unattached and available as I was. That Nancy had never stopped loving Tommy and couldn't look at me without thinking of him. That the daughter *and* the mother might gradually grow to love *me,* maybe even take the Joseph name. That a man with no one but a dog might stumble upon a family.

If I had to stay on that Lincoln Park hillside from morning to sundown tomorrow, so be it. I'd come to see Joni, but all I could do was try again later.

SIX O'CLOCK. Balboa Street. On a short strip of blocks that was like a colorized photograph in the cold, dead center of the mostly muted Outer Richmond. A hodgepodge of commerce amid the neighborhood's suffocation of homes. I was sitting at the back of Simple Pleasures Café with finger-combed hair, waiting for Marina Katanova—and asking with each passing no-show minute how I'd let my true mission get derailed by this honey trap.

Simple Pleasures was a coffee shop, but they also had food and beer and wine. All I'd bought so far was a water. At the table to the right of mine a man was giving chess lessons to a schoolboy. The man was different looking but in a rock singer way, and the boy's manicured, wedding-ringed mom was across from him with her arm around her son. I watched them and noticed that whenever the boy pondered a move the chess instructor and the woman would smile at each other. Eye-fucking, really.

And I was musing about how it was the mom who was actually playing a game when a girl in a blue nursing uniform said, "Excuse me," then squeezed through the foot or so separating my table from the vacant one to my left. She was Indian, the overseas kind. She sat down next to me with a glass of red wine, and I put my hand under the table so she wouldn't see my bird claw. All of these people—the innocent boy and the handsome chess instructor, the good-to-go mother and the nurse with the speck-of-ruby nose stud—were close enough for me to reach out and touch.

"Checkmate," said the boy.

"Word," said the chess instructor, fist-bumping the boy.

"That is awesome," said the mom. "You're a *fantastic* teacher."

I just stared ahead and listened, but the nurse was looking across my table now, watching the chess lessons. After a while I noticed a guy in medical scrubs and plastic clogs angling our way. He was cradling a pint glass of beer like it was filled with nitroglycerin, and he kept shuffling toward me in his orange shoes but then sat opposite the nurse.

"Hi, Radha," he said. "Oops for ordering without you. Didn't see you when I came in."

"That's okay," she said. "Hi."

"Thanks so much for coming. And sorry. Dr. Weiss made all the residents stay a little late today." He pointed at her wineglass. "Vino. Cool. Cheers. You already paid for that?"

"Uh-huh."

Obviously. Great question, guy. He barely looked old enough to drink. "A lot of people in here," he said to Nurse Radha.

"Yeah," she said. "I guess because it's Friday."

"Totes. How was your shift?"

And so on and so on. The flouncy-haired resident would be a bona fide doctor eventually, but he still talked and acted like a frat boy. "So," he said, "have you thought about it?"

He started to say more, but the nurse sighed and cut him off. "I *have* thought about it," she said, "and here's the deal—you seem like a really nice person, but I don't think it's such a good idea. Me being a nurse, us at the hospital every day." A speech spilled out of her, one I could tell she had prepared well beforehand. A speech she'd maybe practiced on her hospital sisters between rounds. It was like there was someone standing behind the resident and holding up cue cards for her to read. He tried to stop her but she rolled on, rushing her words as if now those cue cards were on fire and disappearing. "It's not smart," she said, "with us having to work together, and so, yeah—"

Her voice trailed off, and she looked at her lap. This was a pre-date, a negotiation to perhaps have a date in the future. A powwow not so different from the one Viktor claimed to have organized for me and Marina (forty-five minutes late and counting). There you go, Radha. Piss on all doctors. May they spend their nights alone in their castles, raping their sterile and perfect hands. I was being shot down, or at least stood up, as well—but we weren't in the same fraternity, me and him.

The resident was trying to save face now. "I understand," he was saying. "I understand totally." Nobody had lifted a chess piece in a long time; we were all listening to this death rattle. "It's just that I dig you," he added.

Suddenly I needed to get out from between those twin soap operas. The scene had snapped into perspective, and I saw how pathetic it was to be waiting to present myself to some Russian woman I'd never even spoken to. I called Viktor's cell, but no one answered. I didn't bother leaving a voice mail. Despite having given him a two-hundred-and-fifty-dollar check in Golden Gate Park, I'm not sure I ever *really* believed he could find a woman willing to have anything to do with me. No Marina. No Joni. One working day in, this trip was already shaping up to be another wrong turn for me.

I jostled the chess instructor's table as I went by, apologizing when a captured knight fell to the floor. It was a downhill mile to my place. Nail salons and dentist offices and markets. A liquor store and a laundromat and an old movie theater. Chinese restaurant after Chinese restaurant. The air was even colder than before, and I pulled up the hood of my sweatshirt as I headed toward the horizon. Through a mesh of phone lines and cable and wire, the western sky was bleeding in pinks and reds.

THE DOOR TO KAREN YANG'S three hundred square feet of San Francisco was cut into the back of a two-car garage I wasn't allowed to park in, and when I got inside Sam started whirling around in a circle, black claws clicking against the apartment's lemon tile. The floor was all that same ugly tile, and I had one room of living space that doubled as a kitchen, plus a bathroom with a shower but no tub. I pushed Sam away, too cross about Simple Pleasures to pet him, then opened the back door. "Go on," I said, and he skulked out into the plot of sandy dirt and brown weeds I shared via a corkscrew of metal stairs with whoever lived in the second- and third-floor flats above me.

The apartment had a small bed with a synthetic comforter that still had tags. Creased white sheets and one pillow. A table and two chairs. A dresser, a desk, and a couch. There was a computer Karen had said I could use, but if she owned a phone or a TV they were both gone now. Her closet was locked and her dresser had been emptied. There was no food at all in the icebox or the cabinets. The microwave was immaculate; the pots and plates and pans and utensils like they'd just come from the store. No pictures, no books, no calendar. It seemed impossible Karen Yang lived there. That anyone had ever lived there. I suspected the computer might contain clues, but I could only log in as a guest. My password was *Visitor0*.

I called Sam in. It was early, but I killed the lights. My sleeping bag was spread across that uncomfortable comforter, and I yanked off my Red Wings and lay down. I had a towel for Sam by the door, but he crept closer, then dropped to the floor beside the bed. I could hear him breathing.

I HADN'T NAPPED for more than an hour when I woke to Sam barking at my phone. I had on jeans, but no shirt, no socks. The room was dark, the tile cold, and I was bumbling around on the balls of my feet. The phone cut off before I could get to it, then someone rang the apartment bell. Again Sam barked, and I stubbed my toe on the doorsill going into the garage. Fuck fuck fuck. Viktor had my address. This must be him.

I switched a light on. It was freezing with the sun gone. A Volvo was parked too far forward, and I slid myself through the narrow gap between the drywall and the front bumper. The bell sounded again; Sam barked again. "I'm coming," I hollered. It was Viktor all right. I could smell his cigar.

To the side of the garage was a concrete room that served as the building's entrance, and an iron gate kept the world at bay.

I stepped out from the garage and saw Viktor on the sidewalk. He was pacing back and forth behind the bars, and though I was the one who was locked away, in his black pants and black jacket he looked like a silver-browed zoo ape.

"Marina didn't show," I said.

"I know this." Viktor pitched his cigar into the street, then grabbed one of the bars with his wide hand. "I have a message from her."

"I need to put a shirt on. I'll be right back."

He latched onto another of the bars. He was twice my age, but even so, it seemed as if he could tear that gate off the hinges. "You are already all the way out here! Let me in."

His stopping-by-unannounced, probation-officer act had me ticked, but I made my way across the concrete to let him inside. He saw me shivering and laughed. I'm sure San Francisco cold has nothing on Russia cold, and when I opened the gate he slapped my bare shoulder, muttered a word I think might have meant pussy.

VIKTOR AND I SAT on the couch while he tried to salvage our partnership. I was fastening the snaps of my work shirt, and he was brushing at the scab on Sam's ear. Marina had told him her phone had died. That she hadn't been able to call him sooner to relay she wouldn't be making Simple Pleasures. That she'd had to run a few unexpected errands for her employers. Right. Even Viktor didn't sound like he believed her. "But come to my home for dinner tomorrow," he said. "You can meet her then."

"What about *your* cell? You couldn't return my call?"

"I forgot my phone in the Mercedes. Sorry. A bad day for phones. I am just hearing all of this. So now I am here."

"That check I gave you? I'd like it back."

"You do not want this anymore?"

"I don't."

"I would not cheat you." He reached into the pocket of his leather jacket and produced my check. "It is two-fifty for each woman you meet. Give this to me after our dinner. Is that better? You have spent much more than that to be here this week. You are upset. And maybe too you are nervous. But you cannot let that ruin everything."

He was calling me a pussy again, basically. His light eyes seemed sleepy but earnest as he pressed the check into my hand. Perhaps it *was* all a lie, a con, but he had a point. There was little to lose.

"You're positive she will be there?"

"I am positive! We will have a very nice evening." He pulled a Ziploc from another pocket and showed it to me. "Some chicken pieces for the patient," he said.

I nodded, and he tossed them to Sam one by one. Sam's tail started whacking against the side of my leg, and when the chicken was all gone Viktor went into the kitchen area and washed his hands. He seemed somewhat disgusted by how small the place was, and even more so by the lack of a TV. Earlier, walking in, that had been the first thing he'd commented on.

"Do you want to hear a joke?" He was opening and closing Karen Yang's cabinets for some reason. "A Vovochka joke. He is a Russian boy. A student."

I sighed. "Go ahead." Malcolm had ruined me on jokes, but at least his were short. I doubted Viktor's would be. It had happened in imperceptible degrees, this transition of his from dour marriage pimp to jovial comrade.

He was looking in the icebox now. Three blocks from the apartment, down closer to the beach, was a Safeway supermarket I'd hit up already. I had a few beers in the icebox, a few groceries, and he took out two Budweisers. "Is okay?" he asked.

"Sure."

He twisted both bottles open and walked across the room to hand one over. I was still on the couch; he was standing in front of me.

"Vovochka is in the classroom. His teacher, she is at the chalkboard." He pointed at me as he paced and then at himself. I was one of the students. He was the teacher. Sam was sitting on his haunches, watching with his head tilted.

"The teacher, she draws on the board." Viktor turned and traced something in the air with his finger, then spun back around and began talking like a woman. "What is this I have drawn, Roy?"

"A heart?"

He gulped at his Budweiser, then set the bottle on the table. "It is an apple. I have drawn an apple for the class." He pivoted and made as if he was erasing the chalkboard. Apparently even in Russia you are required to sit there dumb-faced until the third-act punch line comes. Again Viktor drew in the air, and again he looked to me. "And what have I drawn now?"

"Don't know. A pineapple?"

"No. It is a pear." He stage-whispered to Sam. "Our Roy is not so very smart, is he?"

Then quit, I was thinking, but he spun and drew once more. He called on a child sitting to my right.

"Vovochka?" he chirped. "What is it that *you* see? I will give you a hint. The monkeys, they eat them."

Viktor hurried over and sat beside me on the couch. He was Vovochka now. "Teacher," he said. "Why would you draw such a thing? Monkeys do not eat dicks!"

At last the end had come—but no, instead Viktor stood, waving his hands like a frazzled teacher. "Vovochka! I am getting the principal!" He ran out the apartment, slamming the door. So a *fourth* act, I reckoned.

Sam whined. "Don't fret," I said. "He's coming back."

I took a sip of my beer as we waited for the joke to continue.

In a moment the door opened, and Viktor walked in from the garage. He glared at the couch. "What have you done this time, Vovochka?" He asked this in a serious voice, a man's voice. The school principal. He turned and looked behind him at the phantom chalkboard. "Shame on you! Last week you broke a window and yesterday you started a fight." He pounded at the wall with his fist. "And today—today you have drawn a dick on the board!"

Viktor came closer, leaning over until his face was right in mine, then poked at one of the snaps on my shirt. "Laugh," he said, as himself now. "It was a banana, you see?"

"I do see. Funny."

"Yes," he agreed. "Because nothing was like it appeared."

I 'D BEEN ABOVE THE MARVEL COURT DEAD END SINCE
ten o'clock Saturday morning, watching for Joni, but
also flipping through my copy of *Salted Waters*. What I
was doing was crazy, no story of Russian romance would save me,
but I knew of no other way. I thought of another teenage girl's
house, of Eliza Sprague's parents screaming at me while she cried
on the couch.

Then, two hours in, I looked up from a poem describing a famous ghost ship and saw a magazine-in-hand someone standing
on the small balcony carved into the wall of the yellow stucco.
Not Nancy. A lanky girl wearing red sweatpants and an electric
blue sweatshirt with I ♥ NY on the front. She settled into a cush-
ioned chair, then slid her socked feet between the wooden slats
of the balcony's low railing. I was maybe forty yards away and
level with her, yet she didn't appear to have noticed me. Long
brown hair hid her face, but this had to be Joni. I'd found her.
I ♥ NY. White letters, a red heart. This girl had probably been
to Manhattan—me, Disney World was the farthest I'd traveled
before this trip. My earliest memory of Tommy blossomed in my
mind. I'm cheering mechanical pirates, my brother beside me,
egging me on.

Even though Joni was far away and ill defined, out of reach, she felt like more than a fact confirmed. She was a maiden in a tower. Nancy's tower. For the next half hour I watched her, unable to sneak away, afraid if I even scratched my nose she would detect movement on that hillside. Then the door to the balcony opened, and ice-blond Nancy summoned her daughter inside. Joni closed her magazine, stood, and went into the house, but I sat there, fingers crossed she might come down to Marvel Court. That she would be alone, off to run some errand, and I would have the courage to approach her. She'd glance my way—and calmly, gently, I would tell her who I was.

JONI NEVER REAPPEARED, but she wasn't just a name now. Things were moving forward, and I was excited but anxious. Too anxious. Before very long the apartment seemed like a cage. I had a little time until my dinner with Marina at Viktor's, and though I was tempted to stand *her* up to soothe my pride, I grabbed a tennis ball and took Sam to run around so he'd be good for the night.

Sam and I walked Forty-Sixth Avenue's blanched and lonely corridor, our shadows lengthening with the falling sun, and waited for a break in the traffic on Fulton before crossing over to the emerald tree line of Golden Gate Park. West for a block, then—and at the corner of Forty-Seventh Avenue I considered the killing acre. A woman had died there, but there was no way to tell.

The archery range was a large grass field bordered on three sides by a dense jumble of bushes. There was a sign forbidding dogs, but since it was late I didn't expect to be harassed. I soldiered on, scanning the field for cats, skunks, archers, dead people—then I was about to unclip Sam's leash when something made me stop. One of those sixth-sense feelings. I turned and saw an extremely tall man in dark clothes and a wide-brimmed hat. He was standing within an ivied knot of rhododendrons, an arm held up away from his side, a hefty bird perched on his gloved fist. A falcon or maybe a hawk. Here was Viktor's *sokolnik,* I realized.

In the dim light I couldn't see much of the falconer, but he was definitely watching me. I assumed there were statutes and ordinances and commandments against any form of hunting in the park—but I had Sam on the archery range, so I suppose that made both of us scofflaws. I gave a chopping half wave, but the falconer didn't wave back. Instead he emerged from the rhododendrons and moved away at a quick pace, heading for the street.

Sinister fucker. And the tallest man I'd ever seen in the flesh. Looking at him felt like walking under a ladder. I threw the ball for Sam, lit a cigarette, and watched him do his thing. When he returned I had him make a few more retrieves, then snapped him back to the leash. The sun had set, and it was mostly dark. On the way out of the park we passed alongside a white sedan stopped by the killing acre. The car looked plain enough to be an unmarked police cruiser, but there was just an old guy sitting behind the wheel. He smiled and began flashing the interior dome light, trying to draw me closer. I saw a smiling pervert, then nothing, a smiling pervert, then nothing. I shook my head at him and kept on.

I SHOWERED, then wiped at the mirror with a towel. Shaggy, squinting me. My hair was at least two months uncut, and I shaved for the first time in almost a week. In these moments when I'm cleaning myself up—mowing shaving cream and clipping at nails, spitting flossed threads of blood and gargling mouthwash—I often pretend like I'm carving. Like when I'm done chipping away I'll see some of the boy I was, or even Tommy, hiding under that adult decay. But not now, not ever. So I just did the best I could for Marina, and once I was through I combed my bangs out of my eyes, the wings behind my ears, put on a nicer pair of jeans and a collared shirt.

After his comedy act on Friday Viktor had drunk two more of my Budweisers and talked mainly about Viktor. He was a home-owner, and since I doubted homes came cheap in that city, clearly he was doing something right. His four limos were parked throughout the tumbleweed neighborhood, rotating with the schedules of the street sweepers, and before dawn every morning he drove a master-of-the-universe stockbroker to a building downtown in the Mercedes. Then, after the markets had closed in New York, he headed back to fetch the man. As for those limos, Viktor hardly ever drove them himself. "I have people," he'd said. "But not for Mr. Dworkin. He is a decamillionaire."

Viktor's house was painted an adobe color, and there was a sunken garage I suspected contained the Mercedes. Off to the side, a series of steps led up to the front door—but I was a few minutes early, so I lingered awhile on the sidewalk. And I was still standing there when I saw Marina turn the corner. She was wearing a puffy pink coat, the hood trimmed with synthetic gray fur I think was meant to resemble a wolf tail. I waited for her at the bottom of the steps. Those black boots again, but I still had three or four inches on her.

"Hey," I said. "I'm Roy."

Her short hair was brushed straight back, and up close I could see the copper strands were chocolate at the roots. "I am Maria," she said. "I am sorry for yesterday." Viktor had told me she was thirty, but I was questioning whether she might be a few years older than that. There were tight wrinkles around her eyes and mouth. Her teeth had a yellowish tint.

"That's all right. Viktor—"

"The parents, they know nothing." Marina pressed her hands against her face, and I thought she might scream. "And baby is little Satan."

I laughed, but she didn't. Her accent was very thick, her voice even more emotionless and indifferent than Viktor's had once seemed to me, and though behind her heavy makeup she wasn't quite the same woman I'd seen from across a pond, she sounded like a world-weary femme fatale, a somber Bond girl.

"Must be rough," I said.

"Rough?"

"Hard. No fun. Difficult."

"Oh." She nodded. "*Da*. It is very."

The front door opened, and I saw Viktor's moon face grinning at us from the top of the steps. He was in his work clothes. Black pants and a black tie. A white shirt like mine, but with the sleeves rolled up on his bulky forearms. He called down. "Come," he said. "Come, come."

The pink coat stopped right at the curve of Marina's waist, and her snug white Levi's looked stitched to her wide hips. She started up the steps in a sway, the block heels of her boots slapping one-two, one-two against the concrete, and before she made the threshold Viktor kissed her swiftly on the cheek, then crushed my hand. "The new carpet," he said. "No shoes. No smoking, even."

Marina was already removing her boots. She'd been there before, I guess, or maybe that was just the Russian way. I shucked my Red Wings and was allowed inside too.

The house was warm and smelled like a good restaurant. I saw a white-walled living room with a black leather couch, two identical easy chairs (black), and a coffee table (also black). On one wall was an enormous flat-screen TV and—resting on the snow-white carpet beneath it—a stereo, a DVD player, and a digital-cable box. On the opposite wall was a cross-shaped mirror large enough to nail a Celtic to.

Marina was focused on the TV. There were DVD cases stacked atop the coffee table, and the picture had been paused during some nature video. A killer whale had launched its entire domino body clear of the sea and now hung frozen in midair. The whale matched the white carpet, the black leather. Same with Viktor in his uniform.

"You worked today?" I asked. "On a Saturday?"

Viktor nodded as he loosened his tie. "I had to drive Mr. and Mrs. Dworkin somewhere. I am getting back only now."

"I was in the park earlier. I saw that falconer guy."

"The *sokolnik*? He is very tall, no?"

"Yeah. Very."

"*Sokolnik?*" said Marina.

Viktor hollered for his wife, Sonya, and a heavyset woman in a black velvet outfit came out from the kitchen to meet me. She had pillowy skin and pearly hair. I said hello, but Sonya and Viktor and Marina began talking in the mother tongue. I was feeling ignored until Dina the Saluki slunk in from the hallway. She bumped at me, then went searching for Sam. I watched her check all around the living room before she gave up and lay down behind the couch.

I turned to Marina again. Viktor had taken her coat, and underneath she had on a blue top that shimmered when she moved. She'd brought color to that black-and-white room. I looked away, but Sonya had caught me staring. She smiled. "Welcome to our home," she said.

"Thank you. Whatever you're cooking smells really great."

"*Pelmeni,*" she said.

Viktor was next to Sonya, beaming, and he rubbed his stomach and winked at her as she pulled Marina into the kitchen. He led me from the door, and we lowered ourselves into the overstuffed chairs that flanked either side of the couch. "Put your feet up," he said. "It is nice."

I told him I was content, but he wouldn't accept no. Finally I popped the lever and got thrown back horizontal. My legs were stretched out in front of me, and I felt defenseless, as if he had captured me somehow.

"You see?" he said.

Soon Sonya came with half liters of syrupy Baltika beer and two glasses. She poured a glass for me and a glass for her husband. It was like being tucked into bed, lying there in my gray socks. I thanked her, and she went back into the kitchen. Viktor kicked up his own leg rest, got himself settled, then tapped at the remote control balanced on the arm of his chair. There was a bomb blast as the killer whale came crashing to the sea. My hands bounced, and black beer sloshed in the glass I was holding. I looked around, trying not to spill, and saw small speakers screwed into every corner of the room.

Viktor eased the volume down, but not by much. "A theater system!" he shouted.

Up on the TV the killer whale had paired with another just off some coastline, and an English man was narrating. The man told us these were South American sea lions we saw spread across the beach, that the two orcas were hunting. Four of the sea lions had strayed too far, and the killer whales came surging in on a big wave, their dorsal fins cutting through the water like blades. They caught a sea lion apiece, then swam back out to the deep and began tossing their crippled victims into the air, torturing them.

"And high definition!" Viktor shouted. "It is the finest!"

"Damn," I said. It was as if those playing whales were about to come out of the wall and land on me.

LATER WE TOOK SEATS at an actual dinner table in an actual dining room, and that meal was the best I'd had in a long time. *Pelmeni* turned out to be little meat-filled dumplings, and Sonya served them with mashed potatoes and a cucumber salad, sour cream and dill. Marina was quiet at first, but after a second bottle of red wine was opened she became more sociable. Sonya and Viktor were arguing over something in Russian when she asked me about my finger. I had my left hand in my lap, but she'd either spotted the stump already or Viktor had told her.

"Show me," she said, interested suddenly.

I hesitated but then set my roughneck hand down on the table. So many cracks and scars and calluses. It would have been an ugly hand even with all five fingers.

Marina leaned closer to look. She was wearing a strong, cotton candy perfume. "You must work very hard," she said. "I was warehouse girl before America."

I mentioned I wouldn't be rotating offshore any longer. That in a few months I'd have the money I would need to retire and then some. She didn't seem surprised, so I assumed Viktor had been wise enough to share that part of my essay with her. But *I* was surprised. There's no two ways about it—I was sitting there trying, albeit in a roundabout way, to sell her on the idea of a life with me as a husband.

Marina patted my knee and said I should see myself as lucky. "This is something, but this is also nothing. Do you understand what I am saying?" She had dark, dark eyes. Black, almost. Some Cajun women have eyes that color.

I put my hand back in my lap. "I think so," I said.

"Then good, then."

I wondered if that meant she'd decided to marry me—and whether, once told, she would conclude that me being a registered sex offender was something, but also nothing. "You're from Moscow, right?" I asked.

"Yes. I come here six months ago."

"Only six months?"

"*Da.*"

"And you've been working for that family the whole time?"

She nodded. "The Colemans."

"Where in the city are they?"

"Do you know Presidio? Next to Presidio."

"Your English is really good—especially for just getting to America and all."

"No. But thank you."

"Did you study that in school?"

"Some. Yes."

Marina appeared to be bored again, and I tried to think of what else to ask her. Nothing was coming to mind. For the moment she seemed through with me as well, and we both went back to eating. When everyone had finished she and Sonya cleared the dishes. It was only me and Viktor in the dining room now, but there was vodka on the table. He lined up two shots and raised his glass, waiting until I did the same.

"*Za vas!*" he said.

We touched glasses, then drank the crisp vodka down.

Viktor poured two more and capped the bottle. "Do you like her?" he asked.

"I like her plenty. But if she—"

The TV in the living room exploded to life, and he jumped from his chair. I followed him. Dina was lying in the corner, and Marina was sitting on the living room floor herself. Her white jeans blended perfectly with the carpet, and that made it look like she was melting. Like all that had saved her from disappearing was her shimmering blue top. I'd seen a reverse of this earlier. The sight of Joni's bright blue sweatshirt vanishing into the house on Marvel Court.

Marina had the remote control beside her, and though I could tell that was bothering Viktor a great deal, he motioned for me to join her. Then he left us for the kitchen, and I sat down on the leather couch to watch more of the sea lion hunting. Dina came over to me, and Marina seemed impressed. She dropped the volume. "Dina hates me," she said.

I scratched the Saluki's slender neck. "I doubt that's true."

She shrugged, and I was thinking I would ask if she'd like to go for a cigarette when I heard muffled techno music. She pulled out her phone, and I listened as she spoke some quick Russian. She snapped the phone shut and rose. "I have to leave," she said. "My friend is here to drive me now."

"Where are you going?"

"This I do not know," she said, moving to the door. "*Do svi-daniya*. It was very nice meeting you."

She put on her pink coat and came back across the room. I stood, gave her a clumsy hug before she went to find Viktor and Sonya. I was by myself, all alone in the living room except for wil-lowy Dina.

A minute or so passed, then Viktor swooped in and grabbed the remote off the floor. Marina was with him, but she didn't look at me. A horn honked, and she went outside for her boots. I watched the door close.

"She is sexy, yes?" said Viktor.

"Yes."

"So you would like to have a real date with her? She wants very much to see you again."

"You sure about that?"

"Of course." He had the remote pointed at the TV now; the volume was slowly rising.

"Then okay," I said, almost shouting the words. "But how do you know?"

Viktor laughed. "I know because this is what she tells me!"

I WAS LYING on my sleeping bag in the black dark of the apart-ment, a waking dream of Joni and me visiting Lake Claiborne slid-ing out of my mind like the last scene of a movie. A nice dream, one so pleasant and comforting I didn't want to see it end.

Before I left Viktor's place that Saturday, my two-hundred-and-fifty-dollar check in his pocket once more, he had explained that unfortunately, due to Marina's work schedule, he thought our date might not be until Monday or even Tuesday night. He knew I had to be gone from San Francisco on Thursday, understood there was no way I was going to report as a sex offender just to extend my stay—so again he'd asked if I was interested in meeting the other two women, and again I told him I'd like to concentrate on Marina for the time being.

I closed my eyes then, counting Sam's whistled snores until that Lake Claiborne dream ended and a new one began. I saw some concrete tenement building in Moscow. The night shift is over, and Marina has taken the train home from a warehouse in the industrial outskirts. Dawn soon. It is summer, the middle of a Russian heat wave, and somehow I'm there as well, with Marina in her room. She's wearing gray coveralls, and we're standing together, smoking my Winstons. The building is a big hollow square, and her open window overlooks a courtyard crisscrossed with lines of drying laundry. In the twilight, through that galaxy of damp clothes, I can see into other rooms across the way. People are already reclined on their windowsills, burning their own first cigarettes of the morning. Marina and I finish with ours, and she undresses. Once she is naked I step toward her, but she tells me to sit down on the bed. She is even shorter in her bare feet, her body a soft, rolling flow, her nipples dark against her skin. She carries her socks and underthings to a sink and turns the faucet. A stream of water begins pooling in the cracked basin, and she adds a measure of washing powder. She soaks her small bundle, working the fabric, cleaning it, and I'm wondering whether she still wants me in the room with her. Then she wheels her socks out on a clothesline she shares with someone across the courtyard, returns to the sink for the rest. The sun is up now, and she is sweating. Beads of perspiration have formed between her heavy breasts. Finally she sits in a chair by the window and stares, trying to decide something about me. There's a glass of water on the windowsill, and inside rests the broken half of a plastic comb. She takes the comb from the glass, still watching me as she draws the wet teeth through her hair. I tell her I'm sorry, that it had been wrong of me to believe I could just select her and have her be mine, and at last she comes over as if that apology is what she'd been waiting for all along. She pulls at my boots, then my clothes, until I am naked myself. She's lying with me on the narrow bed now. The plywood under the thin mattress flexes beneath us as we kiss, and the heat makes us slick against one another. My vial of dirt is slapping at her chin, and she takes it into her mouth. I look away. Across the courtyard smokers are peering out from their own windows, but I don't think they can see us in the shadows. When we are done we lie there. I'm thirsty like I'm dying, but I'm not willing to chance the water from that sink. I glance over at Marina, but she says nothing. I'm afraid she wants me gone, and I begin to gather my clothes. After I've dressed I turn back to her. She has fallen asleep, but then she wakes, sees me standing over her, a Cane River swelling between us. "No," she begs. "Swim to me. Take Marina with you." And I do.

OUTSIDE WAS CLOUDLESS AND SUNNY, JEANS-AND-T-shirt weather for my daily hike to Lincoln Park. But it was also a Sunday morning, and Sundays have always depressed me—so even under that Easter egg sky I was feeling beaten down.

My science-teacher mother once told me evolution might account for why many people have a phobia of all snakelike creatures. The smartest cavemen had the good sense to run from everything slithery, and that fear eventually led to the invention of dragons and the serpent that came calling for Eve. Myths that have been around so long we've forgotten our fears, not our stories, came first. Maybe a similar uneasiness is triggered by Sundays. This is a country founded and formed by believers. And maybe generation after generation of our most prosperous and successful ancestors spending the Sabbath feeling guilty became a heritable quirk. Maybe science explains the hitch I get in my chest on the Lord's Day. I've inherited their fears, if not their god.

I stopped for coffee across the street from Lincoln Park. I'd spent an hour in Café Sun on Thursday, trying to read some of *Salted Waters*, but the squat, middle-aged Korean woman who owned the place had chatted me up. Her name was Sun, like the café, and she looked happy to see me again now. "Good morning, Leroy," she said.

My north Louisiana drawl had been a challenge for Sun, so I guess to her I was Leroy. I didn't bother correcting her. Café Sun was empty today. Far as I could tell, it was often empty. I pictured Sun in the kitchen of a small apartment. Cash on one side of a table, bills and invoices collected on the other. She'd told me she was born in Seoul and had come to the U.S. just two years back. California was her first and only stop, and I wondered if she appreciated how big America was. Whether, like me, she now fantasized about places where getting by didn't have to be this hard. I'll make a deal with you, Sun. You leave San Francisco when I leave Grand Isle. We'll go searching together for where the bluebird sings to the lemonade springs.

I filled a paper cup from one of the push-top thermoses, but before I could pay, a man carrying a clipboard ducked inside and beat me to the register. He was a white guy, but his hair was in long Rastafarian dreadlocks. I got behind him, and he started asking Sun if she sold fair-trade coffee.

"Think I can settle up with the lady?" I asked.

I don't go looking for fights, but I realize I have the worn-and-torn appearance of someone who might. And every once in a while that can be to my advantage. The man didn't say anything; he just left. "Thank you, Leroy," said Sun, but she didn't sound pleased. The guy was probably off to hassle someone else, but by her logic that was a potential customer lost. She punched at the register, and I handed her three dollars for her kitchen table.

"Keep them," I told her, when she tried to give me some quarters. She did a slight bow. Sarcasm. I didn't know Sun had that in her.

Then I got dealt a joker. I'd grabbed a seat in the back when I heard the bells on the front door jangle, and a girl walked in. A teenager. Pin-straight brown hair, blunt bangs, tall, very pretty. She was in jeans and, though the day had been steadily warming, a fringed buckskin jacket. The *Midnight Cowboy* Joe Buck kind. A seventies jacket for her seventies hair. And I was feeling thunderstruck even before Sun sang out, "Joni! Oh! Where have you been, young miss?" Marvel Court was two blocks up the road, so I'm not saying it was a complete miracle for Joni to be standing there in Café Sun—but still, I have to shake my head sometimes at how the world works. At the tricks it will play on you.

I thought of Nancy Hammons and her fucking investigator. There were decent odds that at some point Joni had gotten her hands on a picture of me to study on, and though I'd been hoping for a break such as this, my first reaction was to hide. I shielded my face with my coffee cup, watching as Joni paid for a small carton of something. Coconut water, I think. Her conversation with Sun was a murmur, but I could see her much better than the day before. And here, now, was the mind-blowing, heart-stopping, *you are not the last Joseph* moment I hadn't quite felt on Marvel Court . . . because one thing was clear—she looked enough like Tommy (and a lower-mileage Roy Joseph, I suppose) for me to forever quit questioning whether we really shared blood. More than anything, though, this confident, laughing Joni resembled her grandmother. Not the woman who raised me, so much, but the long-limbed girl I'd seen in old photos. The courthouse bride who'd chosen my father over her own family. She had Mom's same high cheekbones and tiny nose. That same glossy hair. Grief never leaves, it just mutates. Time eases pain only because we forget things or learn how not to think about them—but the grief is always there, adapting, metastasizing, and to stare at Joni was to mourn my dead mother. To remember the woman who went from the girl in those photos to the wailing stranger my father and navy men had to carry into our home, me watching from the doorway as she floated down the hall.

JONI LED ME NORTH on Thirty-Second Avenue. I assumed she was aiming for home, and I was hurrying to catch up with her when instead she passed Marvel Court without turning. I lagged back, still caught off guard from Café Sun, thankful for this chance to gather myself, as she walked another block. The street ended, and she went east, entering a neighborhood called Sea Cliff. I began to wonder whether it had been a mistake to leave the FOR OUR TOMMY album in the apartment. Whether it was foolish to be saving that for some second meeting when I couldn't be sure how this first one might go.

The stockbroker Viktor drove around was a Sea Cliff resident, and Viktor had also told me Sharon Stone once lived there, that Robin Williams still did. The decamillionaires of Sea Cliff would piss on my two-and-a-quarter-mil portfolio, and you'd expect there to be a goddamn moat around such a place. A fence tinseled with razor wire. A minefield. But the Sea Cliff mansions only smirked and smirked as I passed them, their lawns all glowing the same nuclear green. A road sign warned TOUR BUSES AND VANS PROHIB-ITED, then a man in jogging shorts and a bicycle helmet overtook me on one of those Segway deals. He went whirring down the sidewalk, a sleeveless emperor on his electric chariot, gliding toward Joni. She was sauntering as if she was on a nature hike, but I kept my distance, steeling myself for the introduction, worried the right words would never come.

We walked and walked, and after fifteen minutes Joni finally waltzed her way through Sea Cliff and entered the dark, cool forest of the Presidio. Somewhere nearabout lived the Colemans and nanny Marina. What had once been an army base was now just their playground.

Joni's route had us going downhill, and I could sense we were running out of land even before I saw the sign for a beach. Baker Beach. I followed her through the forest like a fairy-tale wolf, down a blacktop road that led to a parking lot. She tossed her coconut water into a trash can, and in due course I came along and dropped my coffee cup. We were now level with a portion of beach speckled with sunbathers. The Golden Gate itself—a bottleneck of rough water connecting the bay to the ocean. To the west was the flat expanse of the Pacific, and right there to the east: the crayon-red cables, towers, and deck of the Golden Gate Bridge.

I'd read a poem in *Salted Waters* set here. A poem about a shark attack. "Baker Beach, 1959." Two college students are swimming when a great white slams into the boy. The salted water is pink, and the boy is shouting at the girl to save herself. But she swims to him. The girl is Catholic. The boy has no specific faith. Though she gets him to the beach, he is bleeding out. She baptizes him with Golden Gate splashes, then asks if that is all right. He gives her his permission to continue, and she has him repeat an act of contrition after her. Then, before unconsciousness, he whispers his last words: "I love God, and I love my mother and I love my father. Oh God, help me."

Joni had taken off her shoes, and I couldn't watch her walk onto the brown beach without feeling that day in 1959. I waited in the parking lot as she stopped not too far from the water's edge. Her buckskin jacket was tied around her waist now; she was wearing an ivory tank top. I was afraid she was going to walk right into the Golden Gate, that a descendant of the shark in her mother's poem would be coming for her, but then she sat down in the sand.

I paused at the bottom of some steps that led from the parking lot to the beach. Jammed my socks into my Red Wings. Cuffed my jeans above my calves. The sand was almost hot on my feet, and I got about ten yards from Joni, ready to roll the dice—could see a starry spray of freckles escaping from the scoop of her tank top, even—when her phone began to ring. I slowed down, not sure what to do, as she spoke in a long sigh. "I know, Mom," she said into the cell. "Okay, I know, okay."

Fuck. This was a haunted, bad-luck place. I couldn't very well jump out of the cake while Nancy was on with her, so I veered to the right, made for the tide line to regroup.

I felt close to certain Joni was watching me walk away from her, a boot in each hand, and I wondered if she was sensing anything familiar in how this drifter carried himself. The Golden Gate Bridge was up ahead, and I squinted against the sun, putting my focus there as I marched on. When I at last looked back at her she was a small blur leaving for the parking lot, and I froze for a moment to decide what next. It was only then that I realized the few sunbathers at this end of the beach were naked, that I'd wandered onto a nude beach. They were all guys—all except for a drunk woman sipping from a brown-bagged bottle and glaring at me. Her whole body was tattoos; her head was shaved. I was staring, and that sent her into a fit. "Eat shit," she screamed. "No gawkers."

A harem of muscled, wasp-waisted men were lying on either side of the woman, and one of them sat up and looked at me. "Yeah," he yapped. "Go away." His skin was as orange as fresh rust, and soon other orange men were calling out, supporting and defending their mistress overlord, misunderstanding my intentions. Joni was gone now. I had been robbed of her, and I imagined pulling out a pistol. I imagined watching them scatter.

But with no Walther to wave I did the only thing I could think of to appease them. I threw down my Red Wings and unbuckled my belt, stripped off my jeans and my T-shirt and my jockeys until all that remained was the chain around my neck. The water was too cold to believe, but I went wading into the surf anyway. I was the sole swimmer on a half mile of beach, and that circus-freak woman had gone from cursing me to applauding me. She had her hands up over her hairless head and was clapping. I wouldn't be able to stand that icy Golden Gate long, but despite my misery I must say this also felt nice, proving all of them wrong.

THAT MISSED OPPORTUNITY with Joni—then, on the way back from Baker Beach, anxious for a distraction, an easing of the sting, I wasn't even able to get Viktor on the phone to check about Marina. I needed to right this ship, so after a shower in the apartment to wash off the salt and sand from my lunatic swim, I went to walk Sam and think.

A light fog had rolled into the Outer Richmond. The warm, sunny day had turned nippy and gray. I knew from Nancy's *San Francisco Chronicle* letter I'd found in the Cybermobile that Joni went to George Washington High School, and I was contemplating how I might make use of that information when I saw a jug-eared old man in a beige windbreaker staple-gunning a flyer to the telephone pole out front of the apartment. I didn't pay him any mind until I realized the flyer wasn't for a garage sale or a lost cat or some such. The top screamed REWARD!, and below that was a photo of a guy with sunken cheeks leaned back in an easy chair and grinning at the camera, a wrapped present on his slim lap. I tugged Sam closer and thought of family albums. Of FOR OUR TOMMY in the bottom of my duffel bag, waiting on me still, but not forgotten.

Beneath the flyer photo was a phone number, then a tight brick of words:

> Up to $5000 for information leading to the
> location of thirty-one-year-old Mark Sorensen.
> He was last seen living near the soccer fields in
> Golden Gate Park. Collect calls will be accepted.

I was more or less looking over the old man's shoulder, but he hadn't noticed me yet. That same phone number was handwritten vertically over and over again along the bottom of the flyer, and the spaces between each scrawled set of digits had been cut with scissors to create fifteen or so tear slips. His hands were trembling, and it took him a while to get the final corner stapled. Next, he ripped off a couple of the tasseled phone numbers and put them in his windbreaker. I almost smiled at that, but it probably wasn't a dumb move. Most people hate to be the first to do anything, and I guess assisting a missing person investigation is no different than calling about a used futon.

The old man got everything situated like he wanted, then turned around and saw me and Sam. He was startled to find us standing there on top of him. A sheaf of flyers was stuffed into his brown pants, and the staple gun was aimed at my crotch. He couldn't have been a day shy of eighty. A warship was anchored across the front of the ball cap he was wearing. The USS *Cecil J. Doyle*, according to the gold stitching. Hooyah. A sailor, then. My brother's brother.

I backed up, and the old man patted at the flyer on the telephone pole with his other hand, the one not holding the staple gun. "My grandson," he said. "Mark."

Oh, fuck me. "I'm really sorry," I told him.

"That's from last Christmas." He was still sort of caressing the flyer. "On the farm in Minnesota."

"You came here from Minnesota?"

"Ten of us done flew out." Sam had been sniffing at the old man's Velcro shoes, and he was petting him now. "Police don't seem to care much. We thought we might could help them along some."

The image of a family of grieving, helpful Minnesotans sitting cross-legged on the floor of a hotel room, scissoring slits into the bottoms of flyers—that will be in my stupid head forever.

"Drugs," he said.

"Pardon?"

"Mark and his darn drugs. We've been expecting something like this."

He took out a handkerchief, blowing his nose as I reeled Sam in. At first I thought the old man was crying, but he wasn't. It was chilly and wet due to the fog, and he just had a runny nose.

"Well," he said, and then he ambled off. He was moving very slowly, and Sam and I watched him. This was a tough old bastard. His generation doesn't let life get to them like mine does. I'd probably had more nightmares and mind slips in the past two months than he'd had in his eight decades, and I've never even worn a uniform—or at least not his and Tommy's kind of uniform. As part of a seventh-grade social studies project I once asked three north Louisiana D-Dayers about the war, but all they had really wanted to talk about was how by golly the women in France had been.

The old man skipped the next telephone pole but stopped at the one after that. He fished out another flyer to staple, then all of a sudden he stumbled. The staple gun went clattering onto the sidewalk, and luckily the pole caught him or he'd have been lying on the concrete himself. I ran over, and Sam scampered along beside me, dragging his leash.

"You all right?" I asked.

"You're back."

"Yes sir." I sat Sam while the old man got his staple gun. I sensed that in his prime this shrunken grandfather in a ship-reunion cap had been a stocky farm boy who could have whipped my ass up and down that street, but those were bygone days. He lifted the flyer he was holding, then stapled it flat to the telephone pole.

"Lawrence Sorensen," he said, offering his hand.

"Nice to meet you. Roy Joseph."

"Two first names? You a southerner, Roy Joseph? You sound like a southerner."

"Yes sir."

Lawrence didn't have much of a grip, but he was still clenching my hand. "But you live here?" he asked.

"I do," I said, not wanting to get into it. Sam was on his belly, alert but being good and still, somehow knowing this wasn't a time for merriment.

"Ever run across our Mark?"

"No sir. Never."

"Bet you see this as harebrained." He let me loose. "But they all were set on coming, and I wasn't about to let them do this without me."

I didn't see anyone else out walking in the cold, Sorensens or otherwise. "Where are they now? Your family?"

Lawrence slapped at the flyers pinned against his stomach. "Split up in the park and thereabouts, doing what I'm doing. I made them give me fifty of these, let me cover a few blocks." He shook his head. "I guess they were right. I guess I should've stayed in Minnesota."

Though I had planned to take Sam to the park, I knew what I should do. What Tommy would have done for another navy man. For anyone, really. Even Sam understood. He was on his feet now but sulking.

"Let's go over to the supermarket," I said. "You can get a cup of coffee, and I'll finish this up. Won't take me long."

I could tell Lawrence wasn't too thrilled by the idea of quitting, but his body was failing him and he seemed to recognize that. I left him while I put Sam in the apartment, and when I returned Lawrence had walked to the telephone pole at the corner of Fulton to post a last flyer by himself. I hurried to him, and he handed me the staple gun like he was surrendering a weapon.

"Are you ready?" I asked.

He shrugged, but I started leading him down Fulton, the out-of-commission LeBaron up ahead, already filthy with city grunge, monitoring us as we made the three blocks to the Safeway.

I sat Lawrence on a bench by the front entrance. There was an arcade unicorn plugged into the wall, and a woman was watching her little girl bounce back and forth. "Or would you rather go inside?" I asked. "It'll be warm in there."

Lawrence hadn't spoken since we'd begun our march, but he looked as if he wanted to tell me something now. He pointed across the street. A row of condo buildings blocked our view of the Pacific. "I was in San Fran with the *Doyle* in '46," he said. "Only other time. Did you know this around here used to be an amusement park?"

"No sir."

"I still remember. It was called Playland. Funland, maybe. Me and some shipmates got into a fight with some locals right on the carousel." He laughed, coughed, and then laughed again. "Us brawling as that thing spun round and round. All those civilians frogging off like they were swabbies on a sinking ship."

"Must've been a sight."

"That it was." He was staring at the girl on the plastic unicorn. "Back then a man could fight another man and not get himself killed. People are meaner now."

"You think so?"

"Sure I do."

I slid the staple gun under my belt. They sold to-go coffee over by the deli, and I bought a cup and a Sunday paper. When I went back outside I saw the unicorn had been abandoned. I gave Lawrence his black decaf, then set the newspaper next to him on the bench.

"Thank you, son," he said. "What do I owe you?"

"My treat. Wait right here and don't worry. I'll pound this out."

He was grateful but he was proud, and I could see I had him

feeling a bit like a child. He passed me the flyers, and I walked those same three blocks up Fulton to Forty-Sixth Avenue, stopping across from that last flyer he'd posted. I got to stapling. There were about twenty flyers left, and I zigzagged through the avenues, careening from Fulton to Cabrillo to Fulton until my jean pockets were confettied with tear slips and I was once again at the Safeway. Thank Tommy, not me. I'm just his proxy, Mr. Lawrence. You'll never meet him, but he's behind this.

I had only been gone maybe a half hour, and Lawrence was still sitting on the bench where I'd left him. The newspaper hadn't been touched, and his coffee was resting on top of it. He was sleeping. I sat down on the bench, and when I cleared my throat his eyes flittered open under the bill of his warship cap.

"Hey," I said. "Done and dusted. You're all set."

He looked over at me. He seemed groggy, and it took him a second to sweep away the cobwebs. "You got both sides of the street?" he asked. "I forgot to tell you both sides."

"Yes sir. Both sides. Hope some good comes of it."

"So do we." He didn't sound optimistic, and there was no reason he should have. Mark Sorensen was doomed—destined for some killing acre and as good as dead, really—but the Sorensens had needed to do something, anything, and this hunting trip was the best they could come up with.

I set the staple gun between us. "What now?"

"Nothing." Lawrence reached inside his windbreaker and pulled out a big-buttoned cell phone that must have been meant for seniors. "I appreciate your kindness, but this spud sack is peeled. I'm supposed to call them when I'm through."

I suspected his phone was also a GPS tracker, and that as his mind went from sharp to blunted some son or daughter would activate that feature if they hadn't already. Before long this man wouldn't be able to go anywhere—Minnesota, California, the Persian Gulf—without them being able to find him, and I wondered if he realized that. He was tapping around for some number, and though I was eager to help, I knew he wanted me to let him accomplish this one small thing for himself.

And soon I could hear the phone ringing even from my side of the bench. A woman answered with a loud, Hey, Papa—and Lawrence put the phone to his veiny, jumbo ear, said he was all right and all finished. You guys can come get me. Tell Larry Junior I'm at that grocery store.

Lawrence tucked the phone back in his jacket. He would like me gone before his family showed. Somehow I knew that as well. He wouldn't shake hands sitting, so we stood up together. The light fog had become heavy fog, and I reminded him to wait inside the store if he got too cold.

"That boy is sick, Roy Joseph," he said. "He's sick, and we should've dragged him home when we could."

I nodded. I didn't know if Mark Sorensen left Minnesota because he was running to something or, like me with Dry Springs, *from* something—but, either way, leaving seemed to have been the wrong move for him. I had written off Dry Springs, my own home, years ago, but maybe that was a long and extended mistake. Maybe what I'd always thought of as an exile had in fact been a flight. Then there was gung-ho Tommy, dying on the other side of the planet. It's not just a job, it's an adventure. What if he'd never gone looking for that adventure? Who's to say what might or might not have happened to us? Who's to say we wouldn't all be on the farm together come December? Instead of one Joseph there are six, seven, eight of us. Wives, children. Our parents. We're roasting a Christmas llama as new wars are waged on TV.

LATER, MUCH LATER, I walked with Sam to the Great Highway and watched the sun set into the ocean. I stood there as night fell and people started lighting campfires on the beach. Government-sanctioned fire pits, seasoned oak bought from the Safeway at precious-metal prices, but to me this was like observing the aftermath of some catastrophe that had caused civilization to crumble. A second Dark Ages. The peak oil world or a plague, a thinning of the herd. I saw those five taxpayer campfires, then envisioned not five but five hundred, campfire after campfire all down the beach. Golden Gate Park was now a hellscape of stump-covered sand hills, every last tree cut and hauled off. Sharon Stone was dancing in hobbles. Robin Williams, made to split park wood. San Francisco. About forty-nine square miles. There were nearly a million people crowded onto that rock of a city. It was really only a matter of time.

Lawrence and I had said our good-byes at the Safeway earlier, but then I'd gone by those across-the-street condos and played guardian. And though he had waved at me to move on, I wouldn't leave until I knew he'd be taken care of. Fifteen minutes, then a white minivan pulled into the parking lot. And this had been such a nice thing to witness—the Sorensens piling out of their rental, the smile on Lawrence's face as he forgot me and rose to meet them—that I wish I could have just chanced upon that scene, that I didn't have to know the what and the why of it all.

I N GRAND ISLE I'D DEVELOPED CERTAIN HABITS, CUS-
toms, and rules for simple living, and on Pearl Lane
Mondays I often made a batch of something I could
eat from for the rest of the week. Comfort food. Red beans, white
beans, a basic gumbo. And, seeking comfort, I had short ribs in
the oven now. They were simmering away in one of Karen Yang's
pristine pots.

When Washington High emptied that afternoon I would be
waiting. With luck I'd be able to spot Joni, and finally we would
meet. Though for weeks I had tried to prepare for this day—other
than, Hello, I'm Roy Joseph—I still didn't know what those first
few things I'd say to her would be. If Mom, Dad, Tommy walked
out of that school I'd trip over myself rushing over to hug them,
to tell them I loved them before our window closed and it was
me versus the universe again. There would be no trivial talk, not
before I said the important things.

But Joni? She was like a child left by gods to prove they exist.
A foundling being raised in a temple far from her home, born
into a role she had no choice but to accept. A girl to be revered
by priests and pilgrims not for who she was but for what she was.
So yes, I had thought about this day plenty, but in the end I knew
all I could do was be bold and let the current seize us, hope the

river would eventually carry us away from that temple, that place of surrogate worship, and toward something real.

Yet what would happen once I had told that temple child everything I could about Tommy? Once I'd shared the Gospel of Roy and converted the pagan girl? Maybe at that moment of conversion I would see her as a niece—but when I shed my disciple robe would she see an uncle standing there? Would she have any more use for me at all?

And there was Marina to think of as well. The likelihood something real, something good, could come from that either. Sunday had passed by without any word from Viktor about my date with her, but I knew she took the bus to the park most mornings to see her friends at the nanny pond. I couldn't stay gone too long with those ribs in the oven, but I was restless. I combed my hair and shaved, put on jeans, my Red Wings, a T-shirt. The Loranger Drilling windbreaker I'd poached off some jackup a long, long time ago. As I was slipping out the door with Sam I was reminded of my boyhood hunting days—of me and Tommy in a tree stand together, of the deer whose antlers were collecting dust in Peach City Self Storage. My first rack buck. An eight-point that lived wily and nocturnal all season only to lose his vigilance and cunning during the rut, chasing does across a daytime clear-cut until Tommy whispered, "Take him, Roy," and a bullet fired by a kid drilled through his animal heart. Tommy's hands wet with blood; my face painted red.

A MILKY, SUN-HIDDEN DAY, but several glum nannies were already pondside when I arrived. Sam and I were walking the blacktop path, and I didn't see Marina initially—but then the nannies parted, a woman in pink waved, and I realized it was her. She had revamped herself since our Saturday dinner, had dyed her hair from copper to the color of oil. I waved back, and all of the nannies were looking at me now. Marina said something to them, then pushed her stroller a few feet closer to the group, set the brake, and came over. She was wearing tennis shoes and tight gray corduroys, the same puffy pink-and-wolf coat she'd had on at Viktor's. Sam was watching her approach with his head cocked.

"Small world," I said.

But if Marina was shocked to see me, she wasn't showing it. "This is your dog?"

"Yes. Sam."

She put her cigarette between her lips. "Let him go."

I tossed my end of the leash, and Sam went wiggling to her. She crouched and began smoothing his yellow hide.

"I like your hair," I told her. "It's Elizabeth Taylor-y. You know, as Cleopatra?"

She slapped her hands together before taking the cigarette from her mouth. A smile, then. I'd never seen one from her. A closemouthed, teasing sort of smile. Cleopatra. This looked to be the best thing I ever could have said. "You are here for me?" she asked.

"Maybe."

"Maybe or yes?" She ground her cigarette out on the asphalt. "Viktor knows I am coming here always. He told you this, no?"

"Yes," I admitted. "But I don't want to take you away from your friends."

She stood, satisfied. "Say what is true. At least with me this is how you should be."

"I meant what I said about your hair."

"I could tell this. And you are taking me?"

"For a walk or something. But—"

"Stop. I would like to walk with you."

"Yeah? Great." I pointed in the direction of her stroller. "The little Satan?"

She sighed and gave a slow nod. The other nannies were watching still, and I waited with Sam while she went back in among them. She spoke to the nannies, then retrieved her charge. The big, sleek buggy was like the Cadillac of strollers. She wrestled it over to us, and I saw the sleeping Coleman baby, all bundled and as pink as a piglet.

"He seems calm enough," I said.

"*Da.* For now, yes. You will push him?"

I situated myself behind the stroller, and she took Sam's leash. We kept mostly quiet as we walked, and I decided I liked this about Marina. How she didn't come at me with question after question. We made it to the end of the pond, then turned left onto a path that followed a road. Eucalyptus trees loomed over us, and a salt, icebox breeze was rustling their fingery leaves in a white noise type of way. The park's concrete lampposts looked like the iron ones I remembered from downtown Vicksburg, and a Mark Sorensen flyer was taped to the first of them we passed. A few cars went by, a few bikers, a few joggers, and anyone taking us in would think we were just an American Dream family out with their dog. This Russian woman might actually be my wife one day. She might even have *my* child. I stared down at the baby, but I didn't feel a thing. He was like a plastic doll. Not even an extra in this movie, but a prop.

The baby was still sleeping when we came to the buffalo pen. Shaggy bison were grazing in the middle of about ten high-fenced acres, and Sam barked once at them but then quit, paws on the fence, unsure if he was seeing wild animals or livestock. I'd been by here before, and in a park full of strange things this was one of the strangest. I looked over at Marina, but she was standing with her back to me as she watched the buffalo. There was a small red heart tattooed at the base of her neck, right below her purple-black hairline. I wanted to ask about it but stopped myself.

I got Sam to sit and started telling Marina what my mother or maybe my father once taught me about nineteenth-century market hunters. Part science, part history. How sharpshooters would catch up to a quivering sea of brown and position themselves on a distant rise, then—working methodically, beginning with the outliers and the strays—drop buffalo by the hundreds without ever spooking the herd. "To the buffalo," I explained, "all that shooting didn't sound any different than thunder." And of course, I was thinking of Lionel Purcell too. Of him and his crazy sniper rifle, shelling Himalayan snow cocks.

I wasn't sure if Marina was listening, but then she turned to me. "How do you know what it is buffalo believe?" she asked. "Are you a buffalo?"

We were like Terry and Larissa now, joking in the parking lot of the Sureway in Grand Isle. She seemed interested, so I dipped back even further on the timeline and described a buffalo jump. Imagine a great, loping herd being stampeded through a long chute of rock and willow until bulls and cows and calves plunge over the edge of a cliff. Imagine more braves waiting below with their spears. They move blood-soaked through the broken-legged and lowing buffalo.

Then came Spanish ponies, rifles, railroads. I finished my lecture and asked if she'd like to have dinner. "Only me," I said. "No Viktor, no Sonya."

Marina didn't answer right away. We just stood there, but then I saw her shrug. "Yes. But it cannot be tonight. Tomorrow, Mr. Buffalo?"

We traded phone numbers, and she texted her address to my cell. Then I told her I had something cooking in the oven and needed to head back. She nodded but stayed where she was—on a rise with someone else's baby, watching those city buffalo—

until finally she said she was ready and let me return her to the nanny pond.

ON THE WAY BACK to the apartment I called Viktor, and he seemed annoyed I hadn't waited for him to coordinate with Marina himself. "For what time?" he asked.

"She told me to pick her up at seven."

"Okay. I will make a dinner reservation."

I tried to tell him that wasn't necessary, that I should have the LeBaron fixed by then, but he hung up before I could get the words out. The day was growing colder, and the fog sliding in from the Pacific looked like billowing smoke. I have a talent for layering worries atop worries, and I began to picture a sequence of events in which my unattended oven had set the building, then the block, then the Outer Richmond afire. An earthquake jostles Karen Yang's apartment, and a gas pipe tears lose. A sulfur-stinking cloud snakes toward the open flame of the oven burner, a pilot light.

Earthquakes. I didn't know the first thing. Do I run outside or stay indoors? Fill the bathtub? And there were these signs all through the neighborhood—TSUNAMI EVACUATION ROUTE written across a drawing of a big wave. At least a hurricane gives fair warning. San Francisco sat on a powder keg.

But on this day the earth kept still, and when we got back the apartment smelled only of cooking meat. I pulled a rib bone for Sam, cooling it with water from the sink, then he slurped the bone from my hand and went parading to his towel like a happy thief. In three days I'd have to leave San Francisco. I was feeling restless again.

THE GROUNDS OF Washington High covered at least two whole blocks in the Outer Richmond, and at three fifteen a mob came pouring from the main entrance. The building looked more like a misplaced slice of the Pentagon than a school, and I positioned myself off the fog-socked corner of Thirty-Second Avenue and wide, median-split Geary Boulevard, figuring Joni would probably cross there on her way home to Marvel Court. And just as I was reckoning this was a stupid idea—me showing up, believing I could find her—a black-jeaned, book-bagged, sunglasses-in-the-fog girl with long, straight hair and a highlighter-blue I ♥ NY sweatshirt emerged from the crowd.

Marvel Court was directly ahead, less than two blocks away, yet for some reason Joni turned left. I followed her to Thirty-Third Avenue, then realized she was about to join a crush of students forcing themselves onto a city bus. I hustled over, but the door closed behind her. The 38 Geary was a beast. A long, limited-stops-to-downtown double bus with accordion bellows between the two segments. The rear door was still open, and I jumped aboard without paying. Book bags and teenagers were pressed every which way against me, but I was nothing to them. They went on about their conversations. California slang. *Hella* this and *hella* that. I could see now just how young they were. Damn. They were babies. Is that really what I'd looked like in high school? The ninth grader at Tommy's basketball-court memorial service?

And where was Joni going anyway? We rode east, at each stop exchanging rowdy adolescents for cheerless adults until eventually the bus wasn't quite so crowded. I was still standing near the back, and she was in a sideways row of seats up front. It was no real trick to hide from her, as she seemed to be making it a point not to look from the book she was holding. The librarian posture, the level-bangs-then-sunglasses disguise, the hood of her sweatshirt thrown over her head—she was doing everything she could to make herself invisible as well. No, to make all of *us* invisible. She'd transported herself to someplace where she could forget the garbage bags spilling clothes an apple-gumming man in an oversized WE FEED THE CITY T-shirt had dropped by her leg. Someplace where she didn't have to acknowledge the peekings of those salesmen and blue-collars who, despite the paisley book bag between her feet, appeared to have concluded she was fair game. The pages of her paperback were turning so fast I couldn't help but wonder if she was only pretending to read. If instead she was keeping tabs on everyone. Hoping the grease monkey to her left and the polyester suit to her right would quit hitting their knees against hers, on purpose or otherwise. That WE FEED THE CITY would never get around to asking her whatever question seemed to be forming on his lips. That the nine-fingered sex offender would have a comforting explanation as to why he was shadowing her.

A half hour went by, and we were in a seedy, liquor-stores-and-massage-parlors section of downtown when Joni stashed her paperback. The Tenderloin—a neighborhood that seemed dominated by tenement buildings and dilapidated hotels that looked like tenement buildings. I was certain this couldn't be her destination, but then she shouldered her book bag and stood. The bus stopped, the door opened, and she hopped down onto the sidewalk. Unless I could content myself with a second missed opportunity, another lost day, I had to do the same.

I was behind Joni, on the sidewalk near a cluster of African men divvying up stacks of pirated DVDs. And I was about to say something to her when she went hurrying across the street. No Sea Cliff sauntering, not here, but as soon as she reached the opposite sidewalk she paused in front of a brick building. Crooked fire escapes latticed the narrow six-story, and a neon sign on the first was blinking TAROT READINGS. Joni had a key in her hand and was unlocking a graffitied door. Suddenly I was very, very afraid for her. If I had been her shadower before, I was her angel now, her sworn protector. I wasn't really thinking anymore, just acting. I was sprinting, dodging cars, and I made myself call her name but the honk of a horn drowned me out. The heavy door shut. She had been swallowed up again, and when I tried the handle it was locked.

Then I got the feeling *I* was being watched. I looked back at the street. A police cruiser was parked where the bus had been—a windows-down black-and-white with a cop at the wheel, bulky in his body armor, the visor of his blue service cap aimed my way. He was shaking his head but had an amused look on his veteran face, loving the moment when the perp sees he'd been made. I was trapped—walk off now, I had no doubt he'd be coming to hassle me.

You weren't following that girl, were you? Let's see some identification. My oh my, a Louisiana pervert. How long you been with us here in San Francisco, ace?

The door. I didn't see any other choice. An intercom was bolted against the side of the building. A single button, no room numbers or anything. Some asshole had molded chewing gum over the button, and I pushed at the hardened glob.

There was a long nothing, then a woman's voice came on. "Yeah?" she said. "Who's this?" She sounded faraway and scratchy, as if she was speaking to me from a space pod orbiting the earth. I could feel the drill of cop eyes even worse than before.

I brought my mouth closer to the intercom. It smelled like bile. "Is Joni Hammons there?" I asked.

"What?"

"Is Joni Hammons there?"

"What? Talk!"

"Can you hear me?"

"Fuck. Stay put. I think this cocksucker is broken."

The intercom hushed, and I stood there, nervous and waiting, fighting the urge to glance back for that police cruiser. Long minutes ticked by before the door creaked open, and I saw an enormous woman dressed in purple sweats. She wasn't fat, just large—a true giant of a woman pulling at her curly hair like some frustrated cartoon character. I was guessing she worked as a gatekeeper for this hell, that she was a minion of a slumlord. She was pan-faced and blotchy, had toothpaste-blue eyes.

"Whataya want?" she said.

"I'm looking for Joni Hammons. Do you know her?"

"Daniel's chick?"

I had no clue, of course, but I'd say anything to get off the sidewalk. Away from that cop and toward the unknown dangers Joni might be in. "Yeah," I said. "Her."

"So call them. I'm the super, not a doorman."

"Sorry, sorry. Dead phone."

The woman looked me over, and I was preparing for her to tell me to beat it when instead she moved aside. A lesser miracle, but I felt like I'd parted the sea, calmed a lion—or at least tickled some curiosity within her. I stepped in before she could reconsider, and she closed the door, turned her back to me, went lumbering on. It was like she was daring me to accost her, like she was hoping I might be dumb enough to try something, and I saw now that, of all things, she had an aluminum fish bat in one hand—a sort of billy club sports use to bash the brains of gaffed tuna and whatnot.

We were at the head of a dark and grimy hallway. The floor was carpeted, but a tear ran down the centered length of it like a wound showing concrete flesh. On either side of me unmarked doors led into what could only be very small rooms, and stairs rose up at the end of the hall. Joni was in one of these rooms, a victim of bad judgment, doing God knows what with God knows who. Perhaps this was not about jumping into a river with her and seeing where the current took us. Perhaps the only reason fate had brought me to California, perhaps the only reason I was ever even born, was so I could brave that miserable building and save Joni Hammons from Joni Hammons. She had a curse in her blood. No matter what her name was, she would always be a Joseph.

I followed the woman up to the third floor, then halfway down the hall, before she stopped to pound on a door to our right. I heard the click of a dead bolt turning, and then I saw her—Joni standing between the frame and the cracked door, hair like splayed horsetail, her lipstick a smear of pink. The sunglasses were gone now, and her eyes flicked to me but then returned to the woman. Green eyes. Those didn't come from any Joseph I ever knew. I have plain brown eyes, all of us did.

"Where's the fire?" she said. An uneasy girl trying to sound like a droll adult.

I eased forward. "Hi," I said. "I need to talk to you."

Joni looked back over at me. I was about to speak again, but now she was staring at my face and touching her own. "No freaking way," she said. She staggered, still holding the doorknob. The door swung all the way open, and I saw the room. A guy was in there with her. No shirt, older than Joni was, but not by too much. There was a leather tool belt lying on the floor, and the legs of his torn jeans were tucked into a pair of work boots. Red Wings just like mine.

"Joni," he said, "who is this?"

She'd let go of the doorknob and was twisting at the bottom of her sweatshirt. I ♥ NY was like an eye chart now. "It might be him," she said.

"Who?"

"That man I wrote."

"That's right," I said.

"You mean?"

"Yes," said Joni. "*Him.*"

The no-shirt kid was straw-haired, good-looking. Skinny but strong. A hammer jockey, judging by the gear on his tool belt. I was studying him, being wary, when a jab to my arm spun me around. That mean little fish bat was in the giant woman's hand, and she was squared up, ready to unload if she had to. "You come in here starting crap?" she said.

"No. It's not like that." But I was bracing for her to smack me on the skull like a swordfish when the kid got between us.

"Geraldine," he said. "Wait. I think we know him."

She lowered her fish bat, but Joni only stood there watching. "Dang," I said to Joni. "I'm sorry we had to meet this way."

"Shut up," said Geraldine. "Want me to call the cops, Daniel?"

He didn't seem to love that idea. A furrowed, north-south line had formed on his smooth forehead. He looked like he was failing a math test. There was a small ceramic pipe smoldering atop the radiator in the corner, and I could smell pot smoke. Actually, gang, a cop's right outside. Just drag me down to the street, and he'll be there.

"I'm not sure," said Daniel.

Joni had moved away from us to sit on the sagging edge of a Murphy bed. Daniel turned to her, but she stayed mute. I tried to speak, but Geraldine told me to shut up again. We were all deferring to Joni now, and finally her long hair swayed.

"Really?" Geraldine asked.

"Yes," Joni whispered. She didn't try to explain herself. Daniel was still standing by, hovering, but she was like a statue.

Geraldine poked at my stomach with the fish bat. "You gotta leave right now," she said, each word louder than the last. Her cheeks were as red as if someone had slapped them, and all that anger made me think that, for her, this had quit being about me.

"Let her hear me out," I said.

"Leave or I'm calling the cops whether these two want that or

not." Then Geraldine chose for me. She took me by the elbow and
tugged me into the hall. "They're damn well getting me high for
this trouble," she said. "Don't you be here when I'm done."

My adrenaline was up, but I'd process that shit show later. The
law had chased me into that building, and now the law was chasing me out. Geraldine stomped back inside the room, and I made
my defeated way to the stairwell. I was at the end of the hall when
I heard footsteps and turned. No-shirt Daniel was walking toward
me. "I can't just let you skate," he said. "Not after that."

"Oh yeah?"

He kept coming, but then he went past me and sat on the stairs
leading up to the next floor. "So you've been following her?" he
asked.

"Only to talk."

"But how'd you even find her in the first place?"

There was more concern than hostility in his stoner eyes, and
I felt myself leveling. "I got a phone call from San Francisco, so I
went online, did some digging."

He dropped his head and nodded.

"I'll speak to her mom," I said. "I should have—"

"Don't." He looked up again. "Please. She can't know we're still
together. That bitch has it in for me."

"Hard to believe."

He pointed at my chest. "She'd have it in for you too. *That* you
can believe."

"Or I might change her mind about me."

"Her?" He laughed without smiling. "Never. I love Joni. Don't
fuck us, man."

"All right. So I won't call Nancy." I sat down beside him. The
kid stunk of the workday, needed a shower. "I will be writing Joni,
though. Tell her to watch for my e-mail tonight, okay?"

"You won't stop with this?"

Daniel had thick wrists, cuts and scars on his hands and fore-arms. Despite all his melancholy cool, maybe he was willing to stand up and attack me.

"Look," I said. "I did this in a messed-up way, but I want Joni to know a bit about who her father was."

"I'll kill you if you hurt her."

"You won't have to kill me, boss. I'll disappear forever if she asks me to."

He seemed almost ashamed to have threatened me, so I reached into an inside pocket of my windbreaker and pulled out a photo of Tommy. Before leaving the apartment that morning I had turned to the final few pages of FOR OUR TOMMY, grabbed a 3 x 5 of my brother, then quickly put the album away. He was wearing a blue cap and gown, the cocky smirk of a senior. On his birthday that April he'd drive to the recruiting office in Ruston, that ragged hair soon to be gone.

"This is him in high school." I handed Daniel the photo. "Will you bring it to her? I have an entire album to show her."

"Go," he said. "Just go."

I stood, but before I left I came close to telling him he was sweating the wrong thing. He, not Joni, needed the saving—someone to tell him that eventually she would grow bored with him and set a course for the future she was meant to have. That one day he'd be all but forgotten by that pretty girl down the hall. In ten or fifteen years this life you've fallen into will have taken its toll, Daniel. You'll have a bad back and a roughneck face of your own by then, stained teeth from all the coffee and cigarettes. Your knuckles will always be scabbed. Your nails will always be dirty. Then maybe a circular saw jitterbugs across your hand some hungover morning. One way or another, you *will* be broken. It's already beginning to happen, and it's probably already too late. Too late for you and me both.

I WENT INTO THE YARD behind my apartment with Sam, smoking a cigarette while he crunched at a rib bone. In the quiet cold I could hear the ocean, and I had a stunned, autopilot feeling not so different from the one I'd sometimes get during my last exhausted days on an offshore stint. Like I'm standing outside my body and watching Roy Joseph.

Until I started with these notes of mine, I doubt I have ever put more thought into writing anything than the e-mail I'd sent Joni that night. My best shot at easing the fears of a sixteen-year-old girl and not failing my brother:

Joni,

How to say this? I'm so, so sorry for what happened earlier. I'm in San Francisco to visit a buddy, and I couldn't be in the same city as you and not try to meet you. I've written you before, so maybe you don't want to meet me . . . but in October, someone—you? your mother?—called me and from the cell number I was able to find out your name and address. Today, I'm sorry, but I followed you. My plan was to catch up with you after school—but then you got on a bus and I saw you go into that building . . . I was worried about you. I promise this is the last time you'll ever hear from me uninvited. I have to go back to Louisiana on Thursday. Here's my number if you want to rewind and . . .

I didn't mention Baker Beach or the spying I'd done from Lincoln Park. I tried to tell her what I had tried to tell Daniel. That my memories were the most she could ever have of her father, and I would give her what I could. You don't have to consider me family. That isn't what this is about for me right now either. I'm asking you for him, and I'm asking you for you. Let's sit down together and talk about Tommy, or all I knew of him dies with me.

Then I had closed with the phone number for the chief of police in Grand Isle. From here on out, I wrote, if I ever do the slightest thing to alarm you, complain to that man and he'll have some ideas as to how to squash me. I'd be an easy knot to tie, but I hope you'll call my number instead of his.

A metal ladder fixed to the backside of my building ran from the yard to the roof, and though I don't like heights, I was on that ladder, then, finally, the roof. To the east-southeast, over the tops of the houses across the way and the trees of Golden Gate Park, were the lights of the antenna tower I could spot from all over the city. Sutro Tower, I would come to learn—a gigantic red-and-white fork that sat atop a high hill maybe four miles away, ruling the skyline. Sutro Tower looked a lot like the derrick of a drilling rig, and those lights seemed to be for me. A San Francisco oil rig saying, Go back where you belong.

WHEN I WOKE I WENT STRAIGHT TO KAREN Yang's computer, but Joni hadn't written me back. I was picking Marina up at seven, and how that went, and whether Joni ever wrote me, might determine if in two days I'd be leaving San Francisco as winner or loser of this cosmic chess match I'd found myself engaged in. And unless I wanted to taxicab my date with Marina, then hitchhike out of the city on Thursday, I needed to get the LeBaron running again. I imagined my name being typed into warrants. Forces descending. A strike team assembling down by the Safeway. Big, steel-toothed gears grinding me into bits. Sam will rot in a San Francisco pound while *The People of the State of California v. Roy Joseph* unfolds.

THE FORT MILEY parking lot lay atop a cliff in the northwest corner of San Francisco, at a place called Lands End that looked from on high at the entrance to the Golden Gate. Across all that glittering water began the tan hills of Marin County, and far to the right I could see the Golden Gate Bridge. To the left, the endless shine of the Pacific. Fort Miley was about the last piece of lofty, Lands End ground before the city fell down into the ocean, and at one time all of this—the dirt beneath the asphalt of the parking lot, the acres of surrounding forest—was part of a military post. I wondered what it would have been like to be stationed there, on the lookout for submarines and U-boats, Japanese fire balloons. War without war. Punch a few weeks watching the horizon, then head into town on leave to assault the dance halls and bars, have an affair with some overseas hero's girl.

Coronado Tommy. My brother on the phone telling me how unbelievable San Diego women are. Hurry up and hit puberty so you can come visit me. I could use a good wingman, Maverick.

And it was there, on that sunny Tuesday at Fort Miley, that I went to talk with Joni. I'd just bought a battery at a Geary Boulevard auto-parts store when she called—a short, tongue-tied exchange that concluded with me agreeing to meet her in thirty minutes. She probably should have been in a classroom, but that wasn't for me to worry about. There was no time for a clean T-shirt, no time to do anything but hurry. I caught a bus to the stop at Forty-Eighth Avenue, then lugged my goddamn battery a quarter mile to that magnificent parking lot, not sure what to expect.

A wide concrete walkway capped the northern, cliff-top end of the car-sprinkled lot, and when I arrived Joni was waiting there, on a long wooden bench that faced the Golden Gate. Her back was to me, and except for a few sightseers we seemed to be alone. Still, this could very well have been some sting operation, and I scanned the wishbone of tree line corralling us for lawmen, Nancy, assassins. Daniel with his hammer, perhaps. Nothing appeared out of sorts, so I came up behind her, scuffing my Red Wings on the blacktop so she would hear me approaching. At five paces she glanced over her shoulder.

Jesus Christ. Those heavy bangs. That perfect, makeup-free face. It was only Joni's green eyes I couldn't make sync with Tommy in that moment—and they were fixed on the battery now. Me carrying a fucking battle-ax wouldn't have been much more off-putting. The Car Battery Killer.

"You caught me in the middle of some chores," I explained.

"Oh," said Joni, as if just then remembering that biological uncles toting DieHards strolled cities everywhere. "Okay."

"Thank you for calling." I circled around the bench, thumping the battery down next to a coin-operated tower viewer that was aimed at the water. She was wearing jeans and a denim shirt, newish Nikes with an aqua swoosh, and her long hair was in a loose bun. I wouldn't ask, but my guess was Daniel didn't know she was here after all.

Joni took in a deep breath, inflating herself until she was sitting up straight and looking at me. "I've decided not to be afraid of you," she said.

Much of what had been pressing against my chest fell away. My fear. Was what she said possible? Could you simply choose not to be afraid? If she knew the trick to that I wanted to learn it from her.

"You don't need to be," I said. "I'm sorry for surprising you yesterday. You do know I'm not a child molester, right? That I was in college, and the girl was in high school? That in December the whole thing will be behind me?"

She nodded. "We know all of that."

"Good. Did you tell your mom what happened?"

"Yikes. No." A wisp of hair had escaped from her bird's nest of a bun, and she pegged the fallen strand behind a multipierced ear. Silver hoops at the top and bottom, a couple of gold studs between them. "And I'm sorry too," she said. "It was me who started this."

I shook my head. "Don't apologize. If you hadn't written I never would have known you existed."

But maybe that was her point. I sat down on the bench. I had no idea how to make conversation with any sixteen-year-old, much less this one. All I remembered from that age was feeling as if my real life was being lived in private daydreams. Beneath

Joni's teenage shell was a person, a personality, but by now I understood that I'd be lucky to come away from this meeting—or San Francisco, period—with even a vague sense of the actual her. There was almost a yard of space between us, and it was hard not to picture Tommy sitting in that gap, looking back and forth from brother to daughter, following our awkward talk and coaxing us both to plow forward, to not shut down and run.

"Did you call me in October?" I asked. "In the middle of the night? Was that you? Not your mother?"

The cuffs of Joni's tomboy shirt were frayed, and she pulled at one of the threads, unraveling some seam until she thought better of it and stopped herself. "Me," she said. "I wasn't thinking. Same as when I wrote you."

"But then I wrote *you*. Twice." I tried to smile. "Crickets."

In front of us, just beyond our bench, the land fell in a hard and thicketed slant to a shoreline we couldn't see. I positioned myself so I was facing Joni, and she turned my way too. "I know you did," she said. "But I'd promised Mom."

"So with that investigator she told me about, y'all really were seeking me out only for medical history? That's all?"

"At first."

She crossed her legs, then uncrossed them, tucked her foot behind her knee. For a girl who had decided not to be afraid she seemed pretty nervous—as nervous as me, I'd say.

"I'd been sick all spring," she continued. "Mom was worried there might be some genetic problem or something, and she wanted to learn as much as she could. And I'm still sick, but we didn't for sure know why until right before I sent you that e-mail."

"Sick in what way?"

"I have Crohn's."

"Crohn's?" Clear skin, white teeth. But Joni was a Joseph, so I braced myself for the worst. Cancer. Rabies.

"A kind of bowel disease."

"But you'll be okay?"

"Yeah. Mainly I have to be careful what I eat, what I drink. I'll deal. At least we know what's going on."

"Jeez, though. Are you in pain a lot?"

She put her thumb to her mouth and bit at the nail. "Can we change the subject?" She mumbled the question into her fingers, but then her voice became forceful. "I'm fine."

"Sure. Of course." A bowel disease. That's what it had taken for me to encounter my final living relative. "It's just so great to meet up," I said. "Properly, I mean. Imagine what this is like for me, sitting here with you."

"Unreal?"

"There's the word."

A day-roaming moth landed on Joni's wrist, wings flexing, lapping at salt, and she cupped her hand over it. "And my mom and your brother. Like, did she even tell you she's gay?"

"No."

"She says he was her last guy. Calls him her omega man."

"Do you know anything more about them?"

"Only that she was at a party and asked him for a ride home. It embarrasses her to go into it. I've never experienced *that* Nancy." Joni moved her hand, and the moth fluttered off. "She was twenty-nine, but I'm only four years younger than he was when he was with her. That's so insane."

This slightly more relaxed Joni had a sleepy, laid-back way of talking, but if she would have grown up with us in north Louisiana she'd have had an altogether different type of drawl. And that bothered me somehow. "My parents should've been told about you," I said.

Joni dipped her head as if to tell me I was preaching to the choir, but the behavior of adults was beyond her control. Look at you, Roy. My cross-country-driving uncle. "Mom really believed it was the best for everybody," she said. "Please don't be angry with her."

"I wouldn't say I'm angry," I lied. "Don't think that."

"It was a car accident with them?"

"It was. I guess you were five when that happened."

But I couldn't go down that road with her on this trip. Speaking about Tommy would be difficult enough. This was the communion I'd come all those miles to have, yet the suspense and intrigue of my quest to find her was leaking out of me like air from a worn tire, and I was already feeling a little blindsided and buckled. The thirteen-year-old on a porch once more. The nineteen-year-old in a dorm room.

I rattled my pack of Winstons, dropped them on the bench, picked them up. I'd yet to see Joni with a cigarette, but she asked me for one now. She was trying to make a connection, I realized, and an odd memory came to me: my father telling of Civil War sentries in no-man's-land, of Rebs and Yanks trading tobacco and news. The history teacher in him had been fascinated by that sort of thing. Richard the Lionheart losing his horse in the fighting at Arsuf and Saladin sending two replacements. The Christmas Truce on the Western Front.

"Should you?" I asked. "With the Crohn's?"

Joni began to fiddle with her shirt cuff again, then peeked at me. "Probably not."

Still, it would have been weird for me to say no, so I lit hers, then mine, watching as she took a quick drag and exhaled. I could tell she didn't smoke much, if at all. Pot perhaps, but not cigarettes. "You don't have to finish that," I told her.

I don't think she even heard me. She was focused on my hand, her eyebrows in a confused scrunch. The *is he a mutant?* look I get sometimes from children and strangers. Whenever I forget about that lost finger someone comes along and reminds me.

"A wire cut it off," I said. "I work offshore, on oil rigs—but maybe you knew that?"

Her mouth tightened and she nodded, solemn as an empress. "Do you really have a friend in San Francisco? That's for real why you're out here?"

"Yep. Viktor. I rented an apartment over by him for a week. Near Golden Gate Park." But she wouldn't get the unabridged version of my cover story. A marriage broker? A Russian bride? I couldn't share any of that with her. "Got my dog with me," I added, wishing I had Sam now.

"Okay. I was just—" She didn't complete the thought. "A dog?"

"A yellow Lab. Do you like dogs?"

"Definitely." She tapped her nose. "But I'm allergic. Sucks. No puppies for me."

"Oh. Gotcha."

"You said you have to leave soon?"

"Thursday." I couldn't admit the entire truth on that front either, couldn't humiliate myself like that. "It's about the finger," I said. "Workers' comp stuff."

Then came the rattling clatter of a diesel. I twisted around on the bench and saw a beaten school bus roll into the parking lot. Some hippie or other species of wanderer had converted the bus into a camper and painted it black. The bus stopped in the center of the lot, engine dying as a pair of long, buggy-whip arms unfolded a sunshade and blocked out the windshield. There were more cars in the lot now, people gazing at the infinite, unfathomable view like it was an enormous drive-in movie.

I turned to Joni again, watching as she reached into her shirt pocket and took out the photo I'd asked Daniel to bring to her. Seventeen-year-old Tommy was staring at me from her lap.

"Thanks for this," she said. "Everything changed when I saw it."

"You'd never seen a picture of him?"

"No, I had—but yours was different than the ones our investigator found. With yours I could see . . . me. Does that make sense?"

"Sure it does." Same as how I'd felt in Café Sun, basically, seeing *her* up close for the first time.

"We both only have one dimple." She held the photo next to her face, forcing a grin as she pointed at her cheek. The cherry of the cigarette I'd given her was inches from her eye. "Here on the left," she said.

I hadn't noticed that, but she was right. Before today I'd mostly seen my mother when I looked at Joni—but Mom and Dad were also the Josephs I remembered best. Upstream from that river of pain was the River Tommy. The master river. He was sitting on a heart-of-darkness bank, waiting for me to reach him.

"You could almost be his twin," I said.

"That's what Daniel thought. And you look like him too, we agreed."

"Still?"

"Yeah. I bet this could have been you in high school."

She put the photo back in her pocket, and as she pecked at the cigarette I envisioned me and Tommy and her somehow all young—triplet teenagers living in San Francisco together. My brother and I pay a visit to Daniel, tell him to leave our green-eyed sister alone.

"Daniel said you have a photo album?"

I pushed my hair back and nodded. "Mom had us settle on three pictures from each year of his life. She wanted a book like that. Something we could keep out."

"Wow," said Joni, speaking more to herself than to me. "I'd love to see it."

"I thought you might. Sorry, but I was at the store when you called." Though, to be honest, I was somewhat glad for that. Sixty photographs of Tommy to walk her through? Fuck. "Maybe tomorrow?" I offered.

I paused, waiting, but she didn't say anything. I was making her uncomfortable by letting the question hang there, so I figured I'd move on, get another subject out of the way.

"You probably want to know about his death," I said. "But I'm afraid that's in large part a mystery."

She shook her head, then leaned over to slip the cigarette into a Coke can someone had left on her end of the bench. "I want to hear about his life first. About what he was like."

Yes, Joni had Tommy's looks, but he didn't have patience like that. So maybe I was seeing her mother in her then, the soul of a poet's daughter. It was good I wouldn't have to begin by choosing between some *he went out like a hero* line or the facts Joni deserved to leave there with, yet now I was worried I was going to disappoint in other ways. She wanted to dig at bones I'd kept buried since I was a boy—but I was a roughneck, not a poet.

I took a drag from my Winston. "Here's the thing," I said slowly. "I was younger than you are when it happened. I've been more years without him than with him."

But her bit was fixed, and she was ready to drill. She shrugged. "Just tell me as much as you can. I'm sure you know plenty." Then she produced a small notebook and an ink pen from under her thigh. A good-student truant, Joni. "I have questions written," she said, flipping the notebook open. "They're kind of lame, but would that be okay?"

I looked away from her. A massive container ship was churning toward the Pacific. A floating, Golden Gate city-state trailing a westward-bound rainbow of catamarans and sloops, ketches and cutters. If Joni could have sung across miles she would have been a turn around, turn around siren-on-a-cliff to those speedy sailors. "Fire away," I said. But I felt like I was on a witness stand.

"Cool," she said. "So, ugh, what were some of his favorite foods? See? Lame."

"No. That's easy. Fried fish. Fried chicken. About anything fried, really."

She had the pen in her hand, and she jotted that down. A small marble notebook for her, and a big gray binder for me. So somewhere there is another page containing the words: *Fried fish. Fried chicken. About anything fried, really.* You live a life and get reduced to what you might order at a Shoney's in heaven.

Joni finished writing. "What about movies?"

I thought for a second. "*Red Dawn.* Russians invade America, and these high school kids are fighting them."

She frowned as she wrote. "I don't know that one. How about books?"

"Stephen King. Or maybe *Deliverance.* The book, not the movie. I remember that being in his room, at least."

"Oh my God." Her eyes were wide. "I was Carrie for Halloween. I had a bloody prom dress and everything."

I smiled, now feeling more like a contestant on a game show than a witness in a courtroom. Maybe I could do this after all. Maybe the worst that might happen would be me being exposed for the moron I was when it came to the topic of Tommy.

More scribbling, then: "What did he like to listen to?"

"Music? Loud bands. Def Leppard, Black Sabbath, Mötley Crüe, Guns N' Roses."

She kept on asking her questions, and I tried my best. Some answers were true, but some were just guesses. Some were out-and-out lies.

His first word was probably "Mama," either that or "Daddy." But how would I know? I don't think he took any longer than usual to start walking, and his eyesight was better than average. He was into baseball and football, but hated basketball. He was right-handed. He swam really well and could run for days. He drank

RC Cola and liked to hunt and fish. He was smart, and his grades were a lot higher than he let on to his friends. He was a whiz at geography because he loved looking at maps. His car: a '72 Beetle he bought and fixed up with money he made working at a plant nursery. He didn't have any nicknames until the navy—the other SEALs called him Ahab because he once spotted a sperm whale during a training exercise.

This continued for a good while, and it was only when Joni was out of prepared questions, when her pen had been speared into her bun, her notebook closed and set aside, that I realized she hadn't written down a single thing about me. I'd forgotten I wasn't the one she wanted to know, and I felt all my budding optimism being replaced by the sober reality that I had indeed become my brother's gospel-preaching disciple, spinning my own unreliable account of the life of Tommy Joseph. An answerer of questions and teller of stories in the service of a long-dead man. And though in the beginning that was exactly what I'd wanted to be for Joni, I hadn't appreciated how lonesome that job would prove.

I crushed my cigarette against the heel of my Red Wing, but before I could toss the butt Joni moved closer on the bench and set the Coke can by my foot. A hiss, then a curl of genie smoke rose up from the can.

"Did he always plan to go in the military?" she asked.

I almost laughed before explaining that, decent grades notwithstanding, in high school Tommy was more troublemaker than Eagle Scout. "He had a temper. He was about my size, but he was always getting into fights."

"Was he a jock or something? A bully?"

"No, not a bully," I said, frustrated I'd given her that impression. "And, I mean, he was very athletic, but he quit playing sports in eighth grade. After that I never saw him join much of anything till he signed with the navy."

"Then why did he?"

The wind slacked off, and I thought I could hear faint bark-
ings coming from somewhere far below. Tommy was down there
along the shoreline now, the immortal frogman weaving himself
in and out of the rocks with the sea lions and the seals. The game
show was over. *These* were the witness-stand questions, and I was
wishing I could sprout wings and take a running leap from our
cliff. That Joni would let me glide into the cold ocean and swim
with my brother toward the warmth of a setting sun, currents and
sharks and hypothermia be damned. That I could meet the Underwater Panther once and for all.

"Okay," I said, "first you need to know that Tommy's senior year
he had this girl pierce his ear with a safety pin, so now he's the
only guy in Dry Springs with an earring. Every morning he'd drive
me to the elementary school, and one day he went to grab smokes
from this gas station on the side of the highway. He bought me a
candy bar, and we were walking back to that VW of his when an
older guy standing over by the pumps called him a faggot. Tommy
told me to go on in the Bug and stay there no matter what, then
that guy took off his shirt and beat the piss out of him. Ripped his
earring out and didn't stop hitting him till I ran over there crying."

Joni put a finger to the silver hoop at the top of her ear. "Whoa,"
she said.

"Tommy could scrap, but that was a grown man. A big, mean
guy. Prison tats, Oklahoma tags. Never saw him again. Tommy
picked me up from school that afternoon. He's got purple eyes, a
split earlobe. As soon as I graduate I'm joining the navy, he says.
You watch, Roy. I'm gonna be a Navy SEAL."

"Just like that?"

"Just like that. Ever see that old show *Magnum, P.I.?* Before
your time, but reruns?"

"With the detective in Hawaii?"

"That's the one. He'd been a SEAL in Vietnam, Magnum. I

think that's how they got on Tommy's radar." I shook my head. A death made possible by a TV show. "Tommy was a different person after that fight. There was no talking him out of it. My parents tried, believe me."

Joni sat there stone-faced, and I regretted I hadn't lied again and concocted some nicer story, one that displayed how tender, how incredible and brotherly, Tommy could be. And I was about to start telling her how he'd walked back into that gas station, beaten and bleeding, and bought us both an RC to calm us down, when I saw she was smiling. Not the fake grin she'd flashed to show me her dimple. A real one this time.

"What?" I asked.

"That is great," said Joni. "Really awful, but really great." She reached over like she was going to touch my arm, then pulled her hand away. "Thank you. What you said in your e-mail—you were right. You've told me things about him I never would have known."

True enough. I'd been there with Lionel Purcell. Compared to nothing, anything is something. Even the bad. Even the half-truths. Even the lies. I'd scored points, and so, hoping for a break from Tommy, I tried interviewing *her* some.

"Daniel, he's your boyfriend? He said your mom doesn't know about y'all."

Joni sighed. "He dropped out of school. That's all she needed to hear. To her it's like he's a murderer."

"So you knew him from school?"

"No. Right after I was diagnosed I went to a support group at the hospital. Daniel was there working, installing cabinets in the hall, and we started talking. I was really upset back then, about what Crohn's was gonna mean, and he helped."

The sunlight hit Joni's face a certain way, and I saw crescents like ash smudges under her eyes.

"But I'm a lot better now," she said. "I need to figure out how to tell him that."

"That you're better?"

"That I'm not a mad person anymore. That I'm a different person and doing fab." She rapped at the bench twice with her knuckles, deafening the wood gods. "And he said I shouldn't call you. I didn't like that."

I nodded. Apparently Daniel's jettisoning was on an even faster schedule than I'd thought. "*Is* he a murderer?" I asked.

She laughed. "No."

"So you should just tell him. Date a boy you can go to prom with, Carrie."

She winced like I'd cursed at her. "I've never had to dump someone," she said. "It'll be horrible."

Her guard seemed to be lifting. That was enough about Daniel. "It's only you and your mom?"

"Yeah. One parent, one child, she always says." Joni turned sideways and brought her Nikes up on the bench. "I need to ask you for a favor."

I told her to go ahead, but then she was quiet for so long I began to worry Lionel's trailer prediction had been correct. She was going to beg me for a kidney. She needed Roy Joseph for parts.

"Could we meet somewhere tomorrow too?" she said finally.

I smiled, both surprised and relieved. Though I was also questioning how much more of it I could take: speaking about my brother to a someone who looked like my brother. I was her link to Tommy, but what was she to me? This teenager who never knew him? She was a bucket I was being forced to pour myself into. How long before the well went dry? Forget the law—could I even last until Thursday, regardless?

"Of course," I said. "I'd like that."

"But we can't tell my mom about any of this. We will, but not yet."

"Works for me. Hell, we should probably wait till you're in college for that." I thought suggesting this might relax her again, but she was still sitting there like a clenched fist. "Not that I'd bring up Daniel," I added.

She rubbed at her shins. "It's not just him. Mom can get very stressed. What she found out about you . . . that frightened her."

I sighed. All that talking only to circle back to this. "I was wrong," I said. "But I was a kid. A dumb kid. I can say that and still be sorry for what I did."

"Okay. But I don't think Mom would be able to handle it right now. I know she wouldn't, actually."

I'd given that same tiny *I was a kid* speech on a hundred occasions over the years, but as always with everyone, she hadn't heard anything but an excuse. Joni never once touched me that day, never even shook my hand, but having her so close and studying me, inspecting me, was like having that sweet girl grow vampire fangs and sink them into my neck.

"There was another question I had," she said. "It's sappy, but will you to tell me your best memory of him?"

Lawyer Joni again, springing the *oh, by the way* question that nails the witness to the wall. "Do you want that today or tomorrow?" I asked.

She began to rock from side to side in her cannonball squinch, deciding, and I just knew bolts were working loose from the concrete beneath us. That everything would roll forward. We would bounce a few times, then shatter onto the shoreline rocks before I could catch her or she could catch me. "Well, today, if you can," she said. "Pretend there won't be a tomorrow."

"I can try, I guess."

"Great. Thank you."

It made me self-conscious to look her in the eyes and scroll through memories, so I stared off at the Golden Gate Bridge like Tommy's daughter wasn't right there beside me. What I wanted to tell her was that even my happiest memories of him come served with a powerful dose of pain. That when people die all

your memories of the snuffed-out become depressing if you think
on them long enough. That when you know the sad end of a
story, bittersweet is the best you can hope for. One man sees a
beautiful red bridge—another, the most popular suicide spot in
the country.

But I couldn't tell a kid those things. "I was twelve," I said. "It
was a couple of months before Tommy deployed. He was home
visiting, and we were poaching a neighbor's catfish pond when
a storm rolled in. There was lightning striking on top of us, and
there we are, caught in the open. I thought we'd be killed."

Joni was hugging her knees now, and I tried my hardest to meet
her gaze.

"But there was this big concrete culvert lying in the center of
Mr. Russell's pasture. I don't know how come. It had never been
there before, and when I went back later it was gone."

Then, the rest. How Tommy and I had set off sprinting for that
culvert. How he was a lot stronger, so he was carrying everything.
The tackle box, both our fishing poles, the stringer of gasping
channel cats we'd spent the morning catching. How he stayed beside me. How lightning split a shade oak ahead of us and toppled
two cows. How my shoes were caked with mud. How I felt as if I
was running in place. How the entire racing way I was imagining
the hit, the moment when some dark cloud would put a yellow
finger on us.

Joni shook her head. "That sounds so scary."

"More than scary, at least to me. I can't do it justice. The storm
got even worse, and we huddled there in the culvert for what
seemed forever. Like we were about to be flushed down a pipe."

"But you guys were also safe. Maybe that's what you remember
most?"

"Sure," I said. "Maybe. Not much of a best memory, but I think
that might have been the last time we were together, just the two
of us."

Joni was patient and listening, her green eyes twinkling as she waited for me to finish.

"That's it," I told her. "That's the whole story."

IN THE APARTMENT that night I showered and shaved for the second day in a row, then went with the suavest of what I had in my duffel bag: khakis, a wrinkle-free button-down, and a navy blazer I'd bought at a Men's Wearhouse in Colorado. I hadn't dressed for a date since my year at LSU, but preparing for Marina reminded me more of readying myself, panicky and alone, on the morning of my plea-agreement hearing. Me, home on the farm, fumbling to put on my dead father's tie and wanting to call time-out, wondering whether going with the public defender had been idiotic, wondering whether I was about to make a huge mistake.

Before Joni and I parted at Fort Miley she'd asked if we could meet somewhere after school tomorrow, said she would text me during lunch with the details. She appeared bent on taking command and that was fine by me—because, truth be told, Fort Miley had kicked my ass. I was Tommy, dripping blood in a gas station so he could buy those two RCs.

Sam was in the yard still, and I was letting him in when the apartment bell rang. I bumped my way through the dim garage and saw Viktor standing behind the gate. He had on his black-suit, white-shirt work getup, and he looked down at my leather topsiders and chuckled. "A sailboat man," he said. I opened the gate, and he squeezed my arm. "It is almost time to get Marina, no?"

"I'm leaving in one minute." I returned to the apartment, and he followed. "You were gonna make reservations for me somewhere?"

"Yes. But I am driving you."

I shook my head. "You don't have to do that." My muscles were on fire from hauling that DieHard around, but the problem with the LeBaron did seem to have just been the battery—not the alternator or a short or whatnot. She was back among the living again, waiting to carry me away on that fifth working day. "I got a battery," I said. "My car's working now."

Viktor knelt, and Sam fell into him in a curl, mouth smiling, tail wagging. "I have walked by your car. Good battery. Bad battery." His face brightened as he began to laugh. "This makes no difference! Russian women do not come to America to ride in ugly cars."

THE HOUSE WHERE Marina was staying backed up to the southwestern edge of the Presidio. There was a sidewalk and strip of grass, then a three-story post-and-beam Tudor. Viktor parked his hearse-black Mercedes on the street, and I was getting to my feet when he honked the horn.

"You should have brought a gift," he said. "I forgot to tell you this."

But then the front door swung open, and there she was—the future Mrs. Roy Joseph, perhaps. It was a cool evening, and she was wearing high silver heels. A buttoned black coat stopped right above her bare knees, fitting her body like a wrap dress.

"Ah," said Viktor. "This Moscow lady."

The yard was split by a short concrete walkway that led to a clamshell of porch, and Marina stepped out, waved me toward her. Viktor shrugged, so I closed the door and headed up. She had gone back into the house and was waiting just inside the parlor, the foyer—whatever rich people call the first little room in a house full of large rooms. "Hello," I said, glancing around for any Colemans.

"That is Viktor you are with?" Marina's arms were folded, and her eye makeup had her looking even more like Cleopatra than on Monday. She didn't seem happy. Her cat eyes went to the Mercedes. "Why is he here? You have car, no?"

I nodded. "I don't know what's going on. He said it had to be this way."

Viktor gave the horn another pop, but she ignored him. The small purse resting on her hip was fashioned from woven sections of tiny, chromed chain, and the strap was sashed across her. She was almost tall in her stilettos, but not quite, and she had a different perfume on now. Something more subtle and expensive smelling. Something I was willing to bet she had pinched from Mrs. Coleman.

"*Nyet,*" she said.

"No?"

We went out to the porch, and she locked the door behind us. I was making for the Mercedes when she began to herd me toward the side of the house. "Hurry," she said. "Be quicker."

I couldn't tell what she was playing at, but I did as she ordered. The house was even bigger than I'd thought, about three times as deep as it was wide, and security lights flicked on one after the other as we sloshed down a pea gravel path. Those lights had me imagining phone calls to the police. Tasers and pepper spray.

Marina must have seen I was leery. "No one is home," she said. "They have gone to a baby party."

"What's a baby party?"

"Some party where people bring babies."

We turned the corner of the house, and a final floodlight tripped, illuminating a sweep of flagstone patio. There was a red scooter parked there. A Vespa. Marina freed a key out from under a flowerpot and pointed at the scooter.

"We will take a ride," she said. "See the city. They will never know."

I watched as she wriggled her long coat up around her waist and straddled the leather seat. She was Eliza Sprague, mounting her quarter horse, and beneath that coat Marina was wearing a sparkling silver skirt that matched her shoes, her chain purse. Her earrings were hammered metal squares about the size of postage stamps. She took them off and put them in the purse.

"Viktor won't like this," I said. "And do you even have a motorcycle license?"

There were two helmets hanging from the handlebars, a pink one and a blue one. She pulled the pink helmet on and handed me the other. "You are afraid, Mr. Buffalo?"

In the distance, beyond the glow of the security lights, the trees of the Presidio were just shadows. "Kind of," I said.

"Then be afraid. Be afraid and I will go be by myself." Marina pushed the key into the ignition and started the Vespa. "Have your night with Viktor." She flipped the kickstand with her stiletto and began to hump the scooter backward. The seat was wedged into her silver skirt, and I could see the dimpling on her thighs.

"Wait."

She got the Vespa lined up like she wanted and looked over at me. Fuck it. I slid the blue helmet on, and I was barely settled on the seat when we went wobbling through the pea gravel. I put my hands on her hips, and we crossed the yard and then the sidewalk. Viktor's Mercedes was facing east, but we were hightailing west. Marina already had us two blocks away before I felt my phone vibrate in my pocket.

SOON WE WERE IN THE PRESIDIO—not far from Baker Beach, really—and at a stop sign Marina told me we had to be done by ten o'clock, that she needed to have the Vespa back in place before the Colemans returned home from their baby party. In some ways I was enjoying the sense of freedom that had come with our unexpected flight, but I'd also gone and riled up Viktor in exchange for three hours of tooling around on the back of a toy, staring at the heart tattoo on Marina's neck, breathing her stolen perfume. There are all types of families, and as a teenager my father night-swam across the Cane River fifty times in one summer before Mom admitted she loved him. But this mad dash seemed nothing like swimming the Cane River. It felt a lot like what it was: a man holding on to a stranger.

The Vespa was brand-new. A peaceful, purring four-stroke. But with our helmets on I couldn't make myself heard as we drove. We exited the blackness of the Presidio and passed a sort of Greek temple-ruin. I've seen more old movies than a nursing-home couch, and I was pretty sure I recognized that domed and columned structure from a film in the video collection on the Loranger Avis. *Vertigo*, maybe. I thought of Joni the temple child, alone in her room on Marvel Court, door locked, writing a fresh batch of dead-man questions into her notebook as she prepared to get me on the witness stand again.

Marina turned right at the next street, cruised east for three blocks, then went north again toward the bay. In a scrubbed, SUV neighborhood of pale stucco walls, crimson-tiled roofs, and other Mediterranean pretensions we were forced to take a street called Prado, and another called Cervantes, before we came to a red light at Marina Boulevard. Marina pointed at the street sign. "I have road," she said.

"Yeah you do." I checked my phone and saw I had four missed calls. "I should call Viktor."

The light was green now, but I felt Marina slump. "Fine, then," she said.

We clipped along the bay, the cold wind watering my eyes, but finally she stopped in the parking lot of a Safeway across from some Marina Boulevard boat docks. Even from the outside I could tell this was a much cheerier Safeway than the one in the Outer Richmond. Not a place where felons bought coffee for old men in warship caps.

I hopped off the Vespa and removed my helmet, shook out my hair. Marina left hers on but spun sidesaddle in the seat as I drifted. One ring and Viktor answered. "Explain what it is you are doing," he said.

"She kidnapped me."

He didn't laugh. "We will speak tomorrow."

"So you're okay with this?"

"Tomorrow," he said again.

I put the phone away and walked to Marina. She was perched on the Vespa and watching me. "What did he tell you?" she asked.

I shrugged. "He says have fun."

"Have fun? Like we are his pets?"

She unzipped her chain purse and took out her cigarettes, some foreign brand that came in a thin, flat box. I lit her import, then one of my Winstons, and she asked how things were going with him, whether I'd been on any other dates since coming to San Francisco.

"No," I told her. "Uh-uh. You're the only woman I've met." I attempted to explain, but made myself sound weirder. "And I'm leaving in two days. This is a one-shot deal for me. If it's meant to be, it's meant to be. Right?"

She didn't answer.

"We could go eat," I suggested. "He made us reservations. I can call him back, try to find out where."

"I am not so hungry yet. Let us see more first."

I was game. We'd be moving again, and I think that was all I really wanted now as well. Music, then—the tinkling and clanging ching-chings of halyards against sailboat masts from the docks across the street. A reminder that not every port of call has to be a bruised and blue-collar Grand Isle.

"Do you miss Russia?" I asked.

The helmet had a lock of Marina's black hair pasted across her mouth, and she hooked it to the side with her thumb. "Yes," she said. "I left someone there that I love."

"What?" I assumed this was a conjugation error, that she'd meant to say *loved* and not *love*, but then she looked at me like she was about to apologize and tell me this was all wrong. Like she was about to ask if I'd mind if she just took me to my apartment. "Who?"

"A man."

In that pink helmet Marina came across as much younger, closer to Joni's age than mine. She was a TV movie runaway, a heartbroken lost innocent, and I'd been cast as the redneck detective hired to find her. *Miles from Moscow*, tonight on Lifetime. "Do you want to talk about it?" I asked.

"No," she said. "Please."

FISHERMAN'S WHARF. NORTH Beach. Downtown. The high buildings of the city. Union Square was a noisy day of bright lights, a flat of concrete plaza that traffic edged around and around in a snarl. In the square center: a man on one knee proposing to a woman in a Vespa-red dress. Above: a stone goddess-with-trident on a hundred-foot pedestal. I was sure Marina saw them too—the man, the woman, the taunting goddess—but she didn't let on. *I left someone there that I love.* That was still tumbling around in my brain as a nutcase in fatigues went tottering sideways across our lane. "You should be in bed licking that bitch!" he screamed. "You heard?"

AMONG RENOVATED WAREHOUSES of lofts and art and espresso, nightclubs and tech companies, we passed a carousel enclosed in glass. The lights were off, the flying horses a halted stampede for the night. I wondered if this could be the same carousel that had once been out by the ocean—the one Lawrence Sorensen had fought his dizzy brawl with the locals on. I wanted to call him on his emasculating cell phone and tell him. Take a break from the futile search for your doomed grandson and come see, Mr. Lawrence. Maybe not everything is lost. Maybe not everything is gone.

WE WERE DEEP in the bodegas, street murals, and produce stands of the Mission District before Marina stopped again. "I am sometimes here," she said. "My favorite food in U.S. is burritos."

I'd only been through the Mission District during the day, on one of the buses that had returned me from the bayfront shipyards, and what I remembered as a mostly Hispanic neighborhood appeared to have been taken over by elfish, thirty-going-on-sixteen kids in plaid shirts and girl jeans. Marina had parked outside a place that looked well lit and clean—so now there we were in a room with orange walls, sitting opposite each other at a wooden table, helmets at our feet, sipping at tall cups of watermelon juice and eating American burritos.

Marina still hadn't taken her coat off, and even in my cheap blazer I was still chilled from our ride myself. This was my first clear view of her since the Safeway, and all of the spirit that had been in her while leaving the Colemans seemed killed. I let her eat in peace, but once we were done I decided to risk irking her. "Tell me about him," I said. "Your guy."

She rolled her straw between her fingers, then wiped them on her sleeve. "Efim," she whispered, as if that was all she intended to say.

"That's a name?"

"Yes. But there was also Konstantin."

"*Two* men?"

"They are brothers."

The restaurant was crowded but quiet, and an old and stooped man walked slowly by our table. He was selling roses, but his creased face was from some other time and place. His skin was the color of pipe tobacco. A descendant of Aztecs, Mayans. He looked at us, but Marina waved him away.

"You were in love with them both?"

"Just with Efim. I was engaged to Konstantin."

"Not sure I'm following."

"It is simple—I hurt Konstantin, and later Efim hurt me." Then she shrugged like she was admitting it really wasn't that simple after all. "The three of us were children together," she explained. "In same building. My whole life people said I would one day be marrying Konstantin, and I accept this. But then night before wedding day, Efim, he comes to the door of my family. He is drunk. He is telling me he loves me. He is saying this in front of my mother and father. I loved him too, and I am telling him when Papa went and brings Konstantin."

"Big fight?"

"*Da.* Yes, yes. And no wedding. Next morning Efim told our families it was all from drinking, and they believed him, even Konstantin—but me, I had not been drunk. I said what I said and no one forgives Marina."

"And that's why you left Russia?"

She nodded. "My father put me out of apartment. I cannot sleep, I am missing work. Boss at factory, he fires me. For more than year I have no money or family. In Moscow everyone calls me *shlyukha*. Whore."

She began to cry, and I handed her a napkin from a stainless dispenser. Her chin was wrinkled like a peach pit.

"I know even Mama calls me this," she said. "So I find these jobs, and I come here."

"But you still love him? Efim?"

Years and years before, I'd once helped bring a man back from the dead. We fished him from the Gulf, and then Malcolm pushed the water out of his lungs. And that drowned and strangled gasping is as best as I can describe the sound Marina was making now. "He has been sending e-mails," she said between breaths. "Saying these things to me."

"What kinds of things?"

"That he is sorry. That he was afraid but does not care anymore what anyone thinks but me."

"What about you? Do *you* care?"

"Why should Whore of Moscow care?"

"Quit with that, okay?" She dabbed at her eyes with the napkin, smudging her makeup. Cleopatra was gone. "When did he first write you?"

"Two weeks ago," she said.

"Two weeks?" I double-tapped my cup on the table. "Then why let Viktor introduce us?"

"A friend had brought me to Viktor already. That was before I knew Efim would be doing this."

"But then he did. So why go through with these dates or whatever with me?"

"It is stupid. Because I was sad. I was sad, and I did not know what I wanted yet. I thought it might be nice to meet someone who knew nothing about me."

She went still. Without realizing it I had reached my hand, my left hand, halfway across the table. She'd stopped crying, composed herself, and was staring. I caught myself wondering where that missing pinkie was right then. Whether the shards of bone were buried in the sediment of the Gulf—or whether a hungry red snapper or other deepwater creature had darted out from the tangle of steel beneath the Loranger Avis and inhaled that sliver of me, swallowing my bloody finger before it could hit bottom. One possibility seemed so much more tragic to me than the other.

"That's not stupid," I told her.

Finally she took my hand. The rose man was watching us from the other side of the room, and I could tell he was contemplating giving our table a second try.

"What's next for you, then?" I asked. "Russia?"

"Yes. When I have money for ticket, I will go. I am very sorry."

I passed her another napkin. "It's okay," I said. And it was. I didn't want to marry her. I didn't want to marry anyone. Not yet, at least. I could have sat touching hands with her forever, but I wasn't ready for a wife. I could see that now. There was nothing about this entire trip I'd been ready for.

"You think I am fool," said Marina.

"I don't think that. Efim, maybe—but not you."

"Even if you will not say it, it is what you think."

"All right. You're no fool, but yeah, it might be a foolish thing for you to trust someone who treated you that way."

The rose man had indeed shuffled back over, and before Marina could reject him again I pulled some bills from the pocket of my khakis with my free hand. *"Cinco, amigo,"* said the rose man. "Five, *por favor.*"

Marina got her thorn-stripped rose, and he left us. She smiled at the wilting flower. "You should meet Viktor's other girls for you," she said. "I know them. They are both pretty."

"We'll see," I said.

Her hand had remained locked in mine, but I made myself release her. I took our trays to the trash can, and when I returned to the table she was holding that rose like a candle.

She looked up at me. "I was expecting you to be different," she said.

"How do you mean?"

"I was expecting you would be worse than your photograph. That I would hate you. Even though I agreed to meet you I was expecting this."

"Oh."

"But you are good man. A much better man than I thought you would be."

Then she stood and kissed me on the lips. A long kiss that tasted of watermelon juice and had me questioning if that business about an Efim and a Konstantin had only been a test. She kissed me, yet when I tried to haul her closer still she broke free. I collected our helmets, struggling to think of something to say as she wafted back and back toward the door on those silver heels. But before that something came to me she began to sing. The words were in Russian, and there was no way for me to tell if they were even her own words. For all I knew the sole purpose of that song was to save me from myself. To fill that silence so I wouldn't fill that silence and ruin everything. She sang until we were on the Vespa and riding away—and it was almost as though she was thinking what I was thinking. Let's just keep going and going, Roy. There's so much to see, but so little time.

O N WEDNESDAY MORNING I WAS LYING FACEDOWN in bed, not resting so much as thinking, when Viktor called. I didn't pick up, but then, since I was afraid I'd hear him ringing my apartment bell before long, I called him back and asked if we could meet by the beach in a half hour. In the end Viktor seemed to have done right by me at every step, and I felt bad for having wasted so much of his time and energy for nothing but a two-hundred-and-fifty-dollar check. But I was also anxious to be done with the guy. I'd pack up today and see Joni in the afternoon, attempt to last one more round with her before I was forced to hit the road tomorrow and make my San Francisco getaway.

When Sam and I reached the end of Fulton Viktor was already waiting on the sidewalk that ran above and along the beach. A bleak, broken-fog, windbreaker morning. The Great Highway between us. Two hundred yards of low-tide sand and then miles of Pacific behind him. The waves were up, the surfers at battle. A faraway legion of sprites in black wet suits. And farther still: a lone man on a paddleboard, sweeping the ocean. I heard the low rumble of a fighter jet hidden in the clouds, and I thought of Marina, outside somewhere, maybe searching for that jet plane too.

Soon she'd begin surfing the Colemans' Internet for her ticket to Moscow. Soon she'd be like me, packed and about to bolt.

One Viktor fist was clutching a cigar; the other was jammed into his pocket. Dina's leash was winding out from his jacket, and that clover-honey Saluki had coiled into herself like a sleeping deer. A kid walked past them with a loose dog, a pit bull that was clipping at his heels and shark-looking Dina. But Viktor didn't even glance at the pit. I crossed the highway, and we dropped our leashes so Sam and Dina could have their reunion.

"How was the date?" Viktor asked. His voice was flat, his expression blank. He was more somber and serious than I'd seen him since that first morning we met. He wasn't angry yet, but that seemed to be the next click on the dial. And Dina was in one of her moods as well. Sam wanted to tussle and play, but she just lay there as he sniffed at her.

"We had a good night," I said. "She was on her way home by ten, though."

Viktor was about to suck on his cigar, but this stopped him. "So soon?"

"She had to get back with that scooter."

"Where did she take you?"

The cigar had burned down almost to his fingers, and a bitter Pacific breeze was throwing smoke into my face, dancing my hair. I stepped to the side. "We drove around, looked at the city."

"Did you ask her?"

"To marry me? No." In fact she will be leaving both of us, Viktor. But I didn't say that. Her news to share, not mine. "And I'm not gonna ask her. I'm sorry."

He sighed. I got the feeling he'd never struck out with a client before. "What then?" he said. "Now *you* go home?"

Sam had given up trying to rouse Dina. They were lying beside one another. Dina's eyes shut, Sam's open and sad. "Yeah," I said. "Tomorrow. If I don't take off I have to register here. Remember?"

I could picture cops counting days on a calendar, hoping non-resident RSO Roy Joseph would be stupid enough to postpone his departure.

"You could not tell the police you are here." Viktor checked the wall separating the sidewalk from the beach below us for seagull shit, then leaned back against the concrete. "How would they know? Stay another week. Meet more women."

"I can't," I said. "I can't."

The wheels in his head were turning, him attempting to think of a way to convince me not to disappear. And though there was nothing to suggest he knew of Marina's own plans to leave, I couldn't resist prying.

"Besides, why?" I asked. "You said yourself she was the best of them."

Viktor spun to face the beach and the water. "Yes. But some Russian women, they can be—" He stirred at the air, groping for the rest. "Like hummingbirds, is what I mean. All over the place."

"Maybe so, but I'm sort of that way myself."

"This is obvious. Two *kolíbri*. But you, you do not even try." He shielded his eyes as if watching his hummingbirds zip away together. "And now, off, off you hum."

Sprawled out in the sand between us and the surf was a man dressed in cracked and faded leathers. He looked like he had just tunneled up from hell, and I was worrying he might be as dead as the woman they'd found in the killing acre when he rolled onto his side and scratched at his balls. A postapocalyptic foot soldier, but once, a pioneer child. Long ago that man was a boy somewhere near the Continental Divide. His family died in a plague, so he walked alone for a century and a half, came the farthest west he could come. He made it to California, then the Outer Richmond. But he was too late. All he found was block after treeless block choked with square houses. A drab, soul-sucking grid pattern. The man yelled something at us, but the wind twisted his words and I couldn't make out what he was saying. Nothing good, I was sure. I turned my back to him. Golden Gate Park was a green, grandson-swallowing wilderness across the highway, the stuck sails of the towering windmill like the hands of a clock. The lead sky and the gull shit and the trash. The foaming ocean. The traffic stacking up on the Great Highway. That sandy, road-warrior motherfucker. All I could see was ugliness and disappointment.

Viktor threw his stub of cigar down onto the beach. "A ship hit the bridge this morning. Did you hear?"

"Which bridge?"

"The Bay Bridge," he said. "Buy a television."

"That bridge looks pretty tough. It's probably not that bad, right?"

He shook his head but didn't say anything, more concerned with staring at the Pacific than listening to my nonsense. So maybe my guess was wrong. Maybe the city wanted to evict me *and* trap me. Both bridges are out and the airport is closed. Every road leading south has been land-mined.

I kicked at the concrete wall. "How can you live in this place?" I asked.

"What?"

I started to repeat myself, but he stopped me.

"Because it is beautiful," he said. "California."

He didn't see any of it. If he spent much more time with me I'd poison him. He'd turn around and begin to see California as I saw California. He wouldn't buy into it any longer, and then everything he had would mean nothing to him.

"I'd stay if I could," I said. "Promise."

"No," said Viktor, "you would rather be alone, and that is fine. Some men are that way." He shrugged his ox shoulders. "But you are no man, Roy. You are a boy. To become a man, first the child must die."

Then Viktor Fedorov gave up on me. He walked away with Dina—an irritated Russian and a haughty sight hound—and Sam whined as if he knew we would never have another shot at winning either of them over. As if he knew tomorrow I'd pile everything into the LeBaron and we would quit San Francisco. The rest of my life was waiting whether I was ready for it or not, and this is what I imagined that morning by the ocean:

That I would return to Grand Isle, but only briefly. In December I'd be forever off the sex offender list, and when January rolled around and I hit thirty Mr. Donny Lee would switch on the faucet. I'd sell the Airstream and the LeBaron. Buy myself an off-the-lot truck. Have Ruston professionals load up my storage unit. Through with Louisiana, I would move to another small town on the Gulf Coast. Some *Southern Living* place I knew from summer vacations with my parents. A pretty water town like Pass Christian, Mississippi. Fairhope, Alabama. Apalachicola, Florida. My house might be nothing extravagant, but in a large yard hemmed by strong, high fences Sam would be happy and safe. I'd chop my hair short, shave every morning, stop buying Winstons. And if the whispers grew too loud I'd try to explain my side of the story. I'd tell my new neighbors that if they'd give me a chance I would prove to them I was trustworthy and decent. That I was a man who deserved their compassion. I'd worship at a United Methodist, join them all afterwards at the picnic. Corn bread and iced tea and softball. The congregation would at last embrace me, and since there weren't many other single men in the church maybe I'd revisit the idea of marriage and find my wife *there*. A big-haired, bless-her-hearting girl who wore stiff Sunday dresses cut from flowery wallpaper prints. A woman with no desire or reason to ever leave her hometown. Even a spit-and-polished me would be the nearest thing she'd ever known to the soap opera rebels she lusted after. Her family would become my family, and we'd vacation in the Smokies and Disney World. I would fish for trout and reds with her brothers on the weekends, and in due course my right to bear arms would be restored so I could hunt again, shoot ducks for Sam in his twilight years. I'd be rich and wouldn't need to work, so maybe I'd volunteer with the fire department, coach Little League. Gradually even the thought of having children of my own wouldn't seem so frightening. My wife would insist we name our son Thomas, and on birthdays and Christmases we'd send our niece Joni a thinking-of-you Hallmark. At least once every year I would fly to see her, and as our conversations became easier and easier perhaps Joni would sometimes come to me as well. And between those visits she'd live her life on her coast while I lived my life on mine. A life in which I'd wrapped myself in layers and layers of family, friends, and possessions, hoping that trinity would be enough, that all the obligations that come with having people and things to care about wouldn't smother me. That I wouldn't lie in bed at night feeling snared and terrified, a vial of Panther Mound dirt clenched tight in my hand.

But then I realized I was also perfectly situated to break another way. To run to another sort of life. A life that didn't scare me at all. In that life Joni would be more like a pen pal than a niece. I'd give Sam to Malcolm, sell everything in the storage unit, never buy a house or marry or have kids. With no one to please or be accountable for, I wouldn't have anything to lose. That's an opportunity most never have, and I'd spend my days traveling, getting into adventures, seeing the world, my hair growing longer and longer. I'd drive to Alaska, follow the pipeline to the Arctic Circle, trade the LeBaron for an old motorcycle. Border towns, tramp ships. Nothing would be impossible. In the Himalayas a monk would touch my forehead, call me a seeker, and then maybe I'd show up in Russia, track down Marina just to have a hello, see how she was getting along. Efim would be out of the picture, and soon she'd find herself in love with me instead. But one morning I'd tell her I couldn't tarry, that this is where I ride away. You can fall in beside me, but you can't make me stay. And on a school night a few decades distant some child of Joni's would construct a family tree for his class, then obsess over the dead end where the names of the died-young Joseph brothers were suspended like hanged men. His grandfather and his granduncle, the hero and the vagabond, the incredible experiences they surely must have had on this earth. All those ancestors, all those lives, yet ours would be the only two that seemed interesting to him.

IN THE AFTERNOON I drove the LeBaron to Fort Miley to meet with Joni. Lands End: The American Finish Line. That same cliff-top bench. That same awkwardness and dread. The flowing Golden Gate false river more gray than blue in this weather, more dull than shimmering.

But, nevertheless, on our second day at Fort Miley I was a good soldier mostly. I didn't object when Joni asked a tourist to snap a picture of us with her phone, and then I forced myself to linger over the photographs in FOR OUR TOMMY—even after the first of them to capture my brother and me together almost had me crying. I told Joni that all I really knew about her father's death was that somehow, some way, he'd gone out like a hero, and with that lie I felt what Lionel Purcell must have felt in Battle Mountain. That I had given everything I could regarding Tommy. Here I am even now—alone, pen in my hand—but all I want to do is speed up the tape and rush for the exit.

Finally Joni appeared to sense I was done, spent, and she let us sit there on our bench in quiet reflection. Her hair was down, veiling her face, and she was wearing her buckskin jacket. My San Francisco niece. Her Louisiana uncle. There is only so much, so little, you can actually learn about another person, living or dead, and that's a hell of a thing to realize at any age.

Those two sentences in my mother's journal: *To be a parent is to always wonder whether the world sees your children the way you see them. My son is gone.* Joni and I had come to appreciate what Mom meant by that, at least in part. How we are all strangers, mainly. How we all believe we are the star of the same play, but none of us are.

I lifted my Red Wings and clicked them together, Dorothy in her ruby slippers. "So I guess today has to be it," I said. "But we'll talk soon. Write me, call me, whenever."

Joni's hair fell back, her lips moving as she spoke to the sky. "I broke up with Daniel last night."

I let my feet drop. "Really?"

She looked at me, hands in her lap, green eyes chasing mine. I was all pauses and fidgets, but she wasn't ready to let me escape from her yet. "I took your advice," she said. "I just came out and told him." She shook her head. "And he got mad, very mad. So I got mad."

"But that *was* what you wanted, wasn't it? To split with him?"

"I think so."

"Then all right." I smiled. The Golden Gate was vacant now. No ships. No boats. Simply water. "Now don't ever take any advice from me again."

Joni smiled too. Laughed, even. "Do you have an hour, weird uncle? Will you drive us somewhere?"

"Somewhere where?"

"I know a place that's kind of like your Panther Mound. I want to show it to you."

But why? She put one thumb up, one thumb down, waiting for me to decide. This display of interest in me—and trust—could only be a ruse to maybe get me talking about Tommy again. I was trying to remember when I'd ever told her about the Panther Mound. Yesterday? Today? Then there was the LeBaron. The floorboards littered with receipts, napkins, empty packs of cigarettes.

The seats coated with the yellow hairs of a dog she was probably allergic to.

"Say yes," said Joni.

She stood then, and as we made for the parking lot I thought of all the other places I'd been in my life, dreamed about. I was pondering what it was that always made me believe the thing I really had to see was over the next hill, around the next corner, across a Cane River. Why any new place seemed better than wherever I happened to be. Why all it takes to tempt me is to holler, Hey, let's go take a ride. I had been made to leave Dry Springs, and soon I would be made to leave this city as well—but there's never any need to exile me. Just be patient, and I'll run.

THE MONARCH BEAR GROVE was in a hidden, eastern section of Golden Gate Park, along a weave of trails that led from a sidewalk into forest. On the drive I'd rolled down the windows to help Joni with her allergies, and between sneezes and sniffs she told me the Monarch Bear Grove was one of the few remaining oak groves that predated the city. That the Monarch Bear Grove was considered sacred by the Wiccans and whatnot who'd given it that ridiculous name. "Mom used to be into that scene," Joni had said. "She would bring me there."

Hippie silliness, I assumed, but in her buckskin jacket Joni was now a frontier scout guiding me through wilds, a mixed-blood taking me to raid an Indian encampment—and we'd walked a fair ways into the forest when she froze in the trail. I looked past her for napping Comanche, Apache, but all I saw were scattered clusters of weathered, luggage-sized stones surrounded by gnarled and knotty oaks.

Joni pointed. Ashy quail were dusting themselves beneath the low oak canopy of the dark clearing, curled plumes of feathers dangling like apostrophes from their heads. These were California quail. Not the bobwhites Tommy and I would sometimes flush while stomping along fencerows for rabbits—but similar enough to have me recalling those wintry, twenty-gauge mornings with my brother, heart in my throat as birds erupt from the high grass, Tommy firing away, me too startled to even take my own gun off safety.

"This is it?" I asked, and at the sound of my voice the covey went scurrying into a thicket like a herd of pip-pipping mice.

Joni put her hand down and began to walk backward toward the stones, the pulled molars of some diseased giant. "Mom says there used to be a bear cage here," she said. "Like, a hundred years ago. That bear on the state flag—Monarch—he was here."

"No kidding."

She blew a puff of breath into her bangs. "Queen Sierra Club, my mom. For a while every other poem of hers was about the bear grove."

None had been in *Salted Waters*, but a week later I read a couple online in the Cybermobile. A short poem called "The Wild Bear Caught," a long poem called "Modern Druids."

"Come with me," said Joni.

We went into the clearing. There were no plaques or signposts—just those misshapen chunks of cut limestone that looked to have been chiseled from a quarry generations and generations past—and I listened as Joni told me their history. How the stones were from the chapter house of a Spanish monastery that had been dismantled and shipped to America in the 1930s. How, according to her mother, the monks at that plundered monastery had been keepers of "ancient knowledge concerning the earth." How eventually, mysteriously, some of the medieval stones wound up here: the former site of a cage for a bear called Monarch, one of the last California grizzlies.

Joni seemed like she had more to say, but then she was interrupted by the hum of her phone. She didn't answer the call, and from the annoyed look on her face I knew that somewhere, at that same instant, Nancy had a phone in her hand as well. That mother was checking in on daughter.

So the spell had been broken. If I wanted to learn anything else about the bear grove I would have to find it out on my own. A fallen oak limb was propped sideways over two of the largest and squarest of the stones, and I sat down within a skeleton of branches. "This was worth seeing," I said. "Thank you."

Joni sat next to me on the limb. There were tiny red bumps splashed across her once-smooth cheek, and her button nose was as red as a burn. Sam had bitten her without even being there. "It's cool," she agreed.

Then *my* cell began to ring, and the thicketed quail resumed with their warning pips as I dug the phone from my jeans. Several of the tear slips I'd pruned from those Mark Sorensen flyers went ticker-taping through the air.

"Oh fuck," I said.

"What?"

My phone went silent, and I showed her the number. "Tell me that's not your mom."

"Shit." Joni shot from the cracked limb, a flushed quail herself. "Shit, shit, shit. She knows. Daniel did this. He—" And before she'd even finished talking her hand was humming again. She slapped her phone against her thigh as she paced around the bear grove, her white Nikes kicking dead leaves from the dirt. "I have to go," she said. "I have to call her back or she'll do something wack."

I raked my fingernails across the scaled bark of the oak limb. You could have killed me with a touch right then. All of us poor, tragic Josephs. I guess the brooding part of me always suspected my search for Joni would end in disaster for us both. And now that was happening. I shook my head, stood. "We almost made it," I said.

Joni was walking a circle, but then she broke from her orbit and pitched into me, shoved by a ghost. I caught my balance as we hugged, her hands on my chest. She pushed free when our shoulders met, and I don't remember what all was said in those last hurried, frantic seconds we shared. I know she told me she should be alone during her call to Nancy. I know I didn't argue with her. I know we had a sudden and pathetic farewell. She ran from the bear grove on the same trail that had brought us there, melting into the trees as I was left behind. My scout had abandoned me, and I shut off my phone. If there was ever a time for me to run as well, but I was untraceable now. Louisiana didn't want me and California didn't want me—the whole merciless country didn't want me—yet the bear grove felt like a sanctuary. So long as I stayed there only Joni could find me.

And if not, let them come. Let me make my stand in this bizarre, sacred place and go out with some dignity. I waited in the center of the clearing, the occasional pips of one determined quail still scolding, still rebuking, until I heard the crunch of footsteps in the forest behind me. Joni, I thought. She'd gotten lost somehow, taken trail after trail only to get tossed back into the bear grove. Or maybe she understood exactly where she was and where she was going. Maybe she realized I couldn't beat them by myself, and we would see this fight through together.

So I turned, but instead of Joni's Tommy face I saw a skyscraping beanstalk of a man in a wide-brimmed black hat thrash his way past saplings and enter the bear grove. His head was down, but he was moving toward me, a trench coat draping his reedy frame like the ebony robe of a judge. He carried no bird on his spidery arm that day, but I was certain this was the falconer, the *sokolnik*. Of course that spooky guy came here. Of course he worshipped here. And though for a brave moment I held my ground among those old oaks and ageless stones—and though perhaps the falconer only wanted to quickly pray to strange deities and go—any true courage passed down from my parents went to Tommy, not me. That tall man couldn't have been as threatening as he looked, but I just couldn't tell. I have been wrong about so many things.

PART IV

The Africa Notes

But I was there, and there was no way for me to escape, except by water, from the country of nine-fingered people.

—JAMES DICKEY, *Deliverance*

F OR THE PAST EIGHT MONTHS MY NEW AIRSTREAM has been a hotel room in Port Harcourt, Nigeria. I'm two-weeks-on, two-weeks-off again, albeit on some very different oil rigs. A land rig in the Niger Delta to start, but now: my first stint for a London-based drilling company on the Mantis 15, a Gulf of Guinea jackup located due south of Bonny Island. The Mantis 15 pulls crew from all over the globe, but somehow I am the only American hand. To these Europeans and Australians and Africans, I'm just the nine-fingered, soccer-ignorant Yank who keeps to himself. The long-haired *oyibo* with the binder and a backpack full of books. They don't want to know me yet, and I don't want to know them. In a way maybe this is what I've always been meant for.

After those months in the hot, humid interior I'm relieved to be on the water again, and every night I've found time to put down my pen or my book and go outside to look across the black. From the Mantis 15 the gas flares of the African mainland are like far-off torches, the lights of scattered platforms and other jackups like near stars. And though there have been radio rumors of pirates in speedboats, to date they have left us alone. We are untouchable here, a planet unto ourselves.

In January I didn't turn thirty as a rich man after all. Weeks before—just as Louisiana was removing my name from the sex of-fender registry, and at the dawn of the Great Recession—a ruined and vengeful Mr. Donny Lee shot "financier" and fraud Gil Bean in the neck at the entrance to a Dallas courthouse. My incarcer-ated accountant/adviser has become a *Forbes* celebrity vigilante, but most of my money is gone, lost to a Ponzi scheme that stole billions from fish much bigger than me.

So here I am, four days into a stint that will see me through Christmas, back doing the only job I know how to do. But good-bye Grand Isle, and good-bye Gulf of Mexico. Good-bye Airstream, and good-bye LeBaron. Sam is living with Malcolm's family in Louisiana, and there are even more boxes packed into my storage unit now. Leaving that dog was one of the toughest things I've ever had to do, but money can be made sucking dinosaur wine on these West African rigs, and like most of these hands—from the young Brits always chattering about vacations to Costa Blanca and Thailand, to the local-content-hire Nigerians who go on and on about cell phones and marriage—money is what I need. We're all small pieces of this Mantis 15 puzzle, on rent to a Big Oil su-permajor for almost two hundred thousand dollars a day.

I once dreamed I could choose to have a free-roaming life of adventure, but whatever the continent, whatever the gulf, there is no real adventure in busting your ass on any oil rig, and it takes more than long hair to be free. So although I am once again a roughneck, I am also a college student. Nicholls State has an on-line program for rotating offshore workers, and between stints I've been taking classes, plugging away at a Thibodeaux associate de-gree from the desk of a third-world hotel room. The only dream I have now is that maybe I can start over. Riches have been a false god for me in the past, but all I'm angling for these days is enough of a pocketful to truly be finished with oil patches and begin a new path. Even if I don't know where I will go, or even what I will next become.

A slow-typing paralegal, perhaps—because in addition to the weaselings of that Texas grifter Mr. Donny Lee decided to Jack Ruby, there's another stomach punch I've had to contend with. The fucking law. In August Louisiana limited *felony* "carnal knowledge of a juvenile" to when the difference in age between an Eliza Sprague and a Roy Joseph is four years or greater. So the way the criminal code is now I never would have been an RSO in the first place. Lionel Purcell once told me that triumph without struggle means nothing. And though I'm not an alcoholic, and though every Russian novel I've read has been tedious, the past is the past, and I try not to think about what might have been.

Joni, my Gettysburg. After the bear grove I locked Karen Yang's keys in the apartment and didn't turn my phone on for two days. I was crossing arid badlands, bound for Grand Isle, as Nancy's voice mails stabbed at my ear. Dumped by Joni, Daniel had betrayed me to Nancy—betrayed me in the exact fashion I had promised not to betray *him*—and when I finally called Nancy she was still furious, but she was fair. Somehow Joni had been able to convince her I was no monster, and Nancy agreed to give me the opportunity to redeem myself by staying away. This time the terms of my plea deal, my surrender, my retreat, are more reasonable. Until Joni is through with high school I will cut off all contact with her or say hello to a restraining order. But beyond that, I am Joni's decision to make.

Then Joni got on the phone. She told me that a year and a half wasn't that long to wait. That in the interim her notebook and recollections could be enough. And out of respect for her mother, and equal parts anxiety and fear, I haven't bothered her since. I have a number in my head, and when my bank account hits that mark I'll return to America. I will reclaim my old buddy Sam, and eventually—if I'm certain I'll conduct myself better, that I won't act so goddamn cagey and scared—maybe I will make another trip to see her, if she asks.

I hate to admit this, but right now I imagine Joni the same as I imagine Tommy. She is a memory drifting further and further away. But if nothing else, I am a man who can wait.

Months ago I began taking what I call notes. A comp assignment gone haywire for this born-again freshman. I started by telling my life story to myself, but what I really wanted to make sense of was my failed attempt to rejoin the world. The things I might have done differently. The things I couldn't have helped. I felt as if if I wrote that down I could get rid of it, and now those stories are all told. Going forward, the things I write of will be new things.

This morning I spent the first hour of my seven-to-seven tower tripping pipe on the rig floor, then another two assisting with the scheduled maintenance of the mud pumps—and after being holed up in that pump room, on break I needed to be somewhere open to beat back the claustrophobia. And the helideck is the best place for that on any rig. Ours juts from the northwest corner of the Mantis 15 like a big green stop sign, and though hands aren't supposed to be loitering on helidecks, I'll keep going there until they catch me.

I dropped my hard hat and tied my hair back, took off my safety glasses and my gloves. A slanting, wire-mesh fence bordered the perimeter of the helideck, and I walked toward the Americas in greased and muddy coveralls. Close to the edge, but not too close, just enough so I could look down into near waters below. The legs of the Mantis 15 have the jackup pinned to the Gulf of Guinea bottom, and there is always magic in watching bobbing seas slide by all around and not feeling even the slightest of a rocking or a sway. Like the earth is turning without me. The decay of the silted Niger was at battle with the salt of the blue, and cool, dry Harmattan winds were blowing their smog of Sahara dust over everything. The sun was high, the hazy sky the color of pioneer denim, and through the dust-fog of that trade wind I could see the fins of requiem sharks patrolling for mackerel and rig trash. In the daylight there is so much more to look at here, so much more to tell.

I was at the very top of all those stacked things—Gulf, rig, helideck—but soon my break was ending. The seas are always moving, of course, and they were still moving then, the waters that had been under me before now far, far away. My face was gritty with dust swept from a distant desert I would probably never see, and I thumbed at my eyes. I was hunting my hard hat. I was ready to continue servicing our mud pumps. Hour after hour of replacing worn gaskets and valves, liners and pistons.

My life has been a series of flights in search of safe havens and culverts, and I can feel something coming for me even now, actually. But I'm trying not to be afraid anymore. It doesn't always have to be something bad, I keep telling myself. For once it might just be something beautiful.

AFTERWORD

And then, three years ago, on that Christmas Day off the coast of Africa, Roy vanished. A war came for my brother like a war came for me.

According to a senior Nigerian naval officer generous enough to correspond, the pirates selected December 25 for reasons both practical and symbolic. First and foremost, Captain Bolewa surmised, their leaders—secretive figures viewed as warlords by some and Robin Hoods by others—likely presumed, not altogether incorrectly, that the pirates would encounter a distracted and somewhat reduced crew as they attempted to seize the Mantis 15, the last known place Roy was seen alive. And although no one ever took official credit for the Mantis 15 assault, Captain Bolewa was confident the pirates were aligned with the Movement for the Emancipation of the Niger Delta. This militant group claims to oppose the exploitation and oppression of the people of the Niger Delta, and the devastation of the natural environment, by partnerships between the government and oil corporations, and months earlier MEND had initiated Operation Hurricane Barbarossa—an ongoing string of actions intended to bring down the oil industry in the region pursuant to an "oil war" targeting pipelines, facilities, and work sites. In Christmas,

Captain Bolewa speculated, MEND saw an occasion to send a message of defiance to the West.

Which returns me to Roy, Christmas Day, and the Mantis 15. An Australian named Liam Simms remembers tranquil seas and a battered twenty-foot panga with a two-hundred-horse outboard. The speedboat came in fast out of the setting sun, and there were eight pirates in total. Fatigues and bandoliers. Black balaclavas. They carried Kalashnikovs and machetes and, on the shoulder of a pirate in the bow of the now-idling panga, an RPG he kept leveled on the Mantis 15 as another man spoke broken-English, surrender-or-be-fired-upon demands through a bullhorn.

BSX Drilling had employed a tactical security team to provide for the safety of the Mantis 15—as was done for most, if not all, significant drilling rigs in the Gulf of Guinea—and the Mantis 15 team was comprised of four former special forces types of various units and nationalities, led by Simms, an ex-sergeant from Australia's 2nd Commando Regiment. It was Simms who went on the loudspeaker to direct the crew to collect on the far side of the rig while the security team took defensive positions. And it was Simms who presented himself unarmed at the railing, shouting down to the bullhorn man as he tried to calm the masked, faceless pirates in the speedboat fifteen meters below.

The primary, immediate threat was the pirate in the bow with the RPG, as a well-placed warhead would have unleashed hell on the Mantis 15. But to surrender the rig to pirates was only a slightly less frightening prospect. Accordingly, Simms continued to buy time until—and I am speculating here—a corporate office monitoring the situation from thousands of miles away radioed in orders, and a member of the security team shot the RPG pirate in the chest with an M4.

The fighting ended quickly. Two pirates who opened up with Kalashnikovs were also killed, and a fourth was shot as he lifted the dropped RPG. He fell forward with it into the water, and seeing the RPG lost overboard, the other pirates chucked their weapons. Simms had his men hold their fire, so what would have been a turkey-shoot massacre was avoided. Still, three pirates lay dead in the speedboat and one was in the Gulf, hurt and bleeding, fighting to keep his head above surface, treading water but only barely.

But the pirates had a contingency plan, apparently—because then a man sitting on the gunwale of the panga began popping and tossing floating smoke canisters to provide cover. The orange smoke billowing from the gap between the speedboat and the rig, as well as the fading light of sunset, made it difficult for Simms to describe what happened next. What he does know is that my brother and another crew member, a Nigerian cook, came alongside him at the railing. Simms warned them back, fearful there might be more shooting, but Roy, and the cook, stayed there with him, looking into the darkness and the smoke. Almost zero visibility, yet they could hear the splashings of the pirate in the water. The cook and then Roy grabbed life rings and threw them blindly into the Gulf, but the wounded pirate was screaming now. Simms moved over to the cook, about to push him out of harm's way, when he saw the American with hair "like a Gypsy Joker" biker climb the railing and point down at something.

The pirate in the drink had gone quiet, and Simms recalls Roy glancing back twice before flipping off his hard hat and jumping, disappearing, into the orange of that smoke cloud. "He seemed angry," Simms told me. "Not afraid, not crackers—cut-snake mad. And then he went over like he was a bloody lifeguard." Maybe a minute later, Simms heard the speedboat's outboard throttle up and drone away.

The search for Roy Joseph was called off the next day. There were no ransom demands or hostage videos, and Simms was considerate enough not to mention sharks to me. He said only that he believes my brother drowned trying to save the life of a pirate.

LIKE ROY, I too have known the ends of the earth. And during the summer of my year one as a prisoner in the desert, already driven desperate by agonizing solitude and boredom, but also seeking to perhaps earn some sympathy from my invisible and enigmatic captor, I persuaded a guard to submit my request to receive instruction in Arabic and Islam. For this I expected to be ignored or even punished, a return to the terrible months that had followed my arrival at that remote, secluded compound, but a week later a man in a blinding white head scarf and thawb appeared in front of my cell. Ahmad. My tutor was much older and spoke crisp, perfect English. And he was kind. Ahmad whispered that it would be prudent if I didn't tell him anything I wouldn't want passed along to "others" beyond those sands, and then we began to talk. A single visit that was never repeated. Not once did I meet the fiend who held the key to my cage, but early on such seemed to be his psychopathic way. To give and then take. To find amusement in relayed accounts of my sufferings.

But I did get that lone visit. Ahmad told me he had been pleased to learn my name, explaining that the Joseph of my Book of Genesis and the Yusuf of his Quran were one and the same. Consequently, he announced, we shall open your lessons there. Over the next hour, the first pleasant hour of the twenty years I would spend in that earthbound limbo, I listened as he shared the story of the prophet Yusuf with me. The story of a dreamer who was thrown into a well by his own brothers, enslaved and then imprisoned for many years before becoming favored by a king and set free, reunited with his family. Yusuf's life was a splendorous life, my tutor contended, and as he said this I knew he was trying to give me what I needed. A way to look at my circumstances and not lose hope.

Neither my brother nor I have been very likely prophets, and no one would call our lives splendorous, but I see us both as that dreaming brother of legend. As that Joseph in a well, waiting for what might come next. That day in the culvert, Roy, you were shaken and afraid, but what you did not know, what I wish you could have known, was that I was also so afraid. And the only thing keeping me stable was having you there with me, riding out that storm. "Be careful, Tommy," you said to me then, a soaked twelve-year-old speaking not of a storm but of war, and I should have done more than act brave for you. That wouldn't have changed our destinies—destiny is destiny—but there in that culvert, yes, I should have given you more.

After Ahmad I found strength in meditation and in books, in the scattershot prayers of an agnostic, in the eventual, startling gentleness and even friendship of my guards, but above all it was the dream of my homecoming that sustained me during my years of captivity. The dream I might one day hobble down the steps of a plane and see my family on the tarmac. On the final night in my cell I heard the explosions of mortar rounds, then the rat-a-tats of firefights, and in the morning the compound was taken by rebels. With the Arab Spring my dream seemed inevitable. There was the crossing of that golden desert on motorcycles and in cars for a rendezvous with amazed CIA spooks, and three days afterwards, like an offering from a god, nighttime helicopters filled with brother SEALs descended onto a road near a seaside date palm grove to help bring a long-haired and bearded scarecrow home. A C-17 flew me from a secured airfield directly to Germany, and I was a week at Landstuhl before the med/psych experts came clean about my parents, then Roy. As I wept I remember feeling as if the world had finally broken me. I was the last of the Josephs, and having a sense of the loneliness my little brother had been living with felt like more than I could bear.

Then, later . . . America, Walter Reed, and the visit from Margaret Mokwelu. Poring through Roy's binder introduced me to a new level of pain, frustration, and anger. And there was astonishment but no joy even in knowing Joni and Nancy were out there because, unfortunately, I was famous by then, so this much was clear: they must have heard about my return from the dead, yet they had chosen not to contact me.

But Margaret was persistent. Due to those notes she knew things about me and my family no one else knew, so in certain ways she was my only friend. For several days she would come and we would talk, and she pleaded with me to summon the strength to do what Roy had done and go to Joni. The strength to eventually make the San Francisco phone call Margaret had never been able to make. I failed in that, she said, but that was also not my place. Please take this burden from me. Then she asked me the question Roy once asked himself. What would your brother want from you?

My reassimilation and reintegration was meant to be a long and ongoing process of closely supervised mental and physical healing, but after three months of military bases and medical centers—and a time-served, photo-op promotion conferred by the president—I'd had enough. Following my surgery and rehab at Walter Reed, and another month as an outpatient, I was allowed to walk away, and since then I've been an expeditionary, retired-navy traveler and tourist, moving through this country and this ghost story. I remain astounded by the Internet and the price of gas and the phones in everyone's pockets, but otherwise I still recognize America.

In Louisiana I found Sam. His muzzle was gray, his body stiffening, but when I spoke his name he rose and came to me like a fighter answering the bell. Get yourself an address and send for him, Malcolm said. Have some time with the old rogue—even if it'll make this coon-ass cry to give him up.

And in Nevada, Lionel Purcell. Battle Born Outfitters is in

business again, and he says his outlaw days are over. Almost all of my SEAL platoon had been through Walter Reed to see me at least once, but Lionel just waited patiently until I wrote him, in that knowing and reclusive way of his. Yup, Ahab, your brother was out here. Yup, you might have a kid. When I arrived in Battle Mountain he brought me to the Rubies, and I told him that what happened to me in the Persian Gulf—the agony I've caused for so many, the guilt I'll live with forever—was not anyone's fault but my own. This first Joseph to jump before he should have.

But I also told Lionel that on my swim I had felt something with me in the dark water. Something that had awoken me from my slapped sleep. Something the fishermen who found me on the beach seemed to have a name for. And although I'll never know what he was, exactly, that something was definitely there. Confusing me, watching me. A panicked, disoriented boy, alone and swimming. A boy mistaking the lights of an underway trawler for the lights of a search vessel. A boy realizing his mistake too late for that mistake to be corrected. Too late for him to do anything but push on for the shore.

California. I regret Nancy Hammons probably comes off as the villain of Roy's pages, as a shadowy presence to be avoided and feared, because the actual Nancy is thoughtful and caring. A woman who once kissed me on a beach and told me I was too much of a kid to be the warrior I thought I was then. A mother who would lay down her life for her daughter. She was dumbfounded to hear from me, could never have expected that binder, showing me the way, but she has been a lighthouse in all of this as well. I retraced Roy's pioneer trail, driving from a trailer in Battle Mountain to a hotel in San Francisco to meet her, and we talked in my room for hours. My memories of our night in San Diego seemed to be from another lifetime, but I did remember her. She was the last woman I'd been with, just as I had been her last man.

In San Francisco Nancy told me that, as reports of Thomas Joseph began to flood the news, she and Joni had read of Roy's death in one of the many articles written about me. And they had been as surprised to learn of that as they had been to learn of my resurrection. Even the fact Roy had been in Africa was a revelation to them. Nancy explained that after months and then years passed, Joni finally accepted Roy had decided to turn away from her. No private investigators this time, only trust, a conviction Roy would find her again when he was ready. But Joni knew the truth now, and Nancy said they'd still been discussing how to best approach me when, instead, I had called them. Nancy insisted all blame for their delay lay on her. She had been worried I'd never be able to forgive her for shunning my brother.

So it was for me to tell Nancy to put that aside. I wish she would have told my parents about Joni, that they could have known her and loved her. And yes, Roy had deserved better. But any bitterness I might have been holding on to went away when Nancy drove me to the yellow house on Marvel Court. A star-spangled WELCOME HOME balloon was tied to the tucked balcony. The same balcony where Roy first saw Joni.

"No more secrets," said Nancy. "This can be our beginning."

And then: Joni. She was standing in the center of a living room with two framed photographs in her hands, pictures Roy had given her. "Hey," she said, shy and shaking, and I told her that one of the photos was of a day I still remembered. A bright hospital room where brothers are meeting. I am a child, and Roy is the infant cradled in my skinny arms. And, blurry in the background yet certainly there, a mother and father are watching their sons.

But the other photograph, the other photograph was Roy's notes come alive. He and Joni are sitting on a bench, a photo album resting between them. A young man and a teenage girl looking about as related as an uncle and a niece can look. My brother's hair is untamed, his brown eyes shining, nervous, and wild.

As it had been for Roy, seeing Joni was enough to assure me she was mine—but Nancy wanted me to have no doubts, so we'd already confirmed it with a DNA test. I had a daughter, and suddenly nothing seemed more important to me than that. Joni is the same age now as I was when I swam off the face of the earth. A twenty-year-old college student who loves children and intends to be a pediatrician someday. Things are still clumsy between us, but I can feel that changing. On my most recent trip to San Francisco she brought me to some of the places Roy spoke of in his notes, places he once wandered himself. The Outer Richmond and Baker Beach. Fort Miley and Golden Gate Park. The Monarch Bear Grove. For now he is what we have in common, but that has provided us with a foundation to build on, a history. I'm limping into middle age with poor health and a bad leg, but Joni has given me a purpose. And Roy is to thank for that, of course. For bringing us together. He carried the torch for his older brother for as long as he could manage, and ultimately that did as much for me as any Arab Spring.

I WROTE PEACH City Self Storage as soon as I found out about the unit Roy had rented, but the contents were sold at auction when his checks stopped coming. The buyer was a man from Grambling, and all I can hope is that by some miracle he is indeed the hoarder the owner of Peach City described in her e-mail to me. Please don't hang up, I told that Grambling man. I will pay you five times what you paid for whatever is left.

Although I'll never have that reunion of Josephs I had longed for, I have an updated dream to sustain me. I like to think of a morning when my new family will gather at a cemetery in north Louisiana. A small ceremony. Joni and Nancy and I in the shade of a water oak saying words for my mother and father—then, for Roy. I'll stand at attention by that empty space between my parents as workers, laborers like him, replace one stone for another so our switch is made complete.

And I will drive to Dry Springs for a pilgrimage to the old home. Res Ipsa Plantation llamas will watch me and Sam pick our way across the pasture to the Panther Mound, and there I'll make it known to the Underwater Panther that my own vial of stolen dirt has been lost, taken from me like that dirt was once taken from him. I will apologize for us ever having disturbed him, and I'll pray the curse has been transferred, the Josephs' debt satisfied. That perhaps he will finally let us rest.

I should stop there, but I won't. Because if Roy's notes taught me anything it is that things aren't always as they appear, and that lesson, that gift—a religion, almost—has given me the faith to believe whatever I choose to believe. For example, still another dream. The dream of a stubborn and hopeful disciple that my brother is alive. He was pulled from the water by pirates who treat him as a hero. The good man who fell from the sky to rescue their friend. Roy is with them but not as their prisoner. The pirate life. One of his escape fantasies made real. He's free to leave, yet for these three years he has remained. Often thinking of Joni, but seduced by adventure.

But maybe news of me will somehow reach him and give him a second reason to emerge from the mangroves of that sweltering delta maze. A half-land, half-water place where hundreds and hundreds of creeks flow into the sea. He will steal a boat and slip down one of those tributaries, his journey resumed until we are reunited at last.

Or maybe you are already here, Roy, watching over me from afar. I can settle for that dream, if I have to. Brothers. I am for you as you are for me. My past, my present, and my future. My past, my present, and my future.

—T.J.

ACKNOWLEDGMENTS

The author wishes to thank Lee Boudreaux, Megan Lynch, Janie Yoon, and everyone at Ecco/HarperCollins and House of Anansi Press. My deepest appreciation also to Kimberly Witherspoon, David Forrer, and the team at Inkwell Management, as well as to the Stanford University Creative Writing Program, Florida State University, Auburn University, the University of New Orleans, Halawakee H.L., and the Martha Heasley Cox Center for Steinbeck Studies at San José State University.

In addition, thank you to the following individuals: Molly Antopol, Lyndsey Blessing, Eavan Boland, Steven Boriack, Suet Yee Chong, Meredith Dees, Gabriella Doob, Jim Gavin, Lauren Groff, Dan Halpern, Scott Hutchins, Adam Johnson, Jamie Kornegay, Eleanor Kriseman, Sarah MacLachlan, Tom McGuane, Michael McKenzie, Emily Mockler, Ted O'Brien, Allison Saltzman, Jack Shoemaker, Pauls Toutonghi, David Vann, Greg Villepique, Ryan Willard, Charlie Winton, Tobias Wolff, and Craig Young.

This book never would have been possible without the knowledge and guidance of my cousin John Burnham, retired U.S. Navy captain and SEAL, as well as that of my old friend Avis Bourg and Bobby St. Pierre of Offshore Marine Contractors, Inc. in Cut Off, Louisiana. A huge debt of inspiration also to Andrew Holzhalb and my brother Matt Horack, who both left us too soon. Finally, as always, my deepest thanks to my parents, family, and friends—and most of all to Sylvia, my amazing wife, for always shining so bright.

Author photo: Sylvia Horack

SKIP HORACK is a former Jones Lecturer at Stanford University, where he was also a Wallace Stegner Fellow. His story collection *The Southern Cross* won the Bread Loaf Writers' Conference Bakeless Fiction Prize, and his novel *The Eden Hunter* was a *New York Times Book Review* Editors' Choice. A native of Louisiana, he is currently an assistant professor at Florida State University.